# SOULS FORSAKEN

## THE DARKWORLD SERIES: BOOK FOUR

EMMA L. ADAMS

*'Hell hath no limits, nor is circumscribed*
*In one self-place; for where we are is hell,*
*And where hell is, there must we ever be."*
Christopher Marlowe, *Doctor Faustus*

# 1

## FREEFALLING

I looked down at the ocean, fourteen thousand feet below, and wondered how in hell I'd let Cara talk me into this.

The land had shrunk to a patchwork of greens and yellows, dark forests hugging the Australian coastline. The sea was a brilliant blue, flecked with tiny white patches where boats passed, skimming the water. Turquoise marked the reefs, treasure troves beneath the waves. Wisps of cloud floated past.

Then the plane's hatch opened, and a blast of frigid air swept inside, numbing my bare arms instantly. A roaring filled my ears, and my heart beat so fast it felt like it might escape at any moment. At once, I became aware of how tiny, how insignificant, we were, minute figures in a hunk of metal hovering in the sky.

The first parachutist jumped. One second he was there, the next, the relentless wind swept him away. A gasp escaped me. No freaking *way* was I jumping out of this plane.

The guy I was strapped to gave me a smile. The

harness pinned me in place. When he moved, I moved with him. The second parachutist disappeared through the hatch.

Cara was next. A last grin and thumbs-up, and her tandem partner flung himself out into the air. *Holy hell*, I thought, peering frantically out the window. There was a tiny speck below that might be a person falling—was that her?

More parachutists jumped, throwing themselves over the edge like human Skittles, fearless.

*Shit.* My turn. My tandem partner waved the hand-camera in my face. I was pretty sure I looked like a death-white corpse, but that hardly mattered right now. There was no escaping the drop.

My entire body felt numb, detached. Strapped together, the two of us shuffled towards the gaping hole in the side of the plane. Islands outlined in sandy beaches waited below, in a sea of glittering blue. I had to tilt my head back and look at the postcard-perfect sky. *Not a bad way to die*, said the part of my brain that wasn't frozen in terror.

Then the support disappeared, and we were falling, falling into that perfect sky.

I couldn't even hear my scream; my ears were popping so hard that it felt like something was struggling to burst out of my skull. My eyes were stretched open wide, my arms spread, the air buffeting me all over. My heart leapt, and my scream of terror became a yell of pure delight.

I felt the parachute open, and the fall slowed. I finally drew in a breath and flexed my arms to make sure they were still attached to my body.

The view below was unreal. It was like I was looking at a map from above, a 3D image of the Earth on a high-tech computer screen. But it was real. I was strapped to a parachutist, but other than that, I was unsupported. The guy waved the camera in my face again, and I gave a thumbs-up.

*This is surreal.* I tried to take it all in, as though by staring hard enough I could imprint it on my mind forever. Given that eighteen years' worth of memories in my nineteen-year-long life were a total lie, I needed as many of those moments as I could get. The landscape could have been a painting, it was so beautiful. My eyes ached to look at it.

"How do you feel?" asked the guy strapped to my back.

Grinning at the camera, I said, "Awesome."

"TOLD YOU IT WAS AWESOME," said Cara later, when we were back at the skydiving hub. "Man, I admit I freaked a bit when that guy jumped out, though!"

"Me too," I said, sitting back in the comfy seat. It still felt weird to be on solid ground. "These guys do that every day!"

"Must be pretty fun!" she said, looking up at the pictures of posing parachutists and the video of the day's skydivers playing on the flat-screen TV. "Hmm. Might add it to my list of possible careers."

"There are worse jobs," I agreed. "Hey—I think that might be us."

A video of an aeroplane taking off began on the TV screen. The scene cut to a view of the people inside the plane, crammed into two rows.

Cara laughed. "Your face, Ash."

"I thought I was going to die!" I said.

"Nothing like your life flashing before your eyes to give you a sense of perspective."

I caught the hidden meaning there. *I get it,* I wanted to say. *But sometimes things are just too big to put in perspective.*

I watched the video instead of answering, laughing at Cara's facial expressions as she fell out of the plane.

"Dignity fails again!" she said. "Man, we've got to buy these."

"We get some included with the video," I reminded her. "And, no, I don't want my *I'm-going-to-die* face forever immortalised on a key-ring, thank you very much."

"I prefer the fridge magnets," said Cara. "Or how about a T-shirt?"

"Definitely not," I said. "Haven't we spent enough on cheesy souvenirs?"

"You can never spend too much on souvenirs," said Cara firmly. "Besides, you're loaded."

Right. Of course I was. It was just too bad that the money had come with the cost of almost everything else I'd ever held dear to me, because it had come from the woman who'd ruined my life. I focused my gaze on the souvenir display instead of replying, hoping she'd pick up the hint.

"Well, okay. Maybe the T-shirt's a bit much. I'm getting the photos, though."

"Same," I said. "Oh, don't forget the certificate. It's proof."

"Proof that we were crazy enough to jump out of a plane," said Cara. "You sure you don't want to do the bungee jump, too?" She waved her arms in the direction of the leaflets nearby, advertising more crazy adrenaline-high stunts.

"Definitely," I said firmly. "I'll do the cable car thing again, if you want, but no cliff-jumping."

"Spoilsport."

There were reasons for my reluctance to fling myself

from a cliff. For one, I'd taken an unplanned, no-para-chute fall from the sky in the middle of Manchester *and* a tumble off a bridge into a frozen canal only a few months ago. For another, things tended to happen when I fell from high places. I'd barely held my connection to the Dark-world in check when I'd been terrified on the plane. It tended to respond to strong emotions. Even when I was ignoring it, I could never entirely forget it was there. Plum-meting 150 feet into a pond was toying with more than one kind of danger, and it wasn't a risk I wanted to take right now.

When we left the hub, carrying bags of goodies—Cara convinced me to buy a T-shirt after all, but not one with my face on it—I saw the first dark space I'd seen since leaving England a week ago.

It looked like a black hole in the universe, a blank space that wasn't supposed to be there. A familiar chill crept up my arms, although the space looked empty of any life. I never trusted the dark spaces, even the empty ones. Holes to the Darkworld could hide anything.

Even here, ten thousand miles away from home, I couldn't escape them.

Cara, of course, could see nothing. She hopped into the minibus, which waited outside to drive us back to Cairns. It was bright red, decorated with photographs of screaming free-fallers. The ground felt strange beneath my feet, as if I hadn't quite adjusted to no longer being airborne. There really was no feeling like it. It was like being on a sugar high, and even the dark space couldn't spoil the mood.

"What next?" said Cara, leaning back in her seat and pulling her own Skydive T-shirt over her other top. "I'm thinking we could hit the town again tomorrow. And the beach."

"Sounds good to me," I said as the minibus growled to life. "I need to get something for Sarah and Alex."

"A peace offering?" said Cara, giving me a curious look. She knew I hadn't parted on the best terms with my friends from university.

"Yeah, I guess. I don't want to fight with anyone next term. It's stupid."

Privately, I hoped that three months apart might give my flatmates something new to talk about other than a breakup that had happened nearly five months ago. I'd expected Alex's anti-male rants to step up after Leo had broken my heart, but I hadn't expected her to turn so *hostile*. Hi-jacking my Facebook account to send him sarcastic messages had been way out of line, in my opinion. Not to mention it had forced me to have to talk to him again and apologise.

I didn't know where Leo was now. He and his older brother Cyrus had taken off back in April on a wild round-the-world trip. They'd only come home briefly in July for Cyrus's graduation, which was just after the holidays had started. Leo had dropped out of university, deciding that he'd rather do his own thing. I'd have respected his choice under normal circumstances—which was more than I could say for my flatmates. Of course, they had no idea of the real reason we'd parted ways, nor could I ever tell them. Only Cara and Claudia knew the full story. I hadn't had the chance to speak to Cyrus before he'd left, so I had no idea what Leo had told him, and I wasn't about to confide anything to Berenice and Howard.

But I wanted to make it up with Alex. Sarah and I were okay, but she was one of those people who shied away from conflict, even though she agreed that Alex had taken the revenge thing too far. It was pretty much me versus the most stubborn person I knew—except possibly Cara—and it wasn't any wonder neither of us had apologised yet.

I stared moodily into my handbag. I'd left my phone behind, locked in the safe. I knew better than to check for messages, but I guessed it was up to me to initiate an apology to Alex. *Be the better person. Right.*

"Anyway," said Cara. "What about tonight? It's Tuesday, should we ride the party bus again?"

"Again?" I zipped my bag closed, our provisional schedule opened on top with a colour-coded list of activities—Cara had raised her eyebrows at it, but hadn't said anything. She knew I'd planned out every second of our trip in an attempt to gain control over *some* part of my life.

"The guys are going tonight."

"Not sure if I'm in the mood," I said. I wasn't really a clubbing person, but Cara and I had gone on the "ultimate" night out the first night in Cairns. It was hard to avoid, given that it took place on an open-top bus that blasted clubhouse music whilst driving around town, dropping the riders off at different bars and nightclubs throughout the night. Each bar boasted drinks offers and challenges, and it had been entertaining, to say the least. But tonight I just wanted to relax. Unfortunately, Cara tended to interpret "relaxing" as "moping" and wouldn't stand for it.

The minibus dropped us off a street away from our hotel. We'd got used to navigating the winding streets over the past week, although it had been confusing to begin with. Every building in this area seemed to be either a hotel or a tourist office, but once we knew where to go, we worked out how to find bars and restaurants and just about every activity possible, from quad biking to boat trips out onto the reef.

Cara spread her arms wide, grinning up at the still-impossibly-blue sky. "What d'you fancy for tea? There's a Nando's around the corner."

"There are Nando's in England," I pointed out, steering her onto the other side of the pavement before she skipped headlong into a group of other tourists.

"Yeah, but. Everyone's going."

By "everyone" she meant the other tourists sharing our dormitory. Fiona, Mike, Ryan, and Clare were travelling together as part of their gap-year trip, and we'd hit it off right away. Ryan had even asked me to dance on the big night out, and Cara kept encouraging me to take the next step. But I wasn't sure I was ready for that. He lived in London, anyway, and was leaving in a couple of days. I didn't want a relationship, and I wasn't the one-night-stand type, however many girls Leo had hooked up with since starting his travels.

Not that I knew for sure. I hadn't been outright stalking him, but Cyrus kept updating Facebook with photos of their latest adventures. Last time I'd checked, a couple of months ago, he'd been on a beach in California surrounded by gorgeous supermodel lookalikes. That particular photograph, incidentally, had been what prompted Alex's Facebook Vendetta.

"Who needs him anyway?" had been Cara's response. "If he's that focused on looks, he clearly wasn't right for you anyway. Not that you aren't gorgeous anyway. You can do a million times better."

But even when dancing with Ryan, it hadn't felt *right* the way things had with Leo. More like awkward. I *was* awkward, and I wasn't naive enough to assume every relationship would be the same, but I needed stability, not a mindless fling, and I'd all but begged Cara not to keep shoving me at every available guy.

There was no shortage here, since our hotel was a

popular choice with students because it had a nightclub and bar downstairs as well as a pool. It wasn't even overpriced, considering we were right in the middle of the tourist district. I'd never before been to a hotel that functioned as a twenty-four-hour fun house, with neon lights on the floors and clubhouse music blasting from the walls. I'd learned to sleep with earplugs in.

We dropped off our bags in the dormitory and headed down to the pool to catch the last of the hours of sunlight. Despite being the middle of winter in the southern hemisphere, it was warmer than an English summer here, even if it did get dark earlier. The lights never went off in Cairns anyway; most of the shops were open night and day.

It couldn't be more different from Blackstone, the quiet Lancashire village that was a ghost-town outside of term time. My home. I'd needed a change of scenery, and losing myself in the noisy, crazy tourist city on the brink of the Great Barrier Reef was about as far from what I was used to as possible. It was the trip of a lifetime, and the perfect way to forget, even in the darkest hours of the night.

The nights were the worst at home, because there were no arms to hold me when I woke screaming, no soothing voice to wash the nightmares away. No one to stave off the crippling coldness that came in with the dark and froze me from the inside out.

It never got dark here. It was perfect. And yet no matter how long I lay out in the sun, I could never really get warm. Coldness followed me everywhere I went, a faint chill that clung to me like an unwanted shadow.

Since I'd first seen the demons, it had been like I'd been thrown into a dark, icy fog, left to find my way out alone. Leo's had been a hand that reached out of the darkness and held on to me tight, bringing warmth that spread through me and made me feel alive. Without it, everything had spun back into chaos, and as much as I tried to keep going, I felt like I was back in the fog, stumbling towards a future that held no certainty, from a past built on lies. Nothing was the same.

I opted for an early night, declining Cara's and the others' invitation to drinks in the bar, and returned to the dormitory alone. I fell asleep almost instantly, despite the discomfort of the rickety metal bunk bed—and found myself in a familiar place.

Leo stood on the edge of a cliff, his back to me, staring out at the raging waves. Behind me, I knew, a winding path led through the forest to Blackstone, to home.

I stepped up behind him. "Leo," I whispered, my voice caught in my throat. He didn't turn around.

"Leo," I said, louder.

He turned. The eyes that stared into mine weren't his, but the violet eyes of a demon.

I took a step back. "Mephistopheles," I said. My heart hammered in my ears, and my fingers itched to close around the demon's throat, to punish him for what he'd done to Leo and me. But I knew I was dreaming. Leo wasn't here.

"The one and only." The demon's voice had a bitter edge. "It's taken me a while to find you, Ashlyn. Your *mother*"—his mouth twisted into a smile—"did a good job of sealing my heart."

"That was the point," I said. Trapped in the Darkworld with his demon heart under lock and key, Mephistopheles apparently had nothing better to do than to stalk my dreams in the shape of my ex-boyfriend and try to destroy my peace of mind.

"Why do you deny yourself, Ashlyn? You could have it all."

"Why don't you stop stalking me?" I countered. "We've had this conversation before. Too many times. I'm. Not. Interested. Not in being your pawn, or host, or whatever it is you want."

"I never said it was about *you*, Ashlyn."

I stared the demon down. I knew precisely who he meant, and it changed nothing. That part of me was locked away. The demon inside hadn't stirred since the night Leo had almost died.

"Lucifer would like very much to speak to you also, Ashlyn."

"I'm not interested in anything Lucifer has to say."

"His time is coming, whether you like it or not, Ashlyn. Soon, all things will end."

"How so?"

"Lucifer is rising. You'll hear from him soon…" Mephistopheles looked up, as though something had distracted him. I turned my eyes up to the cloudy sky but could see nothing, not even a harpy.

"Well, now," he said softly. "This is an interesting turn of events. I think it's time for you to return to the waking world, Ashlyn."

"What?" I said. "Wait—what did you mean about Lucifer?"

But the dream was slipping away. Leo gave me one last smile, and the gleaming demon eyes were the last thing I saw before my vision clouded over.

Then I awoke. I rolled over, pushing my covers off. The dim light cast the dormitory into shadow, but I saw someone else moving about. They looked up at me, and my heart stopped in my chest.

Leo.

## 2

### DECEPTION

I couldn't speak. I could only stare as Leo walked over to me. His dark hair was tousled, like he'd been running his hands through it. He smiled at me, his eyes shining with that look that made my insides melt. It told me he thought I was the most beautiful person in the world, that there was no one for him but me.

"Leo?" I whispered, my heart thudding like a jackhammer.

"Ash."

It *was* him. Impossible as it seemed. What the hell was he doing here? I sat up, aware that I was only wearing my pyjama shorts and a vest top, but I couldn't take my eyes off him. He looked real, solid, but after my dream, I didn't trust him not to melt into shadows.

"What—what're you doing here?"

"I came to see you, Ash. I've missed you." He reached out to stroke my face. "I want you."

Ice shot up my spine as his eyes turned violet.

"Leo!" I shouted, jumping up.

"Fuck!" he said, in a voice that didn't sound like

Leo's anymore. I stared as his appearance blurred before my eyes—for a second I looked into a whirl of blackness, like a dark space—then he was someone else entirely. Ryan.

"Shit," he said. His eyes turned to pale blue, with no hint of violet.

"What the hell?" I said, scrabbling away from him. "What did you just do?" Blind shock gave way to something else. The pain stabbed through me like a dagger. Leo wasn't here. He'd never been here.

Ryan was too busy cursing to notice that I'd spoken. Through the pain, I felt a surge of rage. The Darkworld responded, and my vision turned purple, as though I looked through someone else's eyes. I seized him around the neck with hands that were suddenly coated with ice, and jumped off the bed and slammed him into the wall with a strength I'd never known I even possessed.

"What—in—hell?" Ryan choked. "You're a demon!"

"No, I'm—*not!*" I shouted, more at myself than anything, willing the demon to go away. The violet tinge faded from my vision, but I still gripped his throat with a demon's strength.

"What *was* that?" he said.

"Tell me what you did, first!" I said. "You looked—you looked just like my—"

I broke off. I didn't want to say *ex*. Truth be told, I had no idea what Leo and I were exactly. That was the worst part.

"Your boyfriend?" he said. "*Dammit.* I was so damn close."

"What the hell do you mean?" I demanded. "Tell me, or I'll snap your neck."

Or rather, the demon would. She'd never responded to my emotions before, but I'd felt her rage alongside my own. I might not be capable of cold-blooded murder, but she sure as hell was.

Ryan's pasty face went positively grey. "Jesus. Shit, I had no idea you were... one of theirs. I don't deal with demons."

"Then what was with the demon eyes? You're a shape-shifter, are you?"

But I'd thought only ghouls could shape-shift, and not usually very well. The doppelgänger who'd imitated me had been an exception. Only higher demons could truly take on the form of a human, and Ryan definitely wasn't one of them. So what the hell *was* he?

"I'm an incubus," he said. "You're not a succubus, are you?"

*Incubus? Is every supernatural creature I've ever read about real, now?*

"No, I'm half-demon," I said—slightly disarmed by how easily the truth came out, considering I'd kept it from everyone for so long, and only a handful of people knew about it. "Surprised?"

If anything, *I* was the most surprised my voice was steady. An incubus? What next? Was the Darkworld going to stalk me until I finally lost it?

"Half-demon? You don't meet many of those. I thought they'd died out, actually." He made an attempt to smile, even with my hands still wrapped around his throat. Objectively, he was good-looking, but trying to seduce me in the form of Leo had put him low enough in my esteem that he'd ruined any chance he might have had to win me over. Could I not even enjoy a holiday without the Dark-world interfering?

*This isn't a coincidence. They're watching me.* In the dream, Mephistopheles had seen him coming. And I knew better than to believe in coincidence where Lucifer's right-hand demon was concerned.

"Yeah." My hands felt unsteady, but the ice held them in place. I didn't know too much about incubi, but I knew better than to trust a demon. "So what do you want from me?"

He raised an eyebrow. "I thought that was obvious."

*Oh. Right.*

"You feed on what? Lust?" The question came more from morbid fascination than anything.

"You've got it. I take the form of the one you most desire." He tried to squirm free of my hand, but the ice kept him pinned in position.

"Seriously?" I said. "It can't be coincidental that we're both here at the same time."

"Says who?"

"Are you in league with Mephistopheles? Or Lucifer?"

The instant the words escaped, it occurred to me how bizarre this would look to an outsider: me pinning him against the wall and interrogating him about biblical monsters. But my heart continued to pound against my ribs, and if not for the ice, I was sure my hands would be shaking with fear for what the demon inside me might do.

"What? Who the hell is that?"

"Don't play dumb with me," I said, the demon's presence pushing me forward. "You're an incubus. You must know about demons."

"Never heard of those two," he said. "I try to keep a low profile. I don't mix with demons if I can help it."

*Really, now?* The one book I'd read that mentioned incubi had talked about both in the same chapter. Incubi and half-demons were related, in some twisted way. Inwardly the thought made me shudder. "Don't you have any idea about what happened a few months ago in Manchester? The demon attack?"

"I don't keep a record. I live in London, anyway. Demon attacks every day. They kind of merge together in my head."

"Great," I said. Apparently my luck was so terrible that I attracted trouble from the Darkworld on the other side of the Earth, when they weren't even looking for me. What were the odds of that? Even the thought of Mephistopheles and Lucifer having nothing to do with it didn't unknot the tension coiled around my spine. *He's still dangerous.*

Then again, so was I.

"You live right near the Venantium, don't you?" he said. "That place. I can never remember the name."

"Blackstone," I said, searching his face for familiarity. No. He might be related to demons, but he was a stranger to me. "So do you know any magic-users?"

He half groaned, hands rising to push mine away, but the ice stopped him. "London's full of people who believe in magic. It just depends who you talk to. I don't really associate with sorcerers, but yeah, I know a fair few."

I didn't move my hands. I wasn't sure I *could.* "So you just live a normal life, except when you decide to turn into people's boyfriends? Is that how you pick up girls? You must make a lot of enemies."

"Nah. I don't usually go for intelligent girls. Most people don't notice the difference—" He choked again as my grip tightened without me consciously trying. A flash of fear shook me—what if the demon inside me refused to stop?—but righteous anger doused that feeling pretty quickly.

"You make me sick," I said. "What made you think I'd *ever* go for someone like you?"

"It—it was worth a shot," he wheezed. "I saw you by the pool earlier. Couldn't resist."

For a heartbeat, I thought the demon was going to go ahead and kill him—my hands felt like they were stuck to his neck—and then the spell broke. I pulled back, my grip slackening, and he sank to the ground, massaging his throat.

"Get out," I said, ice dripping from my hands to the floor.

"Huh?" He coughed. "But I'm staying here. I paid for the room—"

"If you don't get the hell out of here in the next sixty seconds, I'm calling the hotel staff."

He paled. "You wouldn't. Don't you want to talk? I've never met a human-demon before—bet you've never met anyone like me, either—"

I gave a humourless laugh. "Oh, I've met my fair share of dickheads, Ryan. Out."

He scrambled up and started shoving things into his suitcase. I watched him, making sure he didn't try anything else. Icy droplets fell from my fingers, and my heart still raced. I'd scared *myself* a bit, let alone him, but he'd struck on the one nerve everyone else had learnt never to touch. I felt the demon inside supporting my actions, but that didn't make me feel any better about almost strangling him. Mostly because in some part, the demon *was* me.

Ryan all but fled the room, just as Cara came in.

"Where's he going?" she said, raising her eyebrows as he let out a frightened noise and barrelled past her. "Ash? What's going on?"

I told her, and by the time I'd got to the end, I had to restrain her from going after him. At least my body temperature had almost returned to normal—which for me, was still freezing cold.

"What a dick," she said, throwing her bag across the room and spilling makeup everywhere. "I'd never have thought it. Jesus. And he's a sex demon?"

"Basically."

"And I thought the world was messed up enough already." She marched across the room and grabbed her bag, haphazardly throwing lipstick back into it. "Do you want to move to a different hotel? I'm cool with spending more for a private suite if it means avoiding twats like him."

"It's fine, he's gone," I said, brushing my hair from my eyes, partly to reassure myself I was still present, still human. "I don't think he'll be coming back."

"Good." She shuddered, walking over to her bed and shifting a pile of souvenirs onto the floor. "Creep."

"Sorry," I said, sinking back onto my own bed and knocking slivers of ice off the covers.

"What're you sorry about?" said Cara.

"Weird shit always happens to me. I did warn you." I massaged my forehead.

"I don't care. I told you, it doesn't matter. What's with all the water?"

The ice had melted to a puddle on the floor.

"Magic," I said, sighing.

"I keep forgetting about that," said Cara, eying the puddle and the scattered ice slivers I'd knocked onto the floor. "Mad, isn't it? My best friend's a sorceress."

I didn't say anything. Using magic had reminded me of how *not normal* I really was. I'd avoided it for a time, fearing it would bring out the demon. The idea of being able to summon ice-fire, freeze things, make shadows dance around me, sounded awesome in theory, but it came with a price. Add in the total train wreck my life had turned into over the past few months, and I'd have traded in magic along with every penny in my bank account for the life I could never have back.

"Could you freeze that water again?" said Cara. "Or is there some kind of limit?"

"Normally there is," I said, struggling to drive the thoughts away. "But I froze a canal once."

I pushed away the memory of cold hands scrabbling from the darkness, and a face both familiar and unfamiliar at the same time.

"Epic." She grinned. "So normal people can definitely not do it? For sure?"

"Only people with a connection to the Darkworld can," I said. "If you're extra-sensitive to it—can you see harpies?"

Her lips pursed in clear confusion. "Harpies? I don't know."

"Massive ugly birds. Some people can see them if they're sensitive to the Darkworld. Lots of people at my university can, but they just think they're really big ravens, I guess. Probably part of the Venantium's tricks."

Cara walked around the pool of water. "Hmm. I might've seen one when I was staying at yours. Can you show me how to use magic?"

"That... probably isn't a good idea. It attracts demons." I sat back on my bed. "Trust me, the last thing I want to do is give them a reason to target you." *Besides... you probably can't do that.* But Cara's bright, interested eyes and willingness to listen tempted me to tell her the theory. I'd already told her about the Darkworld, and the other messed-up things in my life. It was pretty unlikely she was a magic-user—she hadn't commented on the harpies in Blackstone that time a flock of them showed up, for one thing.

Maybe I was selfish for wanting to offload the burden

onto someone else, but I really didn't want to speak to the other magic-users I knew right now. Cara was safe.

Cara sighed, perching on her bed. "You're right, but it sucks."

It did suck. I thought for a bit, wondering if I *could* teach someone the theory who didn't have a connection.

"Tell you what," I said, inspiration striking. "I could teach you how to make a demon-proof shield. I can't guarantee it'll work, but if you can do it, it'll keep you safe."

"Seriously?" Cara's eyes lit up. "Demon-proof?"

"It wouldn't work on the higher demons, but it makes you invisible to anything else. Even other magic-users. I'm wearing one right now."

Cara scrutinised me. "I can't see anything."

"That's the point." I smiled, or tried to. "It's invisible. If a member of the Australian Venantium walked by, they'd not be able to tell I had a Darkworld connection."

"You can tell when people do?" she said, blinking at me.

"I would, if they didn't wear shields. All the *venators* do. If they didn't, I'd be able to see... like, a shadow, all around them." In fact, thinking about it, I'd never actually seen another magic-user on the street. And I hadn't been able to sense anything off about Ryan, so someone must have taught him how to conjure a shield. Interesting. And scary. How many people walked around under shields, even here?

Cara bounded to her feet. "Okay. So how do you do it?"

"It's like this." I paused, thinking how to put it into words to someone who couldn't see the darkness. I barely needed to *think* about contacting the Darkworld for it to answer me, shadows coming away from the walls like living vines, swirling around me. "Can you see that?"

"See what?" She blinked, confusion furrowing her brow.

Maybe it wouldn't be possible for someone without a connection after all.

"The shadows." I held up a hand, from which shadows trailed like a long sleeve. "When I contact the Darkworld, I can make the shadows move, come over to me." I pulled the shadow straight and it spread out, like a veil before my body. Moving my hands, I made the veil stretch around my whole body, covering me from head to toe. Cara's eyes widened.

"I saw something then!" she said. "You're kind of... glowing."

"Glowing?" I echoed, glancing down at myself. *Glowing isn't exactly a word I'd use to describe the Darkworld.* But I'd never asked what it looked like to outsiders.

"Kind of. Like... you know when it's so hot the air looks kind of hazy? That. You've got this kind of glow around you. Like a halo?"

I couldn't help but laugh at that one. "I look like an angel?"

"No..." She looked confused at why I was laughing.

"Sorry," I said. "It's just, you know. The Darkworld. The demons. It's like the opposite. People think it's like Hell."

She gave a short laugh. "Hmm. I guess it does look a bit shadowy. Turn around."

I turned to the side, and she exclaimed.

"I definitely saw it then! It's like you're under some kind of... like, veil."

"You *can* see it!" I let the veil drop to the ground, where it joined back with the shadows across the floor. "Okay, you try grabbing them."

"Grabbing what?"

"The shadows. It's trickier if you can't see the Darkworld, but watch me."

I reached down and the Darkworld practically rushed at me, shadows flowing through my hands in a thin stream.

Cara couldn't keep a tinge of scepticism out of her expression, but she did the same as me and reached toward the shadows gathering on the floor in the gaps between the sunlight streaming through the blinds from outside. The shadows didn't respond to her the way they would to someone with a Darkworld connection, and she picked up a handful of nothing.

"Did it work?"

"Not exactly," I said. "Maybe it only works for people with the connection."

She tried again, and the same thing happened. Again. And again. Her forehead wrinkled in concentration, and she grabbed at the air over and over.

"I look like a complete twat," she muttered, with another swipe of the hand. "Tell me there isn't a demon, sitting laughing at me right now."

"Nah, you'd have heard me talking to it by now."

Cara's hands dropped, and she visibly shivered. "That's so… intrusive. I can't believe they just won't let you be."

"It's not so bad now," I said, with an offhand shrug both of us knew I didn't mean. "There aren't so many here, anyway. Guess it's because the population's lower."

"Huh?"

"Demons hang about where there are a lot of people," I explained. I kept forgetting which particular pieces of information I'd told her, since I was used to talking about this only with Claudia and the others, who knew more than I did, if anything. Just thinking about our old meeting room made my heart squeeze.

"More victims?" said Cara, with another shiver.

"More magical energy. And more chance of there being sorcerers, I guess. But they're really not bothered about ordinary people, or even most magic-users."

"They're bothered about you."

"Yeah… but like I said. Used to it."

Cara's eyes narrowed. "Doesn't mean I have to like it. Creeps."

I gave a faint smile. "Really, it's nothing. Compared to everything else… a drop in the ocean."

Drunken singing echoed from outside. Cara jumped. "The others'll be back soon," she said.

"Yeah, maybe we can try again some other time?" I said.

"Sure thing, but I guess I'll have to stick to rereading Harry Potter for magic." She smiled. "Anyway, it's our holiday now. Nothing's going to ruin it."

I managed to return her smile, pushing the darkness away. "Damn straight."

SEX DEMON ASIDE, the rest of the trip was just as fun as the first half, and for a wonder, I did manage to put demons out of my mind. I'd been dreading my birthday for months, but thanks to Cara's expert planning, she'd managed to book us a scuba diving trip that day on the Great Barrier Reef. We had a whole day in paradise, lounging on an ocean liner in the pure blue sea, watching for dolphins, and snorkelling on the pristine reefs, where we only had to put your head under the water to be greeted by a scene straight from a wildlife documentary. Everything was crystal clear through the water: the vibrant corals and the shoals of glittering fish. I wasn't too comfortable with depending on a tank for air during our twenty-minute scuba diving session, but it was worth it to have a close encounter with ocean wildlife.

The next few days passed too quickly for my liking, but we were busy all the time, riding a cable car over the rainforest, taking tours, rafting, learning to surf. But all too soon, we were boarding our flight to Sydney and facing a thirty-hour journey home.

Except I didn't have a home anymore.

I'D NEVER HAVE PREDICTED that at nineteen, I'd be living alone in a single bedsit the size of a kitchen cupboard in Manchester. Most people my age, at least those who'd gone to university, still lived with their parents. But since my entire life had shattered last April, I didn't have anyone I could call family anymore—and I couldn't just move in with Cara, even though she'd told me I was welcome to stay at any time. The people I'd called my parents had moved away from their old lives, now, after their house had burned down in a fire. A fire that was my fault.

They'd left the city. I didn't know exactly where they'd gone, but I'd heard people talking. I'd only gone back once, to the place where I'd spent the first eighteen years of my life. Just to find out what was the latest. To make sure they were okay. Even if it broke my heart that Mum and Dad were happy without me in their lives.

Erasing a life is complicated in this modern world. Every stage of your life is on record—birth certificates, school reports, ID. It ought to be impossible to do what *she* had done, and make a couple raise a child who wasn't theirs, a child who shouldn't even exist. Yet she'd done that, and erased the evidence when it suited her. I could only assume she'd made everyone else who knew me or my parents forget, too. Or maybe that was why they'd moved.

That woman. And yet… she'd honoured her last promise. One night last term, I'd sent her a message, even though I'd sworn never to have anything to do with her again. I'd pleaded with her to do one thing for me—to give me back my own memories, even if she couldn't give me back my life. Living with half memories that hurt to think of was worse than living with the truth, however painful it might be. I wanted to remember my parents, even if they would never know they had ever had a daughter. Call me a masochist, but I wanted to *feel* the pain. Not an echo of it. If nothing else, it might give me a shot at coming to some kind of peace.

My last month at home passed in a blur of mindless routine, and I counted down the days until the beginning of term from the instant the plane touched down on English soil. I kept busy as best I could. I'd never had much luck with part-time jobs, but I did luck out and find an editorial internship with an online literary journal. I also posted on my blog about Cara's and my adventures in Australia, which proved a hit with the small tribe of readers I'd accumulated, especially the snorkelling videos.

I also joined the gym, although I'd once shunned exercise of any kind. Running on the treadmill drew my concentration away from brooding, usually because I had to concentrate on not making an ass of myself and face-planting. Then I spent my evenings on my laptop, reading books and writing reviews. I went out with Cara a few times, but I wanted to avoid running into people from school. There was a reason I'd opted for accommodation on the other side of the city; I didn't want to become the object of gossip. I could hardly tell them the truth; that my parents weren't actually my parents but had lived with false memories for the past eighteen years. I'd debated going back into therapy, but while I had the money for the best therapists in the world, there was nobody on the earth who would understand that my mental state was not down to my breakup with Leo, but the foundations of my life being yanked out from underneath me. I'd end up committed if I told anyone the truth.

According to the doctor's records, I did still exist, so I pretended to be stressed about the start of term in order to tick the right boxes to get back on medication for the first time in over a year. I never should have stopped taking it in the first place, but learning demons existed had made my diagnosed clinical depression seem like a minor inconvenience. Meds helped. Having my parents back would have helped more, but you couldn't have it all.

On my last night, I finished packing up all my possessions and tried to figure out how I was going to carry them. I'd spent the last few weeks of summer term frantically trying to sell things off; my new cupboard-sized flat barely had space for me, let alone all my possessions, and carrying a stack of boxes on three trains and a bus was impossible even for a magic-user. In the end, I'd had to put most of my essentials—mainly kitchen stuff—in storage at campus like the international students did. It was either that or hire a removal van. So many ridiculous complications to worry about. *If this is what being an adult feels like, they can keep it.*

A year ago, the people I'd thought were my parents had driven me up to Blackstone in the car, helped me unpack, hugged me goodbye. A year ago, I'd thought—bar a few demons—that my life was normal. I'd wanted a new start, an escape from the demons I didn't understand. And for a brief time, I'd got that. I'd made friends, made a life I'd never known I was missing back in the city.

And then the demons had smashed into that life and reduced it to shreds.

I tried once again to repack my case. My souvenir collection from Australia filled half a suitcase, but I didn't regret it. I also had hundreds of photographs on the new camera Cara had bought me for my birthday. I was glad I'd spent that particular day out of the country; it would have just been a self-pity-fest otherwise, given that no one except Cara had even acknowledged the day.

In the end I managed to get everything into a large suitcase and three bags. I collapsed onto my bed, which creaked in protest. The crappy old mattress had given up the ghost years before. It was my own fault for opting for budget accommodation, but I hated spending money that I didn't feel entitled to. Especially when it came from the one person to whom I didn't want to owe anything more.

I logged into my laptop to check my emails for the last time. A couple of comments on my blog, some spam telling me I'd won the lottery—and a message from Cyrus.

I hadn't heard from Leo's brother in months, unless you counted a "happy birthday" post on Facebook. I'd tried to avoid social networking sites—overtly optimistic updates and petty whining grated on my nerves equally—so I had no idea whereabouts he was right now.

**"Hey, Ash. Hope you enjoyed your trip. I checked out your blog, and it looked amazing!**

**I hope you don't mind me contacting you, and I understand if you don't want to talk about what happened with my brother. But I'd like us to be friends, if that's okay? :)**

**You're going back to uni soon, right? Would you be able to keep me updated on what's**

**happening in Blackstone? I don't like asking favours, but after all the crap that happened last year, I'd like to know everything's fine and if you need any help with anything.**

**Hope to talk soon,**

**Cyrus."**

I HESITATED. He was right; there was no reason why we couldn't be friends. I wondered what would happen to our group this term, now that Cyrus and Leo were gone. I'd never particularly liked Berenice and Howard, and that just left Claudia. Aside from a few shared experiences, most of which had involved demons, Claudia and I weren't really close as friends. We'd drifted apart after Leo had left, which was partly my fault. We couldn't seem to be together without painful subjects coming up.

But I decided to reply to Cyrus's email, anyway.

**"HEY CYRUS,**

**I'M happy to stay friends. I'd like to keep in touch. I'll be sure to update you if anything happens in Blackstone. Something did happen when I was in Australia. I met an incubus from London. What are the odds, right? But it seemed to be a genuine coincidence. He said he generally avoided sorcerers.**

I NEVER MENTIONED this last year, but the demons have been getting into my dreams for ages.

Usually they're trying to freak me out, but sometimes they speak to me through my connection to the Darkworld when I'm asleep. I didn't mention it because I didn't want Berenice thinking I was in league with demons or anything, and it didn't seem important. But the other week I dreamt about Mephistopheles and he said that Lucifer was going to make a move soon. He kind of let it slip, I think. I don't know what he meant, but it sounded like the demons were planning something. It was just the one dream, though; I haven't heard anything since.

HOPE YOU'RE ENJOYING your travels. Where are you heading next?

BEST,
    Ash

## 3

## HOMECOMING

Blackstone University was, as usual, huddled under a raincloud. When I finally dismounted the bus at the student village on campus, I ran right to the porter's lodge to collect my keys, ducking under my hood to avoid the pelting raindrops. Alex, Sarah, and I had applied to continue living together before the argument last term, so now was as good a time as any to make it up to avoid an uncomfortable year. New keys in hand, I searched for House 23.

"Ash!" shrieked a voice, and Alex threw herself at me.

I staggered backwards. Alex tended to move with a ceaseless energy that made everyone else feel exhausted just watching her. Her vibrant red hair and bright clothes matched her personality, and she'd acquired a nose piercing since I'd last seen her.

"I'm sorry!" she said. "I'm sorry I was such a bitch. Please say you aren't still mad at me."

*Well, this'll be easier than I'd expected.* "I'm not mad at you," I said. "Where's our new flat?"

"You're telling me you don't know the way?"

"Everything looks the same in the rain," I said, gesturing at the identical blocks that housed most of Blackstone University's students.

"Yeah, but still. Common sense. It's this way." She steered me along the path. "You might be an academic genius, but honestly, Ash, you've got the memory of a goldfish."

"Cheers," I said. "It *has* been three months, though. Is Sarah in?"

"Wait and see!" She used her fob to open the door to the block.

I heaved my suitcase over the threshold and dropped my bag of souvenirs on the floor.

"Oops. Here, have a koala." I gave her one of many cuddly koalas I'd brought back from Australia.

"Cute! I'm so sorry I missed your birthday. I have your present in my bag somewhere! I'll get it when we get to the room. We're on the third floor this year!"

"Too many stairs," said another voice. Sarah came down the stairs. Her mousy brown hair was plastered to her forehead with rainwater, and she wore a pink rain poncho.

"Hey," I said. "Want a koala?"

"Thanks, Ash!" She beamed at me, putting the koala into her coat pocket. "I've missed you guys so much! Things are so *boring* back home."

"Sarah, are you coming?" her mother called from outside.

"I'm dying," said Sarah. "And I've only got half my bags up those stairs. This is torture."

"We can do it!" said Alex, as though we'd been conquering Everest or something. I laughed. I'd forgotten how much I liked talking to my flatmates. They were the epitome of ordinary and just plain *fun*.

I went to pick up my other possessions from storage, after deflecting Alex's and Sarah's questions as to why I'd left them behind. I told them my parents had moved south and hadn't been able to pick me up, to explain why I'd been in Manchester on my own all summer. It was hard coming up with an explanation that would make sense to ordinary people. *My parents forgot I existed because I wasn't really their daughter* wouldn't go down well. It didn't help that trying to avoid memory triggers was like dancing blindfolded on a minefield.

*I definitely need to work out more,* I thought as I heaved the second load of boxes upstairs, wondering why no one had thought to install a lift. A gym membership had been far out of my budget last year, but now I had a small fortune in my bank account, I could even fork out for a year-long gold membership and still be able to afford to eat.

As I surveyed my new room, the irony of it all struck me head-on. I was surrounded by material things—television, games console, iPhone, digital camera, e-reader—and yet what did any of that matter, when I could never have my old life back? I'd trade it all in a heartbeat for one chance to forget that I'd lived a lie for most of my life. One last night watching TV with my parents, listening to Mum chat about customers who'd come into the shop where she worked, to Dad complaining about clients. One last holiday to Windermere, and my aunt Eve's cottage. One last chance to believe I was normal.

*Stop that.* I blinked away tears. It wouldn't do any good to go back to moping now.

All the same, it was hard, when I was unpacking, not to think about last year. Saying goodbye to my parents, reassuring them I could look after myself, that I'd follow my mum's instructions on how to cook and clean. At the time I'd barely been a legal adult, living away from home for the first time. Now I felt a lot older than nineteen, like I'd mentally aged ten years in just one.

The walls in my new room looked bare without my collection of landscape paintings—they'd been one of the first things I'd been forced to sell, along with most of my ornaments. I'd donated a lot of things I'd owned to charity. Even my old television had gone; it was far too heavy for me to transport back home on the train, and in the end, I'd decided that it wasn't an unreasonable idea to buy myself a new flat-screen model that was compact enough to carry in my rucksack. And the e-reader I'd purchased had enabled me to download most of my books for cheap or free, so I could sell the physical copies. There was no shortage of prospective literature students looking for discounted classics and textbooks.

Still, the purchases had taken a chunk out of my savings. I needed to look for a job: that was first on the agenda this term. I felt tainted every time I spent any of the fortune-teller's money.

Of course, now I had my student loan. I had no idea how the fortune-teller had manipulated the student loan company into not noticing my bizarre familial circumstances, but I suspected it involved subliminal mind alteration and memory implantation. That woman was nothing if not thorough.

My notice board this year had no photos from before university. There were plenty of Cara and me, and pictures from various socials last year featuring myself and my flatmates, usually with the English Literature Society. Of course, none were of Leo. I didn't even own any photographs of the two of us. Our brief, month-and-a-half-long relationship was nothing more than a tiny part of last year, on the surface.

But for me, it had been the final blow that had splintered my broken heart.

Rain streaked the window in rivulets. Now I was on the third floor, I could see much farther from my window than I could last year. The field that also doubled as a car park ran down to a swathe of trees that sloped down the hillside, turning to fields intersected by country lanes, one of which led to Blackstone itself. It made a change from the shady alleyway just visible from the grimy window in the room I'd been staying in for most of summer. Plus now I was in Blackstone, I would be free to walk around without running into any dark spaces.

Demons couldn't harm anyone from the other side of the Barrier anyway, but I was glad that the Venantium's extra security measures around Blackstone hid them from my eyes. Even if they could still get into my head. *No way am I letting that happen again.* I wasn't going to be at the demons' mercy, not this time. I forced all negative thoughts from my mind, with difficulty. *New year, new start,* I told myself, and went to find my friends.

Alex and Sarah were already chatting to our new flatmates. Within five minutes we'd gone through the standard introductions. There were two guys, both first years. One was an IT student, the other was studying natural sciences.

The girl was Leo's former flatmate, Rachel.

*So much for a new start.* She regarded me with a smile that bordered on creepy, which was pretty ordinary for her. She was a certified stoner with a talent for impersonating voices, and last year she'd freaked me out more than once by seeming to know things she shouldn't.

"I hope you had a nice summer, Ash," she said, her voice slightly dreamy.

"I did, thanks," I said politely. "You?"

"It was quite fun... I'm glad I'm living with you this

year. I was afraid I wouldn't know anyone. It's a shame Leo's gone, isn't it?"

It felt like someone had jammed a wrench into my chest and twisted, hard. I could only nod.

"I suppose he's having fun now, isn't he?"

I nodded again, teeth gritted. I felt Alex and Sarah looking at me, but couldn't bear to see their pity. *Why me?*

"Why don't we go to Bargain Burgers?" said Alex loudly, breaking the tension. "I don't know about you guys, but I really can't be arsed cooking tonight."

"Good idea," said Sarah, catching on. "I need to get some cash out. Want to walk to the ATM?"

"Sure," I said, and the three of us managed to ditch our new flatmates. I felt bad for the two guys, but I couldn't be part of that conversation any longer.

Whether Rachel was doing it deliberately or not, I didn't know. I hadn't really seen much of her last term. It had been Berenice who had been determined to rub salt in the wounds, flaunting her new relationship with Howard in front of me every chance she got.

We huddled in our coats as we crossed campus. Rain lashed the ground, propelled by a strong breeze. Groups of first years were heading for the Great Hall and the obligatory welcome talk. It gave me a rush of déjà vu, not unpleasant, this time. I still had my friends.

The university campus covered a small hill and seemed to slope upwards whichever direction we walked in. Bargain Burgers was under shelter in the central square opposite the on-campus shop where Sarah worked part-time. We ducked out of the rain and into the small restaurant.

Sarah glanced at the shop across the quadrangle. "I'm dreading first shift," she said. "I'm on for twelve hours till midnight again."

"Ugh. That sucks," said Alex.

"I need to get a job this term," I said, scanning the leaflets in the window of the careers' office as we walked past. *More like, I need to get out the flat if Rachel's going to be there.* "Is the campus bookshop hiring?"

"It's shut down," said Alex.

"What?" I looked away from the adverts. "But it's the only place on campus that sells the course texts."

"I know, it's crap. I'm going to have to get mine from Waterstones in Redthorne this week. Want to go tomorrow?"

"Sure," I said. "I can hand out some CVs."

"Did you spend all your money in Australia?" said Sarah. *Oh, crap.* There was no way to explain my bizarre financial gains without lying, and I didn't want to do that any more than I had to. Stupid, given that I had a whole separate existence from my flatmates.

"Yeah, I was wondering about that," said Alex, with a scrutinising look reminiscent of Cara. "I thought you were skint?"

"I saved my scholarship money," I said, then, to change the subject, said, "Are you joining a hundred societies this term, Alex?"

"Five," said Alex. "Hiking and mountaineering kept clashing last year, and I only made it to badminton once. I'm going for self-defence this time. Karate, maybe."

"I might do the same," I said. I couldn't keep relying on magic every time something attacked me, if just because in the real world, freezing someone would attract unwanted attention.

"Sarah's going to join the Singing Club."

"Good on you!" I said. Sarah suffered from even worse confidence issues than I did; Alex forcing her into singing at open mic nights last year had been a real help.

"My evil mission is complete," said Alex. "Next step is to set both of you up. Make it a triple date, I'll bring Rex."

"Not happening," I said.

"Ash, it's been *six months*. Only way to get over a breakup is to date someone else, right?"

"Not necessarily," I said. "I don't need that kind of crap in my life right now."

Like any guy would want to date a girl who couldn't trust her own memories. Not to mention the evil demon in the back of my head who occasionally made an appearance. It might be my imagination, but when things were quiet, I could feel her there, in the occasional flashes of emotion that weren't directly connected to my own thoughts. But demons didn't *have* emotions. Maybe it was different for human-demons. Not like I had anyone to ask about it. Even talking to my friends now felt like waking again after a long sleep.

"Seriously. Double date. Let's see... Jake from LitSoc's single. And Mandeep. You're not living in the same flat anymore," she added to Sarah, who'd started to protest. "Also, the new guys in our flat. But that might be a bit weird."

"Where's Pete living this year?" said Sarah, in an obvious attempt to distract Alex from the subject of our love lives—or lack thereof.

"Back in our old flat. You'll never guess what," said Alex, a grin forming on her face. "They've only gone and put him in Terrence's old room."

"Did anyone ever find out what happened to that guy?" said Sarah, frowning.

"God knows. Maybe he died in there and no one told us. Remember the Ouija board incident?"

*Unfortunately.* I hadn't been there for that particular occasion, but it made me a tad uneasy that so many people had gotten spooked in a place where I knew for a fact Terrence had contacted demons. He *was* dead, but he'd died on a cold, dark night in the Lake District after trying to murder me. The demon possessing him had killed him. No one else knew what had gone down in his old room, but we hadn't exactly had people queuing to move in. When Pete had held a party in our flat last year and a bunch of people had shown up and decided to start looking for evil spirits in Terrence's room, something had scared the living daylights out of them—though since they'd all been pissed, I wouldn't exactly trust anything they said.

We talked of other things for a while, enjoying the chance to properly catch up with what we'd been doing over the summer. I told them stories of my travels in Australia, whilst Sarah made us laugh with her account of staying in London for a work placement, in a hostel she labelled "Hell on Earth."

Alex's summer had been fairly quiet. She'd done a lot of hiking, since she lived in Kendal, in the Lake District. But she'd also been on holiday to Greece with her family. Family holidays. Yet another thing I'd never experience again.

Despite everything, I couldn't help but be reminded of the change. It was stupid. It had been six whole months since my life had been destroyed, and yet some things still hit me like the first time. I guess it took a while to re-evaluate your whole existence.

Still, for now I focused on making plans with my friends, and on preparing to start second year as best I could. This year actually counted towards our final degree marks, which made me a bit nervous, but I was fairly confident I'd chosen the right modules. I just needed to stay on top of the reading, which rarely caused an issue, especially as I had no reason to miss lectures and get distracted due to night time excursions in the tunnels beneath Blackstone with Claudia and the others.

Claudia would be in her final year. So would Howard and Berenice. The past year had gone by far quicker than I'd anticipated, and I felt a brief pang at the thought that in less than two years, I'd' be leaving, too. Unless I did a Masters course. Alex and Sarah had joked that I'd be a permanent student, since I'd mentioned doing a PhD, too. Spending another four years reading books and writing essays seemed like a reasonable life plan to me.

My chest tightened as I remembered how proud my once-parents had been that I'd got into university. I'd been the first person in the family to go. It had occurred to me that I didn't really have anything in common with them, but never in a million years could I have guessed that we weren't really related.

My phone buzzed, indicating a message. I unlocked the touch screen, and my heart sank. It was a familiar number, but not one I'd saved under a name, since its owner didn't really have one.

**"I hope all is well, Ashlyn, and that you enjoyed your travels. I am sorry I have been unable to contact you. I have been staying with a group of sorcerers, and they forbid communication with the outside world. I hope to return to Blackstone soon, and I would very much like to see you. There is one thing you must do, and it's important; as soon as possible, you must purchase a fake demon heart. Any old crystal will do. You cannot afford to lose it to the enemy, and if you wear the fake around your neck and hide the true crystal elsewhere on your person, you will be safer."**

She hadn't signed it, but I knew it was my mother. The fortune-teller. Madame Persephone. Melivia Blackstone. She had a number of names, a number of faces, and every one of them told a lie.

I didn't want to see her. I could feel the dam suppressing my emotions tremble at the thought. She was a liar of the worst sort. She deceived and manipulated everyone she met, and me most of all. Although some part of me understood why she'd made the choices she had, the anger still dominated.

*Screw her.* I left the message unanswered. But I made a mental note to go crystal shopping.

When I switched on my laptop that night, I saw that Cyrus had instant messaged me, asking how Blackstone was.

**"Still raining,"** I replied.

A reply pinged immediately, though my laptop was slow to load the attached image. **"Figures. Check out where I am! I'm sure it's 20 degrees colder here. ;)"**

The photograph loaded, showing an expanse of mountains, snow-capped peaks touching the sky. Cyrus stood on a mound of snow, grinning, wearing a snowsuit and holding a pair of skis.

**"Where are you?"** I typed.

**"Colorado. It's awesome! We're skiing here in the mountains for a bit, then we're heading north."**

**"Seriously?"** I typed. **"Not much happening then, is there?"**

**"Lol, it's pretty insane. We're going to spend another few weeks here, then we're flying back to Europe. Might come and pay you a visit?"**

I swallowed. My hands started shaking at the thought of seeing Leo again.

**"Maybe."**

**"Let me know how things are going. I'll keep you updated. Have fun!"**

**"You too. Enjoy your time in the States!"**

Right now, I wasn't ready to see Leo. I felt grateful to Cyrus for only sending me pictures of scenery, not of Leo. He rarely even mentioned his brother by name, which I appreciated. Cyrus had always been the reasonable one in the group; as the eldest, he'd been the designated responsible adult. Generally he'd been reluctant to go ahead with our ridiculous schemes, but was willing to cover for us and help out anyway. Reading between the lines, I supposed he acted old for his age because he'd been used to looking out for Leo after their father had ditched them.

Leo… Leo was fire and recklessness. He could both drive me to frustration by winding me up, then startle me with his thoughtfulness and sensitivity. He was one of a kind, and if I saw him again, I honestly didn't know whether I'd punch him first or hug him.

And I wasn't sure which would make me hate myself more.

# 4

## AN OFFER

Perhaps Cyrus's photographs triggered that night's dream, where I found myself sunk up to my waist in a snowdrift. Icy water soaked through my clothes, weighing me down; I could feel myself sinking farther, but couldn't pull myself free.

The snow numbed my arms, making them feel like dead weights. I slid down farther, snow brushing the top of my coat. I shuddered as it touched my neck. All my senses were dulled, and I felt like a limp doll, helplessly sinking beneath the snow. The white rose up to meet me, closing over my head, and I heard a roaring in my ears quite disconnected from the snow. I fought to bring my head back to the surface, and choked as half-melted sleet filled my mouth.

The snow began to melt, rapidly, and around me, my prison turned to a whirlpool, catching me and flinging me from side to side. I broke the surface, gasping for breath, and saw nothing but open sea. A colossal wave rose, and a figure stood on the crest, violet eyes staring down at me.

"Long time no see, Ash," said Mephistopheles in Leo's voice. "Have you thought any more about my offer?"

I couldn't have spoken if I'd tried; every breath was stolen between breaking waves over my head.

"Perhaps a change of scenery is in order."

A gasp escaped my lips. The sea vanished in an instant and I now hovered in the air over green fields, but there was no parachutist strapped to my back. The land stretched out beneath me, gleaming vibrant green and yellow with tiny towns nestled between low hills.

"Such a beautiful world you live in," Mephistopheles said. "You humans take so much for granted. Dream manipulation can only bring so much satisfaction. I can see why Lucifer wants to return so badly."

"What's he waiting for, then?" I said, ignoring the warning tug at the corner of my mind. These dreams brought all my pent-up anger and pain to the surface, and the sight of Mephistopheles masquerading as Leo did away with the usual instinct against goading demons.

"Patience, little fledgling. He is looking for something important, as the Venantium know well. It's just too bad that they aren't searching in the right place. Their days are numbered."

"So you keep saying," I said, but my voice sounded small in the endless sky.

"You have little faith, Ashlyn. There are plans in motion that you could never anticipate. The great Seven will rise, with Lucifer at the helm, and all will be cast into darkness."

At his words, a swathe of blackness swept over the land below. I saw houses burst into flames, lights winking out like stars as they were swallowed by the encroaching darkness. Violet eyes blinked into existence everywhere I looked.

"You are in an unusual position, Ashlyn. We have told you this repeatedly. You alone have the luxury of choice. Why support a dying race? You could have it all if you chose the Darkworld."

"A life in darkness? No thanks," I said, keeping my eyes on Mephistopheles rather than the chaos engulfing the world below. "I told you I don't want to be immortal. I don't want you to control me."

"You control your own fate, Ashlyn. That is the human in you. You have the freedom we demons can only dream of."

"Are you dreaming now?" I said. "Or is it just me who's sleeping? How are you controlling my dreams?"

"You are dreaming. I am not. That is our curse," said Mephistopheles. "We cannot choose to dream. Every second in the Darkworld is a waking dream, whether we like it or not."

"Well," I said, "That has me convinced. Not. Seriously, give it up. I'm leaving."

I closed my eyes, concentrating on willing my mind back to consciousness. I felt my eyes slowly flicker, the lids lifting, and blinked awake.

*At least I don't have sleep paralysis this time,* I thought, swinging my legs over the side of the bed. I grimaced as I saw the time on my alarm clock. Eight o'clock was far too early to get up on a day without lectures. Still, I felt wide awake. I pushed open my window to clear the stuffy air, looking out at the light gilding the trees. It had been too long since I'd walked in those woods.

I dressed quickly, opting for my usual hoodie and jeans combo. It wasn't like there'd be anyone on the woodland trail at this time.

A damp chill lingered in the air, and the trail was awash with rainwater from the day before. My feet sank into mud and I almost lost a shoe in the quagmire. *Great idea, Ash.*

I left the trail and walked around the outskirts of campus instead, sticking to the paths. Even part of campus had turned into a swamp. There was some kind of construction work going on around the oldest lecture theatres near the Great Hall, and the cleared area had turned into a pond of murky water.

A loud *caw* split the silence, and I looked up to see a black shape fly overhead. A harpy, one of the spies of the Venantium. I hated the creatures, and not just because they looked like winged, deformed human children with corpse-like features and eagle's talons. They'd attacked me on more than one occasion; admittedly, both times I'd been trespassing in the tunnels around the Venantium's Head-quarters, but I thought slicing my arms open and nearly killing me was a step too far for security measures.

The harpies were just one example of the Venantium's hypocrisy. They were Darkworld creatures, enslaved to act as spies and message-carriers by a group that existed to keep beings from the Darkworld out. Admittedly, they were pretty harmless compared to everything else that lived there.

It was strange what Mephistopheles had said. *We cannot choose to dream. Every second in the Darkworld is a waking dream, whether we like it or not.* He made it sound like demons didn't *want* to live in the Darkworld, something that contradicted everything I thought I knew about them. They thrived in the dark and coldness, fearing light and warmth, and as far as I knew, they invaded our world for malicious purposes alone. Before the creation of the Barrier by the earliest sorcerers, they'd been free to move between their world and ours. But after a series of attacks on humans and several power-crazed sorcerers' attempts to build demon armies to conquer the world, magic-users had used some kind of spell to permanently keep demons out of our world.

Of course, sorcerers could always find ways to summon them anyway.

Truthfully, I had no idea of the mechanics of the Barrier and the Darkworld, only that demons fed on magical energy, and people with the connection to the Darkworld were a target they couldn't resist. Anyone could be possessed, but possessing a sorcerer gave a demon access to their powers. I'd seen this first-hand when Mephistopheles had wreaked havoc by taking over Jude's body. In addition to their own mind-powers—which ranged from telepathy and mind-reading to killing at a touch—they could also manipulate humans and use their own magic. The image of Leo possessed had been branded on my mind, like he'd literally marked me when he'd touched my face, smiling a smile that wasn't his own. Mephistopheles might be imprisoned in the Darkworld, the closest thing to hell as possible, but no punishment could be enough for that demon.

Demons couldn't die. Like all spirits, they were immortal, and could only be sent back to their permanent home. I supposed it did sound like a curse when I thought of the idea of existing in an endless black void, unable to die, unable to dream. Like the doppelgänger. She'd been part-demon, the remains of a human-demon killed, whose anger had brought her back from the Darkworld like a ghost. But she'd been out for revenge and hadn't chosen to come back. Not really.

It baffled me that any human would choose that existence, yet Lucifer *lived* there, even though he was human. As one of very few sorcerers who had worked out how to separate from his body and travel to the Darkworld, he could move between the worlds. When he returned to our world he simply took on another host body, exactly like a demon would. That, as Dr Philips of the Venantium had put it, was the price of immortality. One had to kill to return to life.

The fortune-teller was the only person I'd met who'd done that and survived. Melivia Blackstone had lived in Blackstone over 150 years ago, and had been enticed into being a demon's host by a mysterious stranger, Lucifer. When the same demon had killed her entire family, Lucifer had offered to save her by taking her into the Darkworld with him. The demon, left behind, had wreaked havoc, leading to the Demon Wars, an event which still haunted the Venantium to this day.

Melivia had accompanied Lucifer back to our world twenty years ago, not realising that so much time had passed whilst she was in the Darkworld that everyone she knew was long dead, and the world had changed beyond recognition. From what I conjectured, after that she'd turned on Lucifer and helped bring him down, then decided to devote her life to helping other magic-users. She'd also had an affair with a higher demon, leading to... me.

I'd never have believed it if I didn't know it to fit the facts. The fortune-teller was the person I'd least think would associate with demons, given what had happened to her family, and whatever the Venantium thought of independent sorcerers, she only ever used her magic to help people. Or so I'd thought. Now that I knew she'd used Influence to build a web of lies around my whole life to stop me from guessing who she—and I—really was, I wasn't sure her intentions were always so benign. *It was necessary* was the phrase she used to justify tearing my life to pieces, and even if Lucifer had been out to kill me, hoaxing an innocent couple into thinking I was their daughter, whilst masquerading as my distant aunt, had proven how dubious her morals were. My parents had forgotten the entire deception once it had unravelled; as far as they were concerned, they'd never had a daughter. I alone had to suffer with the double memories. It felt like I'd stolen someone else's life, even though I hadn't a clue it was happening.

I'd started to get headaches whenever I came close to guessing, at the time when the fortune-teller's magic had been limited when she'd been the Venantium's prisoner. Then Mephistopheles had burned down my old house, attracting Cara's attention, and she'd realised something was up. By the time I'd got back to Manchester, she'd seen too much for me to lie. Leo and I had fought against Mephistopheles when he'd possessed a woman in the town centre, and sent him back to the Darkworld.

As it turned out, however, Mephistopheles had played both of us. It was merely a trap to ensure that Leo got hold of the demon heart, which still partially anchored Mephistopheles to this world. Through the heart, he'd possessed Leo, and—

I'd grabbed my own demon heart, and my fist clenched, the sharp edges of the amethyst crystal digging into my palm. I wore the crystal around my neck on a string, so it looked like an ordinary, cheap pendant, certainly not as though it stored 150 years' worth of gathered magical energy. A demon's heart tied it to this world whilst it possessed someone. In my case, it was both the source of my magic—and a means of control. Terrence and Jude had both almost killed me when they'd gotten hold of it.

It was what the demons wanted, a way to control me. No matter how they tried to persuade me to join them, I refused point-blank. For some bizarre reason, all demons adhered to a rule whereby they had to have a person's permission before they possessed them. Like a contract. Except, if the person refused, the demon could kill them, so most people gave in. Even Leo had.

My mind had wandered down dark paths again. I shook my head to clear it and felt something brush against my hair. *Low-flying bird?* I thought, frowning as I looked up.

A harpy circled me, just above my head.

"Shit!" I said. "Get out of it!"

I flapped my hands at it, as though that would encourage it to go away. It continued to circle, reminding me of Edgar Allen Poe's raven.

"You're not supposed to be here," I said, and took a tentative step forward.

The harpy dived in front of me, talons outstretched. Instinctively, I reached for the Darkworld and felt ice coat my hands.

"Don't come any closer," I said, warningly.

Someone else came around the corner of the path. My heart sank. I could lower my hands, but I didn't want the harpy to attack me. But neither did I want any randomer to see me using magic. *What the hell's up with this thing?*

"Ash!" The figure walked toward me. David. Not my favourite person. A year ago he'd been my flatmate, and I'd thought—well, it had been my friends, really—there might be something between us. Then he'd revealed himself as a spy for the Venantium, and I'd found out he'd been assigned me as a target since I was an unregistered magic-user. I hadn't been best pleased to find out, to say the least. We had barely spoken since, which suited me just fine. The last thing I wanted was more complications.

"Hi, Ash," said David. "Have a good summer?" I

couldn't tell much from his tone. A hint of embarrassment, maybe. Considering our history, I wasn't surprised.

"Great, until one of your spies started attacking me," I said, gesturing at the harpy. "What's its problem?"

"Sorry," said David, raising a hand. The harpy swooped off with another *caw*. Horrible thing. "I asked it to find you. I wasn't sure where you were living this year. I need to talk to you."

"What about?" I said warily. *Oh no.* As if I'd let anyone else play mind games with me again.

"I have... well, the Venantium want to speak to you, but I told them I'd ask you first. Um... it was Dr Philips, actually. She wants to know if you'd consider working for us."

"You're kidding, right?" I said, taking a step back. *No way.*

David gave me an apologetic look. "I said I didn't think you'd want to, but I had to ask. They're looking for new people to work in the field, and, well, you've had more experience with demons than most novices. You've fought how many?"

"Only two, and it was the fortune-teller who beat Mephistopheles," I said. The Venantium would have to try harder if they wanted me on their team.

"And you helped take down all those Skele-Ghouls, and the human-demon. You can't deny it, you're a fighter, and we need your help."

"Me, a fighter?" I couldn't help laughing. "I can't even do self-defence."

"You're a natural magic-user, that's what I meant," said David. "I've worked at the Venantium since I was sixteen, and I've never even *seen* a demon." Was that *envy* in his tone? Seriously?

"Be glad you haven't," I said coldly. "I'm not interested

in being the Venantium's lapdog. In case you've forgotten, they locked me up underground, and one of their members tried to bury me alive."

David cleared his throat, shifting from one foot to the other. "Jude was a traitor," he said. "I know you and Dr Philips have never really got along, but... well, this is different. You won't be a spy or an informant or anything. You don't have to tell us anything about yourself *or* your friends. We just need your help with investigating demon attacks, shadow-beasts, that sort of thing. You'll get paid, too." He looked me in the eyes at that point, but I refused to meet his gaze.

"You can't bribe me," I said.

"It isn't a bribe. The pay's good, really good actually."

"Because I'd be risking my life?"

David shifted on his feet again. "It's up to you. It'll help us stop Lucifer. We're just trying to keep everyone safe, Ash. Won't you at least think about it?"

I sighed. As reasonable as his arguments were, I just couldn't picture myself agreeing with the Venantium on any terms, much less fighting for them. It was true that I needed a distraction, and hell, if there was anything I could do to help stop Lucifer from coming back, then maybe...

I shook my head. "I'll think about it. That's the only answer you're getting."

"Okay," he said. "Thanks, Ash. I mean it."

"Whatever," I said. "Can I get on with my morning walk in peace now?"

David blinked. "What—of course. Sorry for bothering you."

"It's okay," I said, suddenly tired. I didn't want to fight with everyone I met. Maybe even David and I could speak peaceably without clashing. I still hadn't forgiven him, but I didn't have room in my heart for any more grudges.

"Come to the headquarters on Monday at seven if you're interested, okay?"

I nodded.

*Yeah. I'll think about it.* I wondered what Leo would think about me fighting for the Venantium. Not that it mattered. *Get a grip,* I thought. *Stop thinking about him. Stop it.*

Coming back to university brought all the bad feelings back. Maybe I needed this distraction. If anything, it'd give me the chance to keep up to date on developments without being blindsided. Besides, I did need a job. And in a way, I'd missed hanging out with other magic-users. They couldn't all be as stuck-up as Jude had been.

Just as long as they never found out I was a human-demon. Because then *I'd* become their target.

**5**

## PIT OF HORRORS

I spent Freshers' Week enjoying myself with my friends —my last week of freedom before second year really started. On the first night out, when my friends suggested taking the bus to Redthorne, the nearest town, and its most infamous nightclub, Satan's Pit, I felt a measure of dread settle in my stomach. I'd avoided the place for most of last term, using revision as an excuse to skip shopping trips and nights out. Redthorne was where Mephistopheles had made his final stand and taken over Leo's body. Even when I'd been forced to go there to get the train home for the holidays, I'd rushed through the streets as fast as I could whilst weighed down with luggage, half-paranoid that the ground would turn to a teeming mass of shadows and clawing hands.

But I'd let the fear of demons trap me before, and it made no difference. It had been months since a demon or shadow-beast attack, and I reminded myself of what I'd vowed a year ago, never to let fear hold me down again. I'd looked into hell itself and come out intact, even though life would never be the same. If something attacked me, it didn't matter. As long as they left my friends alone, I was game.

*That's how people wind up getting killed,* said a cynical voice in my head, which I ignored.

"You look amazing!" Alex shrieked as I came out of my room. I wore the new dark blue dress Cara had coaxed me into buying when we were away. It was lower cut and tighter fitting than I was used to. I tucked the amethyst pendant into the cleavage; I'd rather it wasn't on display.

"Thanks," I said, smiling. "So do you!"

Alex wore green and her heels made me look like a dwarf in comparison. I'd never got the hang of dancing in heels without tripping over or twisting an ankle. Comfy slippers were more my thing.

"Sarah! You ready?" Alex knocked on her door.

"Coming!" Sarah opened the door. She wore a pretty flowery dress with matching earrings. She looked more like she was going to a tea party than a nightclub, but Sarah and I had pretty similar views on our preferred entertainment. Clubbing ranked pretty low on the list.

"Let's hit the town!" Alex said, skipping down the corridor like an overexcited child. Really, I had to thank whoever had been responsible for putting the three of us in the same flat last year.

"You're kind of scary," I commented as Alex swung her handbag a bit too enthusiastically and scattered makeup all over the floor.

"Lighten up, Ash, it's Freshers' Week. Hey—what the hell's she *doing* in there?"

She stared through the kitchen window. I followed her gaze and it landed on Rachel, who stood alone in the middle of the room, gazing vacantly at the wall.

"She not coming?" said Alex, retrieving her lip gloss.

Sarah hesitated as if unsure whether to open the kitchen door or not.

"Doubt it," I said. "She'll be smoking weed and painting weird pictures."

"What's her issue with you?" said Sarah curiously. "I've seen her last year, but I can't think where."

"She used to live in…" This was ridiculous. I had to get used to talking about it. "…Leo's flat. She kept impersonating characters from horror films, and she was always high."

"Jesus," said Alex. "Sounds like a joy to live with."

"Yeah." I opened the flat door, speaking in an undertone in case Rachel could somehow hear us from the kitchen. A chill breeze swept up the stairs, and I shivered in the thin lacy cardigan I'd worn over my dress. Seriously, whoever *liked* going out wearing next to nothing in the coldest part of England?

"She's not as bad as Pete," said Alex. "Yet."

"I kind of wanted to avoid her," I said. "She creeps me out."

The real reason Rachel gave me the creeps was because I'd heard a demon speak when it had been just her and me in the flat, and no human could do that accurate an impersonation, especially one who shouldn't even *know* what a demon sounded like. It hadn't been my imagination, I knew that much.

Still, I tried to put Rachel out of mind. Tonight was ours, and nothing else mattered.

Pete almost drew the bus to a standstill by projectile vomiting everywhere before we'd even left campus. According to a rumour, he'd been arrested over the summer for indecent exposure, which sounded like something Pete would do. The guy was messed up in the head.

When we finally reached Satan's Pit, we found it

packed out, a heaving mass of students in varying stages of intoxication. The fiery strobe lights, fake smoke, and horror-film decorations made the dance floor a good approximation of hell, albeit one slippery with spilled drinks and vibrating with dance-floor remixes blaring from the speakers. Alex, Sarah, and I entered the noisy, unruly melee and were caught in a sea of sweaty, gyrating bodies. The music buzzed through me like adrenaline, making me feel alive, if totally deaf to everything happening around me.

"Ash!" someone yelled in my ear. I turned to see Claudia in her most outrageous getup yet, a silky blue dress that could probably double as a flimsy nightgown. It didn't surprise me at all to run into her; she practically lived here.

"Hi," I said, my voice disappearing into the ear-splitting noise. This really wasn't the place for a conversation.

"Have a good summer?" she shouted.

"Yeah!" I yelled back, ducking aside as someone fell over, nearly knocking me off my feet. I could barely see Alex and Sarah in the crowd, dodging elbows and clumsy feet.

"Wanna go outside?" she said.

I shook my head, pointing at my friends. I wouldn't have a hope of finding them again if I left.

Claudia pulled a face. "It's important!" she yelled, or that's what I lip-read, anyway.

I nodded and pushed through the crowd to follow her. Back upstairs, through the red-carpeted entryway, and out into the street.

"What is it?" I asked, wincing as the icy air outside struck my exposed skin.

"Sorry about that," said Claudia. "Mad in there, isn't it?"

"Yeah," I said, hugging my arms to myself. "First night of Freshers' Week, I guess."

"Still, at least there aren't any shadow-beasts!" She didn't bother to keep her voice down, which meant she was tipsy, borderline drunk. Not that anyone was listening, anyway.

"Don't speak too soon," I said, with a habitual glance around. Club lights spilled into the streets, but I knew too well things could hide in the shadows. Still, I hadn't seen any dark spaces yet…

"There won't be any. The Venantium upped their barriers over summer. Now they cover Redthorne, too."

Well, at least that proved they'd learned from all the disasters that had taken place last year. "Oh. Good. What did you want to talk about?"

"I was just wondering if the Venantium had tried to contact you."

*They must have asked her, too.*

"Yeah, they did," I said. "This morning, actually. David sent a harpy after me."

"Did he? That asshat." She shook her head. "Don't waste any time, do they? They got me, too. What did you say to him?" She tapped her heel on the ground.

"Um… well, I said I'd think about it. What about you?"

"I'm joining."

Whatever I'd expected, it wasn't that. I gaped at her. Claudia might act like an overgrown child at times, but she'd always known the Venantium weren't to be trusted. Hell, she'd been the one to tell me that in the first place.

"What? It's not like we have to spy on anyone."

"Just *kill demons*," I said. "We could get killed."

"I'm in dire need of some excitement in my life," she

said. "It's just you and me now. We're last of the circle of sinners." She laughed. *Definitely drunk.*

"I didn't think that was about looking for danger. It usually found its way to us by itself."

"Yeah, but where's the fun in being normal? We have magic." She gave another drunken titter. "I'm not going to sit around while Lucifer screws with our world. I'm going to fight him."

"You definitely think he's coming back?"

She gave me a *duh* look. "Course he is. He's just like any sorcerer with a grudge."

"Except for being immortal," I reminded her.

"No one," she said, firmly, "is immortal."

"Right," I said. I wasn't sure I wanted to continue this conversation. It had started raining again. The cold drizzle stung my arms.

"Join, Ash, it'll be fun."

"I said I'll think about it," I said, ducking under the shelter outside the club. "We should go back inside. I'm freezing to death here."

"Sure thing. Be seeing you soon!" And she darted back inside.

It amazed me how she could move so fast on those heels, but Claudia had always straddled the line between admirable and insane. Not for the first time, I considered that I might be the only sane magic-user around.

～

A LIGHT FLASHED.

A bare bulb, swinging like a pendulum, sending sweeping shadows over the bare floorboards. Nails jutted out like teeth. The wallpaper peeling like dead skin, hanging in folds. I could hear a faint dripping, feel a cold breeze stroke my skin, although I knew I wasn't really here. I was dreaming.

Too bad I couldn't move. I hovered at the edge of the room, a mute bystander.

And something hung from the ceiling, just above the gaping hole in the wall which had once been a door. A body. Bile rose in my throat. It looked like it had been dead for a while. The skin was greyish, the face sunken in. The corpse's hair looked like seaweed. Its limbs dangled sickeningly, and the rope around its neck was dark with dried blood.

Someone called out, "Is anyone there?" A male voice.

*Don't come in!* Something about that dead body hanging there reeked of menace.

"I can hear something," said a girl's voice. "There's— you don't think—"

I heard a door creak open behind me. Two figures came in, a guy and a girl, probably a couple of years younger than me. Shadows clung to them as they moved, but they seemed not to notice. I couldn't make out their faces, like a mist hung before my eyes.

They both recoiled at the sight of the body.

"Shit," said the guy, covering his mouth. "I think it's Jay."

The girl let out a choked sob. "Why—why would he do that?"

*Get out!* I wanted to shout, but as much as I told my body to move, I remained locked down, a helpless observer.

The guy looked at the girl. "Why would he come *here*?"

*"Because you humans are nothing if not predictable."*

The girl jumped backwards with a shriek; the guy swore.

"Did you hear that?"

"Did someone speak?"

"That wasn't…" The girl shook her head, dark hair hiding her face like curtains. "That didn't sound like a person."

"Well, what else could it be?"

The corpse raised its head, which almost came away from the body. Its legs dragged on the floor. *Something that only exists in your nightmares, humans.*

"Holy shit!" yelled the guy, as the girl screamed again, convulsively grabbing his arm.

The corpse's eyes glowed violet. Its head hung at an angle, and the gaps in its neck showed dead, greyish tendons.

*"You shouldn't have come."*

The corpse opened its mouth. Teeth jutted from grey gums, rotting and jagged.

*"Your friend met an evil fate here. But he was the lucky one."*

The guy found his voice. "Wha—what *are* you?"

*"I am the evil that took root in his soul. I am the voice that whispered in his ear. You didn't believe him."*

"What—you're some kind of demon or—"

"Sam, let's get out of here!" The girl started backing away, to the periphery of my vision.

But it was too late.

The corpse dropped to the ground, eyes aglow, arms hanging. Bare, red flash gleamed where the rope had cut its neck. In a second, it had seized the two victims by one hand each and pulled them across the floor, into the centre of the room.

"Let go!"

"Stop!" The girl sobbed in terror. "Stop—oh, God, please stop, please—"

*"No one is coming to save you, humans."*

The dead body raised its sunken head and laughed, a

horrible, inhuman sound. The demon threw the girl onto the ground, and before the guy could say a word, snapped his wrist.

He yelled in pain and tried to twist out of the corpse's grip, but it held firm, far stronger than any normal human could, alive or dead. The other hand snaked around to grab the guy's face.

*"Hold still, human."*

The guy began to scream. His face distorted, and rivulets of blood began to seep from the corners of his eyes. Darkness clung to him with sharp claws, piercing the skin.

I could hear the girl sobbing behind me, as well as a frantic rattling, like someone trying to open a locked door.

*"There is no escape for you now."*

Then the guy's face… came apart. The skin peeled; the muscles beneath twitched; flesh peeled off the bones. I couldn't look away—I couldn't even feel my limbs to move them.

The demon stood and made a sudden, sweeping gesture. The room began to shake, the walls trembling, and the girl was flung across the floor to land next to the body of her friend.

*"Be still, human. It'll be over soon."* Cold laughter. Not emotionless, like usual for a demon, but a laugh of pure sadistic joy.

The floorboards trembled, and the girl lay still, gaze fixed on the demon. I could see the whites of her eyes. She'd gone into shock.

*"You poor human. You know nothing of the true nature of this world. But I know what you really are."*

He knelt down beside the girl and stroked her face with his horrible, greying finger. Then his hand moved downwards to the crucifix she wore around her neck.

*"You believe in salvation, do you? Let me tell you something. There is no forgiving. There are no angels. There is only the Dark-world. And us."*

He took his hand away. His skin looked like paper stretched over bones.

*"How far would you go to save your own skin? Would you make a deal with the devil himself?"*

She said nothing. He kicked her, hard, in the side. She whimpered.

*"Answer me, human. I am offering you a rare privilege. Do you know who I am?"*

"I... I..." the girl choked.

*"I am Lucifer's second, Mephistopheles, and you have been chosen as my host."*

The girl stared at him, horror etched on her features. She looked incapable of speech.

*"I've decided to offer you a choice. Most humans do not survive an encounter with me, but you have interesting potential. But first: the truth. You are a sorceress. Your family have lied to you."*

The shadows inched further towards her. The mist cleared from my vision, and I saw the girl's face clearly, for the first time.

Berenice.

*"What do you choose, human?"*

The shadows cloaked my eyes again, and I awoke, tangled in the covers.

**6**

DECISION

The first thing I did was run to the bathroom to throw up. Reeling from the nightmare, I pressed my forehead to the cool floor of my en suite bathroom. My head was burning, even though the rest of me was cold as ice. Maybe I'd had one drink too many last night, but I was more inclined to blame the dream. Or vision.

Had that really happened? I'd seen real scenes in a dream before—but only when the fortune-teller was trying to give me clues about who she really was by showing me fragments of the night she'd left this world behind and her family had died.

Of course, it might just be my imagination screwing with me. Or a demon. So much for not falling for demon mind games again.

All the same, I wrote a quick email to Cyrus, telling him about the dream. I had no idea why I felt the need to confide in him—perhaps because he wasn't here. Having Cara in on all the craziness had made summer bearable, but she could never truly know what it was like to have her mind constantly invaded, and I hoped she never would.

If it *was* real, then who'd want me to watch that? Berenice and I weren't friends, and if that had really happened to her, then she'd never told any of us. I hadn't even known she'd been Catholic. If a demon had really killed her friend, it would explain why she hated the world so much, at any rate—I knew she'd had bad experiences with demons before. She was like the rest of us, a victim of circumstance, whose mother, like Cyrus and Leo's father, had disappeared into the upper realms of the Venantium and never come back. Her dad lectured at the university and was the English Department's legendary jerk-ass tutor. That was all I really knew about Berenice. She'd been as hostile to me when we first met as though I'd done something awful to her in a past life or something. She'd never given me a chance, and was still a complete bitch, even though I'd been partially responsible for her and Howard finally getting together.

Howard was just as bad as she was: ready to pick a fight with anyone who looked at him the wrong way. Berenice had always stuck up for him, using the well-worn excuse that his family had been wrongfully imprisoned by the Venantium years before. I wondered how they'd both react when they learned that Claudia had joined the ranks of their enemies.

What had appealed to Claudia, I thought, other than the thrill of fighting back against Lucifer? Her parents had left the Venantium to keep her safe, after all. It seemed a bit of a selfish decision.

Not that I was one to talk. I couldn't deny the twinge of satisfaction I felt when I pictured the fortune-teller's face if she found out I was considering fighting for the Venantium.

That alone told me it was a bad idea.

I went back to bed and managed to get in a couple of hours of dream-free rest. Alex knocked on my door to announce that she was putting on a marathon of Disney films, which seemed a reasonable way to spend the day. As people had been repeatedly reminding us, second year pulled no punches. At least I'd be kept busy.

I made the most of our last week of freedom by spending it with my friends, on fancy-dress pub crawls and nights in watching movies. We also went shopping in Redthorne, and I took a stack of CVs to hand to anyone who would take them. It gave me unpleasant déjà vu; I'd spent almost every weekend since I'd turned sixteen job-hunting, practically a job in itself. Having a tendency toward panic attacks in interviews didn't exactly endear me to employers, especially in retail, despite having perfect grades and ticking all the "key skill boxes" coveted by the careers staff.

*Come on, Ash. You've beaten demons, for God's sake. Interviews are nothing.*

The most I managed to get out of that day, though, was yet another string of "sorry, we're not hiring" from everywhere from the bookshop to the pizza takeout. *So much for that idea.* At least I managed to fulfil the fortune-teller's instruction to purchase a fake demon heart, although I then had to tell a nonplussed Sarah and Alex that I'd bought a tacky fake amethyst-on-a-string necklace for a friend's birthday present.

We went through the standard stuff like course enrolment and signing up for modules. I also applied for a newly vacant editorial position for the student paper, which I'd written some articles for last year. I decided to re-join Hiking and the Literature Society, as well as signing up for a free self-defence taster course. And I joined the gym, though I opted for a basic membership rather than the expensive one with all the extras.

*Keep busy. Don't think.* If I repeated it enough times, maybe I'd start to believe it.

Too bad I couldn't shut off my subconscious. Apart from that dream of Berenice and the house, every dream that week was the same, as though coming back to Blackstone had triggered it. I'd relived that awful night in Redthorne too many times to count, and yet it hit me the same every single time, and I'd wake sobbing in darkness, reaching out for the hands that weren't there. Then I had a moment of self-hatred, wondering whether it was normal, or I was going to be one of those pathetic girls who couldn't get over her first relationship.

I didn't want to be pathetic. I didn't want to be weak.

WHEN I CAME into the kitchen the morning lectures started, I found Rachel sitting brightly at the table, talking to a bleary-eyed Sarah.

"Hi, Ash!" she said. "They've found a dead body on campus."

So much for getting on with it.

"They what?" said Alex, who'd just come in behind me. "Who's copped it this time?"

"Not a *recent* dead body," said Rachel, with a laugh. "A skeleton. They unearthed it when they started the construction work up near the Great Hall. Pretty cool, right?"

"Not really," I said. I'd had enough bad experiences with things that were supposed to be dead. *Please don't let it be Darkworld related.* "Has anyone seen my cereal bowl?"

"I used it," said Rachel. "I hope you don't mind. I'll

clean it up." She jumped up so suddenly it was like she'd been plugged into an electric current. Sarah's cereal nearly went flying.

"You guys read the course book yet?" said Alex. "Well, Ash will have. And probably the whole reading list."

"I had a lot of free time over summer," I said.

"Yeah, so did I. I spent it climbing hills and sunbathing, you workaholic."

I couldn't argue with that, so I shrugged.

"Sarah?"

"Yeah, I looked over it. I'm going to have to give up sleep this term if I'm going to be auditioning for things *and* working at the café."

"You still want to work at that place?" said Alex.

"I need the money," said Sarah wearily; they'd had this argument before.

"You need a job where you're treated like a person, not an expendable robot."

"I like robots," said Rachel, who was now scooping Nutella onto her cereal.

Alex raised her eyebrows. "You want some cereal with that?"

"She's being sarcastic," I said to Rachel, who looked nonplussed. Maybe we'd gotten off on the wrong foot, but I wanted to try to make friends with her. Maybe. If just for the sake of keeping things peaceful.

"You in second year, too?" Alex asked her. "You study art, right?"

"You don't *study* art, you *make* art," said Rachel.

Alex blinked. "Um, okay." She glanced at her watch. "We should go. Ready to face second year?"

Sarah pulled a face. "Not really. Have you seen that week when we have to read five books in seven days? And our marks actually count this year, too."

"We'll be fine!" said Alex. "Ash will get a first, as usual —what was your mark last year again?"

"Seventy-five," I muttered, flushing.

"Holy Jesus. You're going to be fine. Hell, you're prob-ably at a post-grad level already."

"And yet I can't even get a job at Pizza Hut."

"No one can get a decent job these days. You'll end up being a professor of literature, trust me."

"If there was a job that required literary analysis, I'd be set," I said, as we went out of the kitchen, leaving Rachel eating Nutella with a spoon.

"Be a tutor," said Sarah. "Seriously—you can offer your tutoring time at whatever price you want. Ask at careers."

"You know, that isn't a bad idea," said Alex. "You should do the same. It's not exploitative. You can do as much as you want to."

I wondered how I'd not thought of that before. "I'll check into the careers' office after lectures."

Finally, I thought, I might be getting somewhere. Maybe I didn't need to join the Venantium after all.

Still, the offer remained at the back of my mind. Perhaps it was because I'd become accustomed to living a double life whilst at university, but I didn't want to be drawn into a false sense of security while some demon played mind games with me. *Been there, done that.* I wanted to be on full alert, if Lucifer really had some kind of plan.

After lectures, I went to the careers office to sign up for tutoring. On the way out of the building, I almost ran into Berenice. She looked abstracted, lost in thought, but when she saw me, her face arranged itself into her usual scowl. She gave me a death glare and stalked off without speaking to me. *Lovely to see you, too.*

I glanced at my watch. I'd have to leave soon if I

wanted to make it to Blackstone before seven. *I'll just ask some questions,* I told myself. *Find out exactly what I'm getting into.*

It was already getting dark, so rather than walking through the woods, I opted to take the bus from campus. Two pounds for barely a ten-minute drive seemed a bit of a rip-off to me. I had to cling to the railing in front of me to avoid being unseated as we lurched downhill; the drivers took their timetabling seriously here. The bus rattled along the bumpy road, swinging around bends and smacking into overhanging tree branches.

"Hey, Ash!"

I looked up, nearly hitting my head on the railing as the bus took another nose-dive, screeching to a halt at the student village. "Hey, Claudia."

"You decided, then?" she said. In a low-cut red dress, she looked like she'd dressed for a night out, not an interview with the Venantium.

"Um… kind of. I just wanted to see what their arguments were."

She slid onto the seat beside me. "Sorry I talked a bunch of crap the other night. But I did mean it about helping everyone. Not so much the ass-kicking part. Well, maybe a little." She sighed. "I don't know. It's my final year, you know? I have to enter that annoying *real world* in a few months." She pulled a face. "I just want to do *something* before all that getting-a-job crap takes over."

"I know what you mean," I said. "But—well, it just seems too reckless, especially for me. If they find out what I am…"

Claudia looked like she didn't know what to say, and I could hardly blame her. Looking at me, no one could guess I might be anything other than human. That the higher demon Lucifer might be my father.

Needless to say, meeting my own father wasn't on my to-do list. Lucifer, one of seven higher demons, known to some as the seven princes of the Darkworld, or just the Seven. Lucifer, Satan, Asmodeus, Beelzebub, Mammon, Leviathan, and Belphegor. As far as I knew, they were the only demons able to fully take on a human form without possessing someone—according to the *Seven Princes of the Darkworld*, no anchor was strong enough to hold them in this world. But it drew most knowledge of the Seven from guesswork, because they rarely showed themselves in this world, and if anyone had ever known anything, they'd probably be long dead. Asking a demon questions was a surefire way to get killed.

The few history books devoted to Darkworld-related events agreed that it was five hundred years since human-demons had walked the earth in abundance, when someone had tried to build an army of them. It had failed because human-demons were weaker than true demons and once their power source was destroyed, they were as good as dead. Human-demons might have a couple of advantages over regular sorcerers—notably, that we couldn't be possessed—but ultimately, demons would always best us. We had all the weaknesses and few of the strengths.

I hadn't lied to David. I had only faced two true demons, and pure luck had saved me on both occasions. The demon Terrence had summoned that night in the Lake District had turned on him, giving me an opening to send it back to the Darkworld. And the fortune-teller had been the one to kill Mephistopheles—just in time, as the demon inside me had been seconds from killing Leo as well as the demon.

In spite of what I told myself, I feared what I could become if I let the demon have free reign. Demons were seen as pure evil, at least by the Venantium, and my magic mirrored their own. I could summon ice as easily as ordinary magic-users could summon fire, and I had no trouble calling on the Darkworld to shield me from demon magic.

Then there was Influence. But I'd vowed to never use it again if I could help it. It was one thing to unknowingly divert people's attention away from me when I wanted to be left alone—I'd done it unconsciously for years—but it was quite another to fabricate someone's life.

At least I couldn't possess anyone, or read minds, the two traits that made demons truly terrifying. If they wanted, they could get into anyone's head, read their thoughts, and on a whim, end their life.

Claudia and I got off the bus and hurried through the winding streets. Light from streetlamps glinted off the cobblestones and refracted from the puddles of rainwater. Blackstone looked almost too quaint to be a student town; it felt like stepping back a century as we walked through the streets lined with old-fashioned houses and shops and a huge abandoned Gothic cathedral dominating the town square.

Behind that lay the cemetery, which housed the Venantium's dead. The Blackstone family's tomb marked the entrance to the Venantium's Headquarters, which I thought excessively morbid, but they weren't known for subtlety.

Fog snaked around the tombstones like the spirits of the dead. David stood in front of the Blackstone family tomb, shifting from one foot to the other. I guessed even he got spooked out by this place at night.

"You came," he said. He wore a thick coat, and I wished I'd done the same. How Claudia could walk around in a dress on a night like this baffled me.

"Yeah, I reckon I convinced her," said Claudia. "They still have you running errands?"

He didn't answer, but a flush rose up his neck despite the cold. "Come with me."

The tomb's oak doors blazed around the edges, then swung open. I swallowed. This was it.

Claudia went after David. I followed them both into the grave—feeling, ironically, like I was about to sign a deal with the devil.

## 7

## THE DARKWORLD DEFENDS

Dr Philips waited in the entrance hall. She had the severe look of someone who'd never smiled in her life, like my head of sixth form at school. She nodded at me, which might have meant she was pleased or annoyed—I couldn't tell, since her expression didn't change. Her face could have been carved out of stone.

"Miss Temple. Miss Delaney."

The blue flames burning in the brackets along the walls made her fair hair glow and her stern eyes look even more imposing. The Venantium had obviously put the candles down here for show, because I knew electricity must work if they could use computers here, however illogical it seemed.

What with the soaring pillars and glass-framed pictures of demons, it felt like the headquarters of some secret cult —which was kind of true. I had no idea how they'd managed to build this place underground, much less deck it out like a horror-movie set.

Flickering harpy eyes watched me from the walls as I turned my gaze back to Dr Philips.

She nodded to David. "You may go."

He bowed his head and hurried off into a tunnel.

"So, you are both interested in becoming part of our combat division?"

"Yeah, sure," said Claudia. "I'm game."

I hesitated to reply. "I just want to know what I'm getting into first," I said.

"That is what this session is about. I want to give you an overview of the workings of the Venantium, to ensure there are no… unpleasant surprises later."

I nodded. "Okay." Unpleasant surprises sounded like the Venantium, all right. I wondered, not for the first time, if she was intentionally trying to freak me out, or if she just spoke like that to everyone.

"You know by now that this is the main entrance to Headquarters. There are many other routes through the tunnels, but much of the underground area is restricted, and it's in your interest to use the tomb entrance to avoid finding yourself in an area you would rather avoid."

*Like the torture chambers?* said a voice in my head. I didn't know for sure if they practiced torture, but so many of their other ways were old-fashioned that it wouldn't have surprised me if they did. Still, that might have just been Jude trying to scare us. I'd heard a scream underground once, but those cells were a pretty grim place to be imprisoned anyway. Especially if you were scared of the dark.

"Those"—she nodded at the doors set in the walls, each beneath an archway carved with a different pattern— "lead to our various chambers. It's fairly straightforward to remember. First on the right leads to the main offices; that's where I can usually be found. Second door leads to the scholarly division, and if you carry on down the same corridor, you'll eventually come to the library. Behind the third is the combat division—that's where you'll receive much of your training. Meeting rooms are located through the first two doors on the left, and the third you're familiar with."

A shiver ran through me. That particular door led to the interrogation rooms, and farther on, the cells.

"Most of the other tunnels are vacant, but beyond the main hall"—she indicated the heavy iron doors at the end of the hall—"there are the private tunnels that lead to our most secret chambers. Punishment for trespassing is severe." She turned her glare on me. "A night in the cells, if you're lucky."

*Like I ever intend to go snooping.*

"That is all you need to know for now. I am going to take you to the combat arena and run some tests."

My insides lurched. The image of the Angel Box came to the front of my mind, and I clenched my fists.

"It's nothing to worry about. I merely want to see what you are both capable of."

She led us through the door she'd indicated led to the combat zone. The narrow staircase twisted downwards, leading into a stone-walled corridor lined with paintings of sorcerers in combat with shadow-beasts, ghouls, and other twisted monsters. Warmthless blue flames lit the way ahead. There was a set of oak doors, one slightly ajar, and Dr Philips pushed the other open, beckoning us inside.

It was a long, narrow hall, high-ceilinged like the entrance hall and panelled in wood. Dr Philips told me to step forward first, and I felt an instant apprehension as she surveyed me.

"Are you ready to show me what you're capable of, Ashlyn?"

*Hell, no*, was the honest answer, because truthfully, I

wasn't sure I wanted to know myself. Plus, I didn't want a certain demon to make an appearance. But something told me that no matter what pressure I was put under, the demon in me would never expose herself within the Venantium's Headquarters. She'd only surfaced when my life had really been in danger.

I was through with skirting around danger. I wanted to know more about my own magic, and if anyone could tell me, the Venantium could.

Common sense had long since departed, and I almost smiled, something in me rejoicing as the darkness rushed in around me.

If this wasn't really the Darkworld, it sure felt like it. Fear tempered the reckless rush of energy as I saw darker shapes moving within the shadows, and I barely raised my hand to react in time as the colossal form of a shadow-beast leapt out at me like a creature from a child's nightmare. *Go time.*

Ice coated my clenched fist as I sank it into the beast's flank. It roared, and even though I knew it wasn't real, the sound went through me like the peal of a bell. Its skin broke under my fist, revealing insubstantial shadows beneath. Shadow-beasts were semicorporeal, and one good punch could easily send them back to the Darkworld. They relied on strength of numbers when sent to attack, and usually went after lone sorcerers. I'd fought them a few times, and while they were usually stupid, if they caught a sorcerer off guard, they could take a chunk out of his face. Howard had been savaged by one once and had been lucky to escape alive.

This one didn't need much persuasion to send it back into the folds of darkness. The Darkworld was ever-shifting, formed of layer upon layer of shadows, and anything could be hiding underneath. Now, several other shapes jumped out. I recognised them as shadow-foxes—smaller but speedier versions of the shadow-beasts. I summoned ice-fire to my hands and dispatched them easily. Adrenaline sang through my veins, like a magic-induced high.

More shadow-beasts. I wondered what exactly Dr Philips wanted to see. I didn't really have a fighting technique—just punch and duck, throw ice-fire, and try to avoid getting hit.

I grimaced as something gripped my ankle, a long, bony hand. *Ghouls.*

A creature shuffled out of the dark, dragging its abnormally long arms, which had long fingers edged with sharp talons. I summoned two orbs of light to my palms, which sent it scurrying away into the shadows, hissing at me. A ghoul would run from bright light, so I had to catch it before it grabbed me again and started feeding on my life energy. Keeping the light burning above my head like a floating lantern, I threw a handful of ice-fire at its half-hidden shape. An inhuman squeal told me I'd hit my target.

Hands grabbed at me again—human hands. *Shape-shifters?* Surely Dr Philips wouldn't bring a pure demon in, even an illusory one. A shape-shifting ghoul, then. Like the doppelgänger.

I shot ice fire at the hands, which loosened their grip. The figure straightened up, demon heart winking at me between two violet eyes. Myself.

She regarded me silently, but I felt none of the terror that had paralysed me when I'd faced the doppelgänger for real. Perhaps it was because my demon heart hadn't reacted at all, or maybe it was the silence. The doppelgänger would have said something chilling, tried to make me doubt myself. But this demon was silent.

I sent a handful of ice fire at it, but the doppelgänger

moved aside so fast she blurred; next second, she had me by the throat. I choked—it *felt* real—and struggled to break her grip.

Demons did crazy things to human strength, as I knew from experience. I concentrated on the Darkworld, bringing folds of shadow close to me, pushing them upwards beneath her hands. Her grip slid down slightly, allowing me to take a breath—and ram an elbow into her chest.

The doppelgänger hissed, twisting to attack again, but I was ready with a handful of ice-fire, and struck it right between the eyes. The demon heart fractured, and the body collapsed, becoming part of the shadows again.

Then I felt a strange pressure, like something came between me and my connection.

"Enough," said Dr Philips' voice, and the Darkworld faded away, revealing the room beneath.

I hoped for a brief, foolish second, that she might be impressed, but her face was as inscrutable as ever.

"Your turn," she said to Claudia, who *did* look impressed.

Now, she stepped forward as I moved back to the outskirts of the hall, and the darkness descended again.

I'd forgotten how natural a fighter Claudia was. She moved amongst the shadows almost gracefully, like a dancer, hurling handfuls of fire. Shadow-beasts stood no chance; one after another crumbled and fled. Whipping her Japanese fan out of her belt, she raised it in the air, and flames flickered along its length. She whirled and slashed at the colossal shadow-beast creeping in behind her. I looked on, gobsmacked.

Then she stopped dead, as a humanlike figure came out of the fog. It had its back to me, so I couldn't see its face. But Claudia's expression of horror told me it meant something to her.

"Mum?"

I expected her to attack it, but her hands had gone slack, the fire dying. The figure bore down on her, seized her by the neck, and—

"Stop," said Dr Philips.

The shadows vanished.

Claudia turned on her, glaring. "Bitch. Why did you have to drag my mum into this?"

Dr Philips didn't react to the insult. "Demons do not have mercy. They see into your mind, read your deepest fears, and replicate them."

"I know that," said Claudia. "But Ash didn't have to face…"

She trailed off, a flush creeping up her face as she remembered.

*Don't say anything,* I thought desperately, but I couldn't stop the image of my once-parents flashing through my mind. A sharp knife pierced my insides, and I stared at one of the wavering candle-lights, determined not to cry.

Dr Philips said, "The two of you fared better than I expected, given your lack of formal training—normally we recruit initiates who show promise at the age of eighteen, but the two of you have… different circumstances."

Too right we did. Claudia's parents had left the Venantium to keep her out of danger, whereas I hadn't even known they existed, thanks to the fortune-teller.

"You are both capable," said Dr Philips. "But you, Ash, rely too much on the Darkworld to defend you."

I blinked. "I do?"

"The Darkworld itself responds to you in a way that is rare to see in one so inexperienced. You need only move and it moves with you. Why do you think you've never suffered serious injury?"

"Um..." *I just got lucky?* Truthfully, I'd always been vaguely aware that the Darkworld itself had defended me on more than one occasion—for instance, when Mephistopheles had dropped me, it had slowed my fall and guided me to a safe landing. But I'd never questioned before how lucky I was that nothing had ever caused me permanent damage. It must be down to being part demon that the Darkworld wanted to *save* me. Now, it gave me chills to think about.

"You have a natural gift, but you need more discipline. I will find an instructor willing to work with both of you, and we'll work more on natural defence skills—without the Darkworld."

That sounded ominous to me.

"I've never been to a self-defence class in my life," I said. "I signed up for a taster session this week, but I don't see myself dispatching shadow-beasts with a well-placed kick in the near future."

Dr Philips raised an eyebrow. "Perhaps not. But you'll find it worth your while, if you're trapped without access to the Darkworld."

Was there an implicit threat there? She'd been the one to block my connection after I'd been mistaken for a demon...

She turned to Claudia. "You have better technique, but it could use some refining. And please ensure you don't let your emotions get in the way."

Claudia glared at her. "Sure. Whatever."

"You are both dismissed." And she left the room.

"It's like being back at school!" Claudia exploded, when she was out of earshot.

"Shh!" I said. "She might be outside."

"Well, whatever. Who was it you were facing anyway?"

"What, the doppelgänger?"

"She thinks your worst fear is facing yourself?"

"I guess so. Well, that's the worst *they've* seen me deal with, anyway."

As far as I knew, the Venantium didn't know about Leo being possessed. That was one of the reasons he'd left the country shortly afterwards; demons rarely spared anyone they'd marked, and the Venantium would have put him under surveillance, maybe even imprisoned him as a danger in case he became a target again. I was pretty sure Mephistopheles had kept Leo alive only to torment me. The fortune-teller had killed the demon before he could take Leo's life. I was grateful beyond words, even though I'd as good as lost him anyway when he'd said he couldn't bear to look me in the eyes after we'd fought each other.

The idea of facing Leo possessed again scared me far more than my dark "other half" ever could.

"Come on, let's go, anyway," I said.

Several people had gathered in the entrance hall. I hadn't realised how dark it had been in the combat hall, but the brightness of the blue candles disoriented me. It took me a minute to recognise the man speaking to Dr Philips as Mr Blake. Leo's father.

I'd only seen him once before, when he'd delivered a warning about Lucifer to the Venantium. He hadn't even acknowledged his own sons. Like some of the more extreme demon-hating *venators*, he considered family a surplus inconvenience. After Leo and Cyrus's mother had been killed by a demon, he'd dedicated himself to revenge, and gradually withdrawn from his family altogether. After spending a few years in orphanages, Leo and Cyrus had been raised by Bill Melmoth, former head of the Inner Circle—who had later been killed by Jude, a former employee of the Venantium turned into a vicious killer of vampires, which he believed to be abominations.

Mr Blake was one of the Inner Circle, the seven highest members of the Venantium, although few people knew their identities, a practice intended to ensure that demons would be unable to track down the Inner Circle by reading their whereabouts from another member. I supposed it was the best defence they could do when facing an enemy who could read anyone's mind at any time.

Mr Blake looked up as Claudia and I slipped past. His eyes narrowed in a way I didn't like, but he spoke not a word, turning back to listen to Dr Philips. By the sound of things, she was telling him about our tests.

Just as we reached the door that led back to the surface, Dr Philips called out to us.

"Speak no word of what transpired here today to anyone outside of the Venantium."

## OLD FRIENDS

"We aren't imbeciles," Claudia muttered as we hurried up the passageway to the surface. "Like they could stop us from *talking*, anyway."

"We don't know they're not listening in on us," I pointed out.

"Well, I wasn't planning on shouting from the rooftops. Be funny to watch if someone did, though…" She kicked a loose stone aside. "It's so *gloomy* down here. What're you planning to do now?"

I shrugged. "Do some course reading, I guess."

"Boring. Don't you want to come for a drink?"

"Sure," I said. "Just one, though. I have to be up at eight tomorrow, and it'll be a long day."

We climbed the stone stairs to the surface. I breathed in the cool night air with relief. It was cold in the tunnels but also stuffy, like the air had been trapped down there a long time.

"Coach and Horses?"

"Good plan."

But someone else waited for us outside the shadowy gate to the cemetery. My heart sank as I recognised Conrad.

"Ash!" He sounded delighted, pretty much his standard response when he saw me—God alone knew why. He'd applied liberal amounts of gel to his blond hair, making it look like it had been dipped in grease. An appealing image. Not.

"Hi, Conrad," I said.

"I hoped I might see you! You were just with the Venantium, right?"

*Is it cruel to wish a harpy would come down and hit him?* "Um…"

"We weren't doing anything," said Claudia impatiently. "Come on. Let's go."

"No, you can talk to me about it. It's fine. I'm working with them, too!"

*Oh, that's fan-freaking-tastic.*

"What, fighting for them?" I said sceptically. The last time Conrad had been involved in a fight, he'd spent most of the time running away and falling over. It would be suicide for him to go up against a demon.

"No, but they've offered me lessons. I'm working in the scholarly division now," he said proudly.

"Um… well done?"

To be honest, I couldn't picture him in a library, either. It astounded me that someone like him had even got into university, what with his childlike dim-wittedness. Not to mention his propensity for shooting his mouth off.

"I'm looking into records about Lucifer!" he said, on cue.

"Tell the world," said Claudia, with an eye-roll. "Good for you, anyway, but we're off now."

"Um… I wanted to talk to Ash."

I sighed. Again, he had the worst timing. But his kicked-puppy look was even more annoying than his babbling.

"What is it?" I said, resigned.

"Um…"

Claudia rolled her eyes. "I'll wait for you in the pub, alright? Give me a shout if you need me."

*Cheers,* I thought, looking everywhere except at Conrad, although I could feel his eager gaze boring into me.

"I heard you split up with your boyfriend, Ash." His eyes were wide with sympathy.

*For God's sake.*

"Six months ago," I said, sharper than I intended. "And before you ask, I'm not interested in going out with you."

He blinked at me, hurt. "I just wanted to know if you're okay."

"I'm fine," I said. He regarded me as though he expected me to keel over and start sobbing on the floor.

"Well, if you need anyone to talk to—"

"I'm fine," I repeated. "Never better." I started to walk away.

"It was nice seeing you, Ash," he called.

"Pity I can't say the same," I muttered. And then felt like the biggest bitch of the century. *I could give Berenice a run for her money.* I'd never been a particularly bad-tempered person, but lately, the slightest thing set me off. Maybe it was stress. No, it couldn't be the demon.

I found Claudia in the Coach and Horses, talking to Pete, of all people. He staggered away as I approached the table with my drink.

"Pete's found a new target?" I said, sitting down opposite her.

"You know that guy?" she said.

"Yeah, he lived in my flat last year. Spent most of his time wasted and stalking Danielle, this girl from upstairs."

"Yeah, he's not all there. I think he's on drugs or something. He kept saying I was *glowing*." She snorted.

"Weird," I said. "But then, he is weird."

"Weirder than fighting demonic illusions?"

"Hell yeah." I laughed.

"Weirder than Conrad?"

"Well, I wouldn't say that."

Maybe I'd been a bit unfair. For all I knew, he'd genuinely been concerned. But last time I'd had anything to do with Conrad, it had resulted in us both being drawn into a deadly trap and nearly dying.

*Maybe that's why you can't hold on to a relationship,* said a cynical voice inside my head. *You put everyone who shows an interest in you in mortal danger.*

*Cheers,* I replied, downing the rest of my vodka and coke.

SUNSET DESCENDED, spreading arms like angel's wings over the landscape. The sun dipped out of sight behind snow-white peaks, dazzling to the eye. Deep orange-red light spilled out like blood, making the lake before us gleam in the reflection of the glowing orb.

He put his arm around me, lips brushing my ear as he whispered, "I could stay here forever."

"Me too," I whispered, and his hand found mine and squeezed. The constricting emptiness in my chest loosened at his touch, and for the first time in what felt like forever, I felt my heart beat frantically, every pulse of blood through my veins like a shot of pure happiness.

I turned to Leo, and his grey eyes shone silver with love and passion, the way they used to.

"Perfect," he whispered, fingers caressing my hair. I watched the sun sink out of sight, the gleam of light in his eyes bringing tears to my own.

He was back. *My* Leo. Not the demon. Even in dreams, I'd take what I could get.

Darkness fell, like the sun had stolen every drop of light with it. I looked back at the lake, which still blazed—but it no longer reflected the sun.

I saw places familiar to me: the old-fashioned brick buildings of the university; the newer campus restaurants; the university square where students congregated. All burning, all alive with the screams of the fleeing students. The image changed and I saw the town of Blackstone burning, too. The Victorian houses collapsed in on themselves. The cobblestones were wet with blood. The picture changed again, to the cemetery, and the cathedral, its spires alight. One stone stood alone, not burning, merely watching: the Blackstone memorial.

A voice spoke. "The end is coming, and all shall burn. The ground will open. The sky will fall. And darkness will descend."

A curtain fell over my vision and I awoke.

*Well, that was dramatic.* I shuddered to feel the cold pressing in on me again. My hands had frozen in my sleep. *You'd think it was a bit contradictory, considering I was dreaming about fire.* Apparently not.

*Darkness will descend.* I understood that part, but the lake of fire confounded me. I'd always thought demons hated fire, the one sure-fire way to kill one. If the world burned, so would they. So much for dreams having significance.

Despite my best efforts, the image of Leo crept to the forefront of my mind. I hadn't dreamt about him in a while, not as himself. It awakened the old pain, the piercing ache that stopped my breath.

I *shouldn't* still feel like this. Our relationship had been like a brief, vibrant dream. Now dreams were all I had, and they always left me aching like this, because imagination wasn't enough. Even photographs could never conjure the reality, the happiness so intense it was like flying, like not even demons could drag me down.

I groaned as my alarm started bleeping. *Time to join the land of the living.*

Not that anyone was particularly awake in our first Shakespeare lecture, with the exception of Alex, who could function at a normal level even on no sleep. I had to resort to underlining random lines in *Hamlet* to keep myself from dozing off. *To sleep, perchance to dream.* If only. Well, I could do without the dreams.

I downed a can of Red Bull from the campus shop before heading to the library with my friends to prepare for my next seminar. Yawning over my notes, I jerked upright when Claudia walked past the table, casually slipped a note into my folder, and sauntered off.

**"The Venantium want us to come down tonight for our first training session."**

I mentally groaned. *Note to self, buy more Red Bull.*

"What's that?" said Alex.

"Um, I'm joining self-defence classes," I said, the closest to the truth I could get.

"What, the taekwondo club?"

"Nah, somewhere off-campus." I struggled to read my lecture notes. Ink everywhere—not a good start.

"Why not the campus one?" Nothing got past Alex.

I shrugged. "I don't want to make an ass of myself in front of people I know."

Alex's assessing stare never wavered. "You know that girl. Who *is* she anyway?"

"Claudia. From GameSoc." Claudia didn't look at all like the kind of person with any interest in video games— actually true—but Alex didn't need to know that. "She goes to the classes, so she got me enrolled. Did either of you two get any sense out of that lecture?"

"Hell, no. The dude sounded like he was making it up as he went along."

"Probably was," I said. "Hmm. Maybe I ought to be a lecturer."

"You said you didn't do public speaking."

"Yeah, but I could get used to it."

A careers person had come to talk to us after the lecture, to strike fear into our hearts about our futures and the less-than-promising job market awaiting arts graduates. I really needed to come up with some kind of plan. I sure as hell didn't want to join the Venantium permanently.

Alex grinned at me. "Yeah, you weren't too bad when you read out that poem last year. Maybe there's hope."

"Maybe," I said. I'd almost forgotten about the time Alex had signed me up to read poetry at the open mic night.

"Yeah, you should do that again," said Sarah. "Do you write much poetry? I was thinking of writing something for the department's new magazine."

"Sounds like an idea." Not that I wanted anyone reading any of my recent poetry; it read like a cliché teenage girl's diary. *Ugh.*

I looked at my watch and saw that I had ten minutes to make it to my seminar. Shoving my messy lecture notes into my bag, I stood up.

"I've gotta run. I'll be back in an hour."

"Sure thing," said Alex.

The caffeine had kicked in by that point, sending my senses into overdrive, so I all but ran downstairs and out of the library. Despite my hyperawareness of everything around me, I failed to notice the person tailing me until a fist connected with my face.

Too shocked to react, I could only stagger back. I tasted blood as my teeth sank into my cheek, and I lifted my gaze to meet a pair of furious eyes. Berenice.

"You traitorous bitch."

"What the hell?" I said. My cheek stung. All I could think was, *She* hit *me!*

"I can't believe you of all people joined up to spy for those bastards," she whispered at me. "You make me sick."

I blinked, nonplussed, until her meaning sank in. "What—the Venantium? I haven't joined them."

"Liar." This time I stepped out of the way of her fist.

"You're crazy!" I said. I'd taken a shortcut on a less well-known route so no one else was nearby, but I looked around to check no one listened in all the same.

"You're a fucking human-demon. Do you know what they do to people like you if you're found out?"

"I told you," I said, refusing to rise to her bait, "I'm not a spy. I'm just going to fight shadow-beasts. What *we* used to do anyway!"

"They *imprisoned* Howard's parents," she snarled. "They let Jude kill Leo's guardian. I don't suppose you've told him about your treachery?"

"What I tell people is none of your business," I said, but my throat closed up at Leo's name despite myself. *Oh, God. What am I doing?*

"Meaning you never tell anyone anything. Every word you say is a lie. You're worse than the fortune-teller. But I guess bullshit runs in the family."

Ice-fire burned my palms. "Don't you even go there," I said, through gritted teeth.

"You weren't going to tell us that, either, were you? Howard told me. Got it from Leo. Apparently he sure loves to talk about his crazy ex."

"Fuck. Off." I stepped up to her, fists clenched. "You don't know anything about me, so keep your nose out of my business or I'll turn you into an ice statue."

She blinked at me, unconcerned. "Whatever. You'll learn soon. I can't wait to see your face when you're staring down death and the *venators* just look right past you, thinking of you as a sacrifice, nothing more."

And she stalked off, leaving me alone in the alley, angry tears forming in my eyes.

I'D NEVER HAD A MORE stressful beginning of term, and most of that wasn't even down to the lectures. The Venantium were, unsurprisingly, more brutal than the instructor at the self-defence taster classes Alex and I went to, largely due to the instructor, Mr Baruch, or "Brutus" as Claudia called him. I came out of my first session feeling like I'd fallen down a rocky cliff and collected bruises on every inch of skin on my body. The wooden floor was not my friend.

As it turned out, I was even more hopelessly unfit than I'd thought, even after going to the gym regularly for the past month. There were three sessions each week, and each was worse than the last. They invariably started with a demonstration of various techniques, with magic or without. Claudia and I stood amongst a group of other initiates, most of whom I guessed to be around our age and students at the university. The Venantium clearly hadn't wasted any time in signing up new magic-users. I also recognised David, who looked openly relieved when we weren't paired up to practise some of the magic-based defensive techniques. I guess I didn't blame him, seeing as I'd turned him into an ice statue that one time.

I didn't fare any better at magic-based defence, either. First, I had to explain to Brutus in front of the other candidates that I couldn't summon fire, which was met with a look as though I'd declared in an English seminar that I couldn't write. Even my demonstration of summoning ice-fire didn't impress. It was like being back in PE lessons at school, at the mercy of a teacher who was out to draw attention to my inadequacy.

Still, at least I wasn't as bad as Conrad. As it turned out, he'd been offered the lessons in compensation for what had happened to him six months ago, when Jude had tried to kill him. Apparently the Venantium had relaxed some of their stubborn rules, even allowing nonmembers to use the library without fearing attack from one of their harpies. I found out this from Conrad, the eminent scholar. Despite my hostility the last time we'd spoken, he kept trying to speak to me at Headquarters, and always seemed to be in the entrance hall when I arrived.

Still, the lessons did have their benefits. Thanks to a spell all initiates went under, I could now see the level of someone's Darkworld connection just by looking at them, even under the Venantium's barriers. Turned out most people couldn't see that naturally, even, I guessed, human-demons. It was like a veil had been lifted from my eyes, and it was both reassuring and uncomfortable. Uncomfortable because the dark aura that appeared around someone with the connection looked a bit too similar to when I'd seen someone possessed by a demon—and reassuring because until now, I'd never realised just how many people at the university were sorcerers. Due to my prior avoidance of the Venantium, I'd only met a handful of them before, but most were perfectly nice, ordinary people—who happened to spend the occasional evening kicking shadow-beasts into oblivion. I even worked up the courage to tell Cyrus this via email, figuring that he was bound to find out anyway, if Berenice made good on her threat. But I thought of Cyrus as the most open-minded of the group.

He didn't say how Leo had taken the news, but said that he'd actually considered joining himself. He'd decided he didn't want to spend any time near his father. I didn't blame him for that.

I also told him about Berenice's threat, and his reply surprised me.

**"I kind of get why she snapped at you. Please don't tell her I told you this, but she doesn't just hate the Venantium because of Howard's issues. They screwed her over once already before that. Her friend was killed by a demon, and they weren't particularly welcoming of her as a magic-user because I don't think her mother has many friends. She works with Influence, so even most of the *venators* don't like her much. So they shunned a sixteen-year-old girl who needed their help. I think she was a mess after the attack."**

**"Really?"** I replied. **"She told you that?"**

**"Surprisingly, yes. It was when she first came to Blackstone and the demons wouldn't leave her alone when she tried to leave the town. There was this one which was giving her a rough time so I asked her what its problem was, and she finally told me. Obviously, I'm not supposed to be telling you this."**

**"What happened to the demon?"**

"Still out there, of course, but she's learnt to ignore it now. I think she was always jealous of you for being able to ignore them right off."

I remembered something else, then. I told Cyrus about the dream I'd had about the demon, where I'd seen Berenice watch her friend die.

"Shit, that sounds exactly like she told me! She's never told anyone else that. Claudia tried to get answers out of her, but she kept quiet until one night when I guess she needed to vent. She didn't really know me, and I think that helped. But yeah. That's so creepy. Have you seen things like that in dreams before?"

"Yeah—kind of. It's happened before, but only when the fortune-teller wanted to show me her past. I've no idea who might have wanted me to watch *that*. But the demon, the one who killed her friend, it was Mephistopheles. He possessed her friend, made him hang himself. And he threatened Berenice with some kind of choice. I woke up before I saw how it ended."

"Nasty. She never told me it was Mephistopheles, but it sounds like his kind of thing."

"He offered her a choice, but never said what it was. Did she tell you?"

"No, she only said the demon killed her friends. I don't know who'd want you to watch that, though. Probably not Berenice."

"Yeah. I wonder what he offered her. He said she had potential, that's why he didn't kill her."

"Weird. I've never asked. She's definitely not on the demons' side, though, so I'd say someone must have killed him before he could work his

**spell on her. She wouldn't still be alive if he'd
locked her in a contract."**

"True."

It gave me an uneasy feeling all the same. But for the
first time, I felt a bit sorry for Berenice. None of us could
help the hand we were dealt, and I kind of connected with
her prickly attitude, especially as Mephistopheles had
screwed with me, too.

Not like I could tell her that, though. She'd kick my ass.

## 9

### BONE AND CLAW

Three weeks of training later and the Venantium finally let me have a day off. I could barely drag myself out of bed that morning, after my first lie-in all term. Every muscle in my body felt like it had been pulled and stretched and wasn't at all happy about it.

"You okay?" said Alex, eyeing me with concern as I limped into the kitchen. She and Sarah sat there with their books out, even though it was midday on a Saturday—a testament to the level of work in second year compared to first.

"Yeah," I said. "Just a bit achy. I've been going to the gym a lot." I'd quit the campus self-defence club after the first session; the Venantium's lessons had done me in.

"Don't overdo it," said Sarah, underlining something in a weary sort of way.

"Don't tell me this is about that photo thing again," said Alex, looking at me critically.

"What photo thing?" I said, pulling out a box of cereal and a clean bowl.

"You know. The sexy California girls."

I nearly dropped my cereal bowl. I'd thought that particular incident was behind us.

"Of course not!" I spluttered. "Like I'd be that shallow. I've never had the slightest desire to look like a supermodel."

"Good," said Alex. "Want to come for a drink tonight, anyway? We've hardly seen you all week. Rex has forgotten who you are."

"Sure," I said, feeling guilty. My training sessions hadn't left much time for socialising. The last few weeks had been a crash course in multitasking.

I spent most of the day catching up with reading and updating my blog—something else I'd neglected due to being too tired. Still, playing a few rounds of pool in the bar with my friends helped improve my mood, even if I did end up on the same team as Rachel, who'd tagged along, too. Sarah had said it would be rude to leave her out, but I got the impression that she didn't particularly want to be there anyway.

"Rachel," I said, for what felt like the fiftieth time, "it's your move."

It was sort of hard to play pool with someone who kept staring vacantly into space.

"Rachel!" said Alex, more blunt than me, and gave her a poke with the pool cue.

"Huh?" said Rachel, blinking at us. "What is it? You're glowing, Ash."

I looked down at myself. "Huh?" She couldn't see the pendant; I'd tucked it away into my inside pocket and wore the fake one under my shirt, as a precaution. Just Rachel being Rachel, I guessed. I hoped.

"Oh, is it my turn?" she asked.

"Yes," I said, exasperated.

"Sorry. I thought I heard someone calling my name."

"That was us," said Alex, rolling her eyes.

Rachel hit the ball so hard it went flying off the pool table and landed in someone's drink. Sarah winced.

"Oh dear," said Rachel, thoughtfully. "I'm very sorry." She wandered over to the table where the ball had landed.

Alex cracked up silently. "Oh, God, we're cursed with crazy flatmates," she said. "I'm wondering what they'll throw at us next year. Last year we had Terrence the Satanist alien, now we've got her."

"Probably a zombie next year," I said, smiling for what felt like the first time in forever.

"Pretty accurate description of most third-years," said Sarah.

Thankfully, Rachel soon departed saying she needed to go and finish an art piece. My relief, however, was short-lived. As Alex and Sarah set up the pool table again, my phone buzzed in my pocket. The Venantium, who were too self-important to leave their name. Apparently, I'd been put on my first mission for tomorrow *morning*.

"What's up, Ash?"

"Nothing," I said, slipping my phone back into my bag. "I'm a bit tired. Think I might get an early night in a bit."

"Come on, it's only eleven!" said Alex, raising her eyebrows. "It's Saturday night, for God's sake. You've been absentee the last few weeks."

I just shrugged. "I've not had much sleep. Stress of second year and all that."

"Yeah, I get you," said Alex. "But you're coming to the LitSoc social next week, right?"

*If the Venantium don't haul me off on another mission.* "Sure. You guys can stay if you like. I'm falling asleep on my feet."

"See you tomorrow."

At least I only had a short walk back through the

student village. The chilly breeze ruffled the poplar trees lining the paths, lit by lamps on the sides of the houses. I hurried along, wondering why I'd begun to feel uneasy. It wasn't the Darkworld, but something else raised the hairs on my arms, a strange kind of intuition. Possibly the lack of sleep and overreliance on energy drinks.

Then I saw the skeleton.

It sat on top of the stone fountain in the centre of a square of grass midway between the houses, perched like part of the statue. But it was a human skeleton, life-size and earth-stained. I moved closer, reaching out to touch it, following some morbid instinct to confirm that it was real, and not just a life-size model. It *felt* real enough, rough and earthy under my hands.

Who would do something like that? I felt sick, but I knew it couldn't be recently dead. At the same time, it didn't look like someone had borrowed a model from the biology department.

Rachel's words from a couple of weeks ago echoed in my head. *"They've found a dead body on campus."* I looked uneasily at House 23. The kitchen light on the third floor was off.

"What the hell?" I muttered.

I looked back at the domed skull, expecting for one heart-stopping moment to see a flicker of life in its sunken eye-holes. But Skele-Ghouls couldn't get onto campus, not anymore. This was just someone's bizarre prank. I decided to move away before anyone could blame it on me. *It's not my problem.*

But it didn't bode well for tomorrow.

Even though I fell asleep almost as soon as my head hit the pillow, it seemed like only seconds before my alarm went off. I blinked awake from a confused dream about being chased through a forest—thankfully not another end-of-days one—and rolled out of bed.

I found Claudia waiting for me outside the block, dressed sensibly for the weather for once. She wore a jacket with a hood lined with fake fur, fluffed up against the cold —and she stood gaping at the skeleton statue.

"What the hell is that?" she said.

"It was there last night," I said, turning my back on it. "I'm guessing it's a prank."

"Not a great one," she said. "That looks like the real deal. Ugh."

"It is. I checked."

"Shit, really?" It would probably have grossed out any normal person, but Claudia hopped over the grass and grabbed the skeleton's hand with no hesitation whatsoever.

"Yeuch. You're right." She stood back. "Weird as hell, that."

"Should we report it?" I said.

"Nah. People are bound to start noticing it soon anyway. I'm amazed no one reported it last night."

"Weird," I said. "This… kind of reminds me of the Ghouls."

But the Ghouls were gone; Jude was long-dead. It must be someone's idea of a practical joke. Surely.

"Nah," said Claudia, but she didn't sound convinced. "Can't be. Come on, anyway. Let's see what this is about."

"Another graveyard?" said Claudia. "Well, that'd explain why they wanted us here in the day time."

We'd just received the details of our assignment; to investigate reports of disturbances at a cemetery in the coastal town of Shaleport. The Venantium suspected something related to the Skele-Ghouls, even though Jude was dead; they refused to believe he'd acted on his own impulse, and thought he might have been linked with Lucifer. Since speaking to Lucifer had been his plan, I could see where they'd got that idea, but it gave me an uneasy feeling after seeing that skeleton on campus this morning.

"Basically, they're trying to cover their tracks," said Claudia, as we sat on the train, which rattled along like it was about to fall apart. "They won't believe any of their members could go bad, so they're pushing the blame onto Lucifer."

"I thought everyone had forgotten about it," I said. "I mean, it was months ago. No one's linked it to Lucifer before. Jude never even got close to speaking to him, thanks to that higher demon."

"How are we to know what goes on behind the scenes?" said Claudia. "I'll be honest with you, I'm starting to second-guess this whole idea. We haven't learnt anything useful."

"Keep your voice down," I warned, glancing at the *venators* sitting a few rows away. They didn't look like they were listening—all seemed to have their iPods plugged in. Normal students, in appearance. I'd learned that week that not all student Venantium members were as stuck-in-the-mud as David was. And Jude. Though with Jude, it might have just been part of his act.

Conrad peered around from the seat in front. "I don't think they're plotting against us," he said.

Claudia rolled her eyes. I'd forgotten he'd been sitting there. He was even more reluctant to set foot in a cemetery than me, and I couldn't say I blamed him. A few months ago, he'd been tricked by the doppelgänger and abandoned in an underground sepulchre, then forced to witness our fight with the Skele-Ghouls. I was amazed he'd even come, but I'd been getting the impression lately that he wanted to prove he could be as good as the other *venators*.

I couldn't see that ending well. He just wasn't a fighter. He tended to give up rather than try again when he failed at something, and for the last week, he'd been tailing this guy called John around after training sessions. John was pretty much a slightly-more-intelligent version of Pete, my flatmate from last year. He had a skull as hard as a coconut, judging by the number of times he managed to hit it on the floor during training.

The train ground to a shuddering halt in a run-down station. A salty breeze blew over our heads from the coast as we disembarked. There were only around ten of us in total. The two leaders were a twin brother and sister, Jack and Freya, and they were around their midtwenties. I didn't know that much about them and wouldn't have guessed they were twins if Freya hadn't told us. She was the first amiable *venator* I'd met, a round-faced, friendly girl with curly dark hair. Jack was tall and blond and didn't say much.

Freya addressed the group, calling us to order. "Now, this shouldn't take too long. I sent a couple of harpies ahead to scout the area, and there doesn't seem to be anything amiss. I think this one might be a false alarm, but it can't hurt to check it out anyway."

We traipsed out of the station, looking oddly like a group of students on a field trip. We followed a country lane lined with neat little whitewashed cottages. The only sound was the creak of trees bending under the breeze, and I felt a chill as we reached the end of the row of houses and came to an old cemetery, tucked in the shadow of a large cathedral not unlike the one in Blackstone.

Freya looked back to check we were all there, then nodded and led us over the turnstile.

The smell of leaf decay lingered in the air. Fungi grew in clusters on the damp ground, around the crumbling tombstones. None of the graves were recent. I couldn't help looking for graffiti, the message that the graverobbers were here. But there wasn't any. We walked the narrow rows of graves and saw nothing.

"I've had bloody enough of graveyards," Claudia muttered to me. I nodded in agreement. Conrad's knees trembled, but no one else looked particularly cowed.

A harpy swooped overhead to land on a nearby gravestone.

"Anything?" said Freya, with a look at Jack.

He shook his head. "Not that I can see. But something feels off. What about that old cathedral? Can we get inside?"

"Worth a look," said Freya, but there was a hint of uncertainty in her voice. "It doesn't make sense, them sending us on a false trail. Mr Blake himself send the report, and that guy can sense demons from a hundred miles off."

My heart jolted. Mr Blake. Leo's father—not that he gave a crap about either of his two kids. I wondered if all the Inner Circle had sacrificed everything else in their lives to gain power. Even with all the time I'd been spending at headquarters lately, I'd not met any of the others, so I couldn't compare. Though Leo's late guardian, Mr Melmoth, had once been part of the Inner Circle, and from what Leo had told me, he'd been a decent guy.

The rotting wooden pole holding the cathedral door closed collapsed when Freya touched it.

"Come on." Jack stepped up and pushed the doors inward.

It was very dark inside. Freya immediately conjured a light, which hung in the air like an orb, illuminating the fractured pews and collapsed altar.

I heard Conrad moan. Freya's sharp intake of breath drew everyone's attention. She focused the light on the raised platform, and my insides twisted when I realised the wet, glutinous substance gleaming on the floor was blood.

I stepped forward, Claudia beside me. Blood had pooled on the edge of the platform and dripped onto the floor. Across the nearest pew, someone had written the words "THERE ARE NO ANGELS" in blood.

Behind me, I heard someone stumble around and run for the door. *Conrad*, I thought.

But if there was so much blood, and so fresh, whatever it had come from must be nearby…

Freya swore, and the light span around us. She'd focused it on the ceiling, where a broken chandelier—and a figure hung, suspended in the air. Human, a girl. One look at her blank eyes told me all I needed to know.

"This has to be reported," John whispered into the shocked silence.

I glanced at Claudia, who shook her head, speechless.

A screech echoed around us, sudden and sharp. Something brushed my head as it flew past, something large and feathery—a harpy. It landed on the corpse's limp arm and began to peck at it. I gagged.

"Come on, let's go," said Claudia, tugging at my arm. "The others are already outside…"

But we'd only taken a couple of steps when a cry rang out, from outside the door.

"What—"

The pendant in my pocket burned, and the piercing chill of the Darkworld shot through my body. I was running before I was aware that my legs were in motion, but the instant I burst through the doors, horror rooted me to the spot.

Conrad lay on the ground, twitching and moaning. Harpies circled overhead, and the *venators* hurled handfuls of fire at them. Claudia grabbed my arm so tight it hurt, hiding her face. Her reaction confused me—until I saw Conrad's face.

His eyes had been gouged out, leaving holes streaming blood and a jellylike substance. My stomach lurched, and I would have thrown up if I'd eaten anything in the last twelve hours. Claudia gripped my arm, looking as though she might faint. I felt light-headed, too. Harpies were the one Darkworld creature assuredly on the Venantium's side. They might have attacked me in the past, but only when they'd thought I was an intruder.

The *venators* continued to fire at the harpies, which, when hit, exploded into dust. Harpies were semicorporeal, easy to kill despite their deadly talons. But I'd thought the Venantium had them firmly under control. I'd never seen them as harmless, but this…

I stood numb, looking everywhere but at Conrad's ruined eyes. My brain refused to process it.

The last harpy burst into nothingness, scattering a handful of feathers. Freya was already bent over Conrad, her normally composed face distraught.

"What happened to them?" seemed to be the gist of most of the hushed whispers. None of the *venators* seemed to know what to do. I gathered that their messenger birds had never turned on them before, not in the long years they'd served the Venantium.

"He—he's not a rogue, is he?" whispered Claudia, indicating Conrad. Her hands still dug into my arm.

A low growl sounded. Everyone looked around, for the source. *What now?*

But the growling came from Conrad. He rolled over, hands still pressed to his eyes, and let out a horrible moaning sound. His nails dug into his already bloody face as he raised it to the sky, and I saw that his features were stretched in a horrific grimace. My blood froze. I knew what was happening.

"He's a vampire!" Freya shouted. "Get back!"

Jack, quicker off the mark, had already ushered several of the others back into the cathedral, which was a pretty stupid idea. If they were trapped in there, there'd be nowhere to run. Plus, that corpse still hung in there. A harpy couldn't have done that—could it?

We had only one option. Claudia and I ducked around a grave and legged it across the cemetery, the vampire's howls echoing behind us.

Like we'd get away that easily.

Conrad leapt over my head and stood in front of me, face stretched beyond recognition. His ruined eyes streamed blood, and his teeth were elongated and bared.

"Shit," said Claudia.

"Oh, God, Conrad," I whispered, my insides twisting. I had no choice. I called on the Darkworld and summoned ice-fire to my hands. When he leapt again, I was ready, and upon contact with his skin, the ice-fire solidified and encased him like a cocoon. But it didn't stop there. Energy surged through me, an angry wave. The ice continued to spread, coating the ground beneath my feet, creeping over tombstones. I had no control over it, and could only watch as the graveyard turned to ice.

Then it stopped. All the energy drained out of me, and I sank to my knees.

## 10

## THE INNER CIRCLE

Jack and Freya took control of the situation, directing the rest of the shell-shocked group. John and another guy called Louie lifted Conrad, and we were told to use Influence to prevent anyone from seeing us as we carried him onto the train. Everyone obeyed in silence. I felt numb, and not just because of the Darkworld. The ground was still slick with ice from what I'd done.

"We have to get him back to Headquarters," said Freya, as we sat in an otherwise-empty carriage on the train, surrounded by an Influence-generated shadow. "A regular hospital won't be able to treat the harpy's poison. You two take him to the healing room." Louie and John nodded. "Jack and I have to go and tell the Inner Circle what happened."

"You think it's a matter for the Inner Circle?" said Jack.

"Our own harpies turning against us? I'd say so."

"It could have just been him," said Jack, hesitantly. "Maybe… because he's a vampire."

Freya looked uncomfortable. "They've never attacked

anyone before, though. Mr Melmoth never had any trouble with them."

"True," Jack conceded. "Okay. We need to report to Dr Philips first—I was going to send a harpy ahead to warn her, but, well…"

"That's what happens when you rely on creatures from the Darkworld to carry your messages," said Claudia. "Whose bright idea was it to enslave those monsters anyway?"

"The Venantium have always used harpies," said Jack, turning to face her. "We've never had a problem with them before."

"Clearly, none of you ever got attacked by one," said Claudia. "Ash, show them your scars."

"I don't think—" I said, but Claudia had already pushed up my sleeve, revealing the faint silvery lines which marked where the harpy had first attacked me. Even after the ministrations of the fortune-teller, it had still left a mark.

Jack stared. "That was provoked, right?" he said, uncertainly.

"No. I was only going to the library," I said. "I nearly died, actually."

"Seriously?" said Freya, eyes wide. "That's… out of the ordinary. They don't usually wound, let alone…" Her hands moved unconsciously up and down her own arms. "I've never seen them attack anyone. Never."

I didn't feel like telling the whole story. My mind swam with unwanted thoughts, and try as I might, I couldn't keep my eyes from straying to the prone form of Conrad propped up on a seat, still frozen into a block of ice. Small mercy that we'd found an empty compartment. Even the ticket man had passed us by, diverted by Influence. I used it on autopilot;

only the perpetual chill of the Darkworld hovering around me reminded me that I was using its power. *The Darkworld itself defends you.* Because I was part of it. Part of the darkness.

The ice around Conrad was solid as glass. It wasn't even melting. Was I really that strong? How had I turned the cemetery into an ice rink?

My head spun, and I couldn't even shut my eyes because of the images that flashed before me. The body hanging from the ceiling in the cathedral. Conrad lying twitching on the ground. The blinded vampire lunging for me. Blackstone burning to the ground, reflected in a lake. I clenched my grip on the rail, as if trying to root myself in the here and now.

One wild bus ride from Redthorne later and we hurried through Blackstone. John and Louie cursed nonstop as they tried to keep Conrad from sliding out of their grip. It would have been a comical sight, were it not for our knowledge that harpy poison had Conrad in its grip, and we might already be too late.

The medical room was located on the same corridor as the interrogation rooms, which seemed ominous to me. The two guys carried Conrad down there—but for the rest of us, it was time to meet Dr Philips.

For the first time since I'd met her, she looked genuinely shocked when Freya explained what had happened.

"Impossible," she whispered. "The harpies have *never* attacked a *venator.* I must speak with the boy. I need his version of events."

"We don't know how it happened, but we can hardly interrogate Conrad now," said Jack. "He'll be lucky to survive."

Guilt stabbed me like sharp needles in my chest. All the

times I'd wished he'd disappear and leave me alone, and now...

"I must consult with the Inner Circle," said Dr Philips. "Freya, you come with me. And you, too, Ashlyn."

"Me?" I said, stupidly.

"Yes. I think they would be very interested to hear your version of events."

"Ash didn't do anything," said Claudia.

"I never said she did. But several of them have been keen to meet our new recruits, and now is the perfect opportunity."

"I'm not being interrogated again," I said. My voice sounded odd, disconnected from my thoughts. "You can't pin this one on me. I didn't do anything to provoke the harpies."

"I was more interested in your unusual use of magic. We have never witnessed such a display since Jude Anders's initiation test."

A chill that had nothing to do with the damp tunnel rushed up my arms.

"You're saying she's a necromancer?" said Claudia. "I'm getting kinda sick of people watching every time we use magic, and I'll bet Ash is, too. We're not on Lucifer's side!"

Dr Philips gave her a glacial look. "You have no respect, Miss Delaney. We recruited you as a mutual favour and would never abuse our position."

"You're dragging her in front of the Inner Circle!" Claudia said.

"I think Miss Temple can speak for herself."

"I'll go," I said. As exhausted as I was, I wanted answers, and I wouldn't turn down the chance to finally meet the mysterious leaders of the Venantium.

Dr Philips looked at me. "Very well. They may not ask

to speak to you at all; as you know, they are extremely busy. Miss Delaney, you need not stay."

"Like hell I'm leaving," said Claudia. "I'm not letting her face them alone."

The two glared at each other. I wondered if Claudia's issues with authority would even extend to the Inner Circle —the voices behind every threat, the nameless faces behind every act against us. I knew I should feel *something*— scared, angry, even determined—but the shock of everything that had happened that day had dulled all sensation.

Apparently, Dr Philips decided it wasn't worth arguing about. "Both of you, then. Come with me."

She led us out into the entrance hall and through the heavy iron doors at the back, into a wide hallway. Claudia raised her eyebrows when Dr Philips stopped in front of a blank stretch of wall at the end of the corridor, but after a minute, I began to perceive the outline of a door. Gradually, it revealed itself, unnervingly like a dark space. Dr Philips knocked, and the sound rang out like the peal of a bell.

"Enter," boomed a voice from within, startling me.

The door swung inwards. A long table dominated the room, surrounded by high-backed chairs. It looked like any old meeting room, really. Except for the paintings on the walls. They were even more gruesome than the ones in the entrance hall, if possible. One showed a ghoul latched on to the leg of a man dressed in medieval garb. His face was stretched in a grimace of pain. The man in the painting beside it had been possessed. The telltale third eye of a demon gleamed on his forehead, and rivulets of blood poured from behind the violet eyes. Behind, a building burned, and I saw the flames edging towards him. But the painting at the far end, above the head of the table, disturbed me the most. It showed a cobblestone street not unlike the ones outside, lined with old-fashioned dilapidated houses. At first it looked to be shrouded in darkness, but when I blinked, there was a row of people standing there in the distance, in a line spanning the whole street. Even from a distance I could see their gleaming demon eyes.

At once a strange feeling rose inside me, a surge of anger that was both mine and not mine, so sudden it froze me to the spot. Something about that painting resonated in a way I couldn't explain, only that the anger was completely disconnected from my own emotions. *The demon?*

I looked away, instead studying the people in the room.

Only three of the Inner Circle were present. One, a woman, while short in stature, had a presence that made me feel like I was about to be judged in court. I didn't meet her eyes for long. A fair-haired, large man sat at the head of the table, and on his left was Leo's father.

Aside from his slightly unruly dark hair, Mr Blake looked nothing like either of his sons. His movements reminded me of a shark on the hunt, quick and deadly, and his black marble eyes stood out in his chiselled face. He looked at me, and I swear my insides evaporated.

"This is most unexpected," he said quietly.

"We have had… a situation," said Dr Philips. I was astonished to hear the deference in her tone—completely different to her usual brisk manner. "A number of our harpies turned on the group and attacked them. One was gravely injured."

"Is that so?" said Mr Blake, as though she'd merely informed him it was raining outside.

"Yes. They tell me there was no provocation."

"Really?" The woman stood up, which made no difference to her height, but her gaze found mine and locked me to the spot. She and Mr Blake shared the same dead-eyed, marble-like intensity in their stares. Maybe a creepy expression was a prerequisite to join the Inner Circle.

"What have these three to say?" she said, indicating me, Claudia, and Freya.

"Only to confirm what they told me," said Dr Philips.

"You are Ashlyn Temple?"

I shifted, uncomfortable under her stare. "Um, yes, ma'am." I felt like I ought to curtsey or something; she had a regal presence that reminded me of the time a local lord had visited our school.

"I am Ms Constantine, Second of the Inner Circle. What is your version of the events that transpired today?"

"Um." I swallowed. "Our mission was to check out this cemetery where some strange things had been reported. There wasn't anything there, but, um, Freya and Jack suggested we have a look inside this old cathedral."

The images rushed back into my head, thick and fast. I fixed my gaze on the floor to avoid looking into Ms Constantine's eyes. "We found… a body. It was hanging from the ceiling. I don't know who it was. Then the harpies attacked Conrad. We had to destroy them, but they'd already…" I swallowed again. "He started to lose control… He's a vampire. I had to freeze him so we could bring him back to be treated. And that's it."

"Jack went to report the body," Freya added. "They should be sending someone up to remove it."

"So we do not yet know if it was one of our own," said the man at the head of the table. "Was there anyone in the field this morning?"

"Kyra Simmons," said Dr Philips. "She went to scout ahead."

The man nodded. None of the three showed any

emotion at the death of their fellow member. I guessed they just saw them as war casualties.

"And there was no evidence that Lucifer was involved?" said the man.

"It sounds like an isolated incident," said Mr Blake dismissively. I felt something inside me clench in anger. Did he not care about anyone? Stupid question. He ditched his own children, for crying out loud.

"If our harpies have turned on us, it would have serious consequences," said the other. "We rely on them for too much. Perhaps... perhaps it is a message."

"A feeble one, if it is," said Ms Constantine. "We will continue to use the harpies until it is proven that they are not our own. We need them to scour the country and search for demonic activity. We cannot possibly send embassies to all areas. The other branches of the Venantium rely on them even more than we do. It would spark a worldwide protest to stop using them."

"It may save lives," said Dr Philips quietly.

"Be that as it may, we need more proof," said Mr Blake. "I shall question the boy myself if need be. Is he in the medical bay?"

"Yes, but he is gravely injured. He will lose his sight, at the very least. Any other effects, I cannot say. The harpy's poison is lethal, as you know, and he was very unstable. He may also still be under the influence of the Vampire's Curse."

"Then he will need to be restrained," said Mr Blake. "Very well. I will check in with Dr Lewis."

"You want to see him?" said Dr Philips, surprise evident in her tone.

"I do. You should all return to your posts." And just like that, we were dismissed.

I knew that I should feel relieved that no one had

brought up the fact that I'd used demon magic, but I was just confused at the conflicting approaches of the Inner Circle members. I couldn't imagine these people as leaders. Granted, only three of them had been present, but still.

"Disappointed?" Claudia asked me, as we walked back up to campus later.

"Um," I said. "Kind of, yeah. I mean, they scared the shit out of me, but I don't know, there was something about them that seemed kind of… off."

"That's what being head of those lunatics does to you," said Claudia. "I'm seriously thinking of quitting. I shouldn't even have joined. I thought…" She rubbed her forehead with her hand. "I'm starting to think there's something screwy about them. More than usual, I mean."

"Really?" So it hadn't just been me. But I got creepy vibes from everyone connected to the Darkworld.

"Hell, yeah. I wanted to fight shadow-beasts, not our own people. And I can't believe that that Ms Constantine actually wants to keep using the harpies. And Mr Blake. Twat."

"They didn't really let the other guy get a word in edgeways, did they?" I said.

"God, they're worse than I thought. What were they even doing in there? It didn't look like a meeting."

"No clue. I wonder where the other four are," I said. Did the Venantium not even keep tabs on the council?

"Hopefully doing their jobs. I wonder who actually pays them? Seeing as they're the highest ranked?"

"I've no idea. Cyrus would know."

"I haven't heard from Cyrus in forever," said Claudia, still rubbing her head.

"I've emailed him a few times," I admitted.

"Really? I thought you weren't…" She cleared her throat. "I mean, after what happened. I know it isn't

Cyrus's fault, but it was kind of heartless of him, taking off like that. Not that it was his fault really anyway... I'm babbling. Never mind."

"He emailed me over summer," I said, more in an attempt to draw the conversation further away from the Inner Circle than anything. "Thought it'd be nice to stay in touch. He hasn't run into any trouble, anyway. He just wanted me to keep him updated with what's happening here."

"Hell is being unleashed," said Claudia, but in a matter-of-fact tone, not overdramatic. "God knows if it's Lucifer who's doing it, but whoever it is, they have no mercy. Attacking the Venantium right where it hurts. And that poor girl."

*Tell me about it.* Right now, I'd be happy never to set foot in the place again. But still, part of me wanted answers. "Why did the harpies only attack Conrad?" I said. "If they wanted to give the Venantium a message, surely Freya or Jack would have been the more logical choices."

"I have no idea. Maybe they just don't like vampires. There might be another Jude."

"But they killed that girl, too," I said, shuddering at the memory. That could easily have been Claudia... but not me. Never me. Because the demons saw me as an ally. Right now, I felt like I walked on thin ice only I could see. How long before the other *venators* questioned why I could freeze an entire cemetery but couldn't conjure fire?

Claudia ran a hand through her tangled hair. "Yeah. That's why I don't want to be involved. Did you feel anything pushing you to join? I've been thinking... You know when the fortune-teller..." She glanced at me, biting her lip.

"What?" I said.

She took a deep breath. "I think something's been screwing with my head. Not just now. For ages."

I blinked, not following. "How d'you mean?"

"Why did you pick this university? The Venantium draw people here with a connection to the Darkworld, right? But I already knew they were full of shit, my parents told me, and I still came here. I've been thinking that I might not have had a choice about it. I think someone used Influence on me."

"You really think that?" I said. No way. But the point of Influence was that it was unobtrusive. I'd walked under it most of my freaking *life* without knowing.

"I don't know what to think. But it's like there's the part of me which wanted to rebel against my parents for keeping me in the dark... and another part of me that wanted to join the Venantium."

"You said you wanted to help people?"

"Yeah, but... I don't want to be part of their mind games. It's all a mess." She pressed a knuckle into her forehead, lips drawn tight with frustration. "Ever since I started thinking about this, I haven't been able to get it out of my head. If they used a mind-trick on me to keep me under their gaze... like the others. What if they did?"

"I don't know." It amazed me that I'd never considered the possibility before. What if we'd all been drawn here by subliminal magic, after all? Thoughts like that would drive me crazy, but I pondered the odd sense of *wrongness* around the Inner Circle. Had they been influencing us in that very room?

"Well, I feel like there's something in my head. It's like you said, when the fortune-teller screwed with your memories. Only it's been getting worse since I joined up with them. I feel like someone *made* me do it. They barely had to ask and I signed up, and now I feel like a jackass to my parents. They tried to keep me away from it all. Now I'm knee-deep in shit." She gave a brittle laugh.

"We can't know for sure. Maybe they were just desperate. I didn't feel anything like that when David asked me." I was fairly sure I'd be able to tell the difference—at least, I thought so.

But I distrusted even my own memory now, after what the fortune-teller had done. Paranoia threatened to rise again, sending my reality crumbling to ashes.

"Come on," I said. "We've had a really long and messed-up day."

"Yeah. I'll have nightmares."

"I don't want to sleep," I said. "I can't—I can't even shut my eyes."

"Want to go for a drink? It might help you sleep, is all."

"Guess I don't have anything better to do."

But try as I might, I couldn't rid myself of the image of Conrad, blinded and writhing on the ground, and the sickening sense of guilt that it was my fault he'd been there in the first place.

## 11

### PREMONITION

Sleep eluded me despite drinking three ciders at the Coach and Horses; every time I closed my eyes, the rush of images made me open them again immediately. I finally gave up and got out of bed, realising I hadn't eaten anything in over twenty-four hours. I went to the kitchen, yawning, exhaustion dragging at my limbs.

Someone sat there in the dark. I didn't see them until the automatic ceiling lights came on, startling me so much I nearly screamed.

"It's only me!" said Rachel. She sat at the table, scrawling on a scrap of paper, not words but a meaningless scribble.

I stared. She looked ill. Her crumpled clothes were stained with multicoloured paint, and her face was pale and light-starved. Her eyes were bigger than ever, and something flashed in them as she watched me edge towards the cupboard to get cereal I no longer wanted.

"How're you, Ash?"

"Um, fine," I said. "Are you okay?"

"Yes, I'm fine."

"You should get some sleep. What are you doing sitting in the dark?"

"The dark is peaceful," she said, her voice barely concealing an inexplicable laugh.

I didn't know what to say to that. I finished pouring cereal and strode towards the door. Rachel turned around and fixed her gaze on me.

"Do you ever hear voices?" she said.

"Voices?" I said. *Oh…kay. This is out of my area of expertise.*

"Yeah. There's this voice in my head…"

"Have you seen a psychiatrist?"

"I'm not mad!" She jumped to her feet, knocking the paper to the floor. My heart plummeted.

She'd been drawing demon eyes.

"What's that?" I said, indicating the drawing.

"You can't pretend you don't hear it," she whispered, coming toward me, hands outstretched. I stepped back into the door frame, goose bumps breaking out as she stroked my arms with her index fingers.

*This is beyond creepy.*

"Hear what?" I edged away, careful not to spill my cereal.

"Him. He's coming," she proclaimed.

"Huh?"

"Say hi for me," she said, moving away from me in another swift, catlike movement. She picked up the scrap of paper, sat down at the table, and started scribbling again.

Shuddering, I rushed back to my room, seized by the impulse to make sure the pendant was safe. I'd left it tucked into my jacket, which I'd slung over my desk chair last night.

I texted Claudia to ask if she wanted to go back to the

Venantium's Headquarters to check on Conrad. The guilt gnawed away at me. I had to know if he'd survived the night; otherwise it might drive me mad.

Claudia reluctantly agreed, despite our conversation yesterday.

**"I dunno if they're still playing mind games but I can't sleep anyway. Might as well go for a walk. I want to do something, and I sure as hell can't concentrate on lectures."**

She had a point; we'd be cutting it fine to make it back in time for my ten o'clock lecture. But I couldn't even begin to think about lectures after the weekend I'd had.

We caught the bus and walked through the fog-wreathed streets to the cemetery. At least we could use the main entrance at any time now. It opened for us as well as any *venator*. I'd grown used to the disorienting sensation of falling-but-not-falling into the grave, so it barely bothered me—in the split second floating in nothingness, I wondered what kind of magic they used to power it. *Influence*, I thought. Magic couldn't transport anything from one place to another, so it must be a mind-trick to make even the members forget how they got into Headquarters. Which was about level ten on the paranoia scale.

In the entrance hall, several *venators* paced about. David hovered around, probably acting as front-boy, while Dr Philips stormed from the tunnels, looking harassed. Claudia and I made a beeline for her.

"He's alive," she said bluntly before I could open my mouth, "but we've had to keep him isolated. He seems unable to prevent himself from succumbing to the Curse."

"What, you've locked him up?" said Claudia, eyes narrowing. She hadn't bothered to put makeup on and looked as tired and dishevelled as I felt.

"It's for his own safety as much as those around him.

You may ask our healer, Dr Franklyn, if you can see him, but it's unlikely that he will recognise you in his current state."

I didn't feel much like facing a crazed, blinded vampire, but we'd come all this way. So we reluctantly walked down the cold stone stairs that led to the medical bay—and the cells.

The medical bay was two doors down from the room with the Angel Box, where I'd been interrogated three times. Our footsteps echoed in the deserted corridor, and I could hear a faint moaning noise that raised the hairs on my arms. Conrad. It had to be.

The door had been left open. Inside the long room were rows of beds, all unoccupied. The moaning emanated from behind another door at the back, and when I nervously pushed it open, my heart dropped.

Conrad was in a glass case that resembled the Angel Box, backed onto a wall underneath a fluorescent ceiling light. He crouched on the ground, hands clutching his face, and didn't look up when we entered. Blood stained his sleeves up to his elbows, and a jolt of anger shot through me at his being caged like an animal. A woman sat at a desk beside the case, typing away at a computer. She saw us and gave us both a pitying look.

"He's lost all sense of self. He won't talk to you. None of us can get close to him."

I didn't know what to say to that. *I'm sorry.*

Claudia cleared her throat. "Um. Never mind. We'll just be going, then."

"I'm sorry," said the woman, pushing a dark curl out of her eyes. Her face was prematurely lined, even though she couldn't be older than thirty-five or so. "Kids like him shouldn't be out in the field."

I raised my eyebrows in surprise. That was the closest

to compassion I'd ever heard a senior *venator* express. I guessed being a nurse or healer required *some* human feeling.

Conrad let out a whimper. His ruined eyes looked even worse in the glaring overhead light, and even though he could no longer see, he twisted away, trying to cover himself from its brightness.

"Is the poison gone?" I said.

"Yes. I was unable to save his sight, however. He will need to get the proper medical care at a hospital, but as long as he is like this, he can't be around normal people. He attacked everyone who tried to help him, injuring three of my assistants when they were trying to administer the antidote. We barely managed to save him."

"At least... at least he's still alive." Claudia's tone betrayed uncertainty. "So... does he just have to stay here, then? Indefinitely? Couldn't you drug him?"

"That would only postpone the problem."

He'd recovered quickly the last time I'd seen him succumb to the curse, when we'd run into the Skele-Ghoul in the forest, but that had been a minor shock compared to losing his sight to a harpy. I had to stopper another unwelcome memory.

"So you just have to wait for him to snap out of it?"

"I've treated others with his condition, but something is different this time. Perhaps it is because he was injured by a creature of the Darkworld."

"What do *you* think about that?" said Claudia. "The Inner Circle—well, two of them, anyway—say that you're going to keep using the harpies." An undercurrent of accusation ran through her tone.

"Did they say that?" said Dr Franklyn. She shook her head. "It's not my place to question their decisions, but the number of casualties recently suggests that something is wrong with their methods. But they're well set in tradition, as I'm sure you know."

"Yeah," said Claudia. "We know that. And I wanna know something else."

She stepped toward the nurse, who blinked at her, puzzled.

"Are you lot using mind-tricks to make magic-users come to Blackstone? Did you manipulate me into joining?"

Dr Franklyn's eyebrows disappeared into her hair. "You believe you're being manipulated?"

"I wouldn't choose to join of my own free will! My own parents spent their whole lives trying to keep me safe from being drawn into the Venantium."

"Many of us do not know what we are capable of," said Dr Franklyn. "Not all of the Venantium are so set in tradition. We want to protect humanity and save lives."

Claudia let out a frustrated sigh. "I know, but this just seems *off* to me. Why do so many magic-users come here?"

"The Barrier draws them," said Dr Franklyn. "It makes sense, when you think about it. But many magic-users go through their lives without ever setting foot in Blackstone. There's another branch of the Venantium in London and a third in Edinburgh. You have limited experience, I know, but we would never manipulate anyone into joining us."

"Right," said Claudia. "Okay. Just making sure. This whole thing recently has been weird."

"You had a horrible shock yesterday," said Dr Franklyn. "I can give you something to help you sleep?"

"Nah, I'm good," said Claudia. I guessed she didn't trust a *venator* enough that she'd take any medicine from them. Though we'd depended on the fortune-teller enough times.

"Is there anything else I can help you with?"

"I guess not," said Claudia. "We should go."

I nodded. We bade farewell to the nurse and left the room. I felt a fresh surge of guilt as Conrad threw himself at the glass behind us, hitting the wall of the case with a *smack*.

"Poor guy," said Claudia.

I nodded. My throat felt tight, and I had that horrible, cliff-dangling feeling again, the sense of utter helplessness in the face of the monstrosities of the Darkworld.

I jumped about a foot in the air when someone swept past us, heading for the cells. Mr Blake.

Claudia gave me a quizzical look. We paused for a second, and then Claudia turned on her heel and followed him.

"Wait!" I whispered, as quietly as I could.

"What's he doing down here?" she whispered back.

"Probably some secret Inner Circle stuff. Seriously, don't go after him."

She ignored me, edging down the hallway like she'd decided to impersonate a spy or ninja or something. *Shit.* I hovered, indecisive. Should I risk getting caught, too? But curiosity won out, and I hurried after her.

We walked at a steady pace, following close enough to see where Mr Blake was going whilst staying far back enough to keep out of his sight—not an easy task. He passed the rows of cells without pausing. I hated this place, the stone walls exuding coldness and the smell of damp pervading. A skittering sound echoed ahead. *Rats. Wonderful.*

I started to question the wisdom of our decision, but Claudia wore a stubborn expression, and I knew that whatever her reasons for following Mr Blake, she wouldn't give up.

Either side of us, I could see the hunched shapes of

human bodies in some of the cells, but I tried not to look too closely. *This is bloody medieval,* I thought, and experienced another confliction about my moral place in working with these people. Whatever crimes these people had committed, the Venantium's punishments reminded me of societies where tyrants ruled. I wondered if anyone had ever challenged the status quo within the Venantium.

These thoughts occupied my mind as we passed cell after cell. After a while, I started to realise that he had no intention of stopping at the cells at all, but walked toward the deeper tunnels. Curiosity started to creep up on me again. Where was he going? I thought of the labyrinth of passageways beneath the villages beyond, of the sepulchres and cellars and the hidden laboratory Leo and I had never found. It probably didn't even exist.

I swallowed the lump in my throat and pressed on. The candle lights dimmed as we left the Venantium behind—and without warning, everything went pitch-black. Claudia swore.

"Crap. He'll see us if we conjure lights."

"I'm not going down there in the dark," I said. "No freaking way."

"But we can follow his light…" Her voice came from just in front of me.

"Not happening. There could be holes in the ground, or rivers, or God knows what."

She sighed. "You're right. Damn."

So we turned around and headed back.

"Asн, why weren't you at the lecture?" said Alex as I came into the kitchen later. "And why are you covered in mud?"

*Crap.* Mud from the tunnels stained my coat and

jeans. Alex, Sarah, and Rachel all stared at me. Rachel looked marginally saner than the last time I'd seen her, her pupils a tad less dilated, but the memory of her drawing demon eyes made me reluctant to meet her gaze.

"I went for a walk," I said, doing my best to feign nonchalance. "Forgot how muddy it gets this time of year."

"All year round, really," said Sarah. "But you've never missed a lecture before. Are you okay?"

I met her concerned gaze and felt something inside me fracture. What had I done to deserve friends like Alex and Sarah? And what if they were the next victims? I put everyone I knew in danger—even though the nagging voice of common sense told me Conrad had volunteered for the mission himself, that I had had nothing to do with it. But the sense of responsibility remained.

"I'm fine," I said, ducking my head. "I'm gonna go and get my books and catch up. Can I borrow your lecture notes?"

"Sure," said Sarah.

"This is a historic occasion," said Alex, who usually asked to borrow *my* lecture notes when she'd either fallen asleep or not paid attention.

When I returned to the kitchen, arms laden with heavy books, Alex accosted me.

"You've missed some seriously weird shit," she said. "Did you hear about that girl who hanged herself?"

My heart gave an unpleasant lurch. "What? Who?"

Alex shrugged. "I didn't know her, but Pete's freaked. It happened in his flat. *Our* old flat."

My insides lurched again. Our old flat. Where Terrence had contacted demons…

*It can't be that. It can't be.*

"Yeah, it's pretty awful," said Sarah, shuddering. "I feel

bad for the girl who found her. She's in hospital for the shock."

"She was talking about demons," said Rachel.

My heart dropped.

"Huh?" I said, trying to keep my voice even, though my pulse raced and horrible possibilities sprang up in my mind. *Why didn't I hear about it?*

"Demons," she said, thoughtfully, as though pondering something. "She said they talked to her."

"She was in shock," said Alex. "Poor girl. And, yeah, Pete's going around talking nonsense too, but that's because he's wasted twenty-four/seven these days."

"That's horrible." I picked up Sarah's notes but couldn't even bring myself to focus on literary theory. What was the point in having a demon in my head if I was totally unaware when things like this happened? Unless it was coincidence, but I didn't believe that for a second. Not where the Darkworld was concerned.

"Yeah," said Alex, halfheartedly turning the page of her own book. "Plus someone dug up a dead body and left it lying around as a prank. The world's gone bloody mental."

"I saw that," I said—that, at least, I could tell them. "It was just lying in the middle of the village. Did someone take it away?"

"It was a beacon," said Rachel. "A warning."

"Huh?" I said. *A warning?*

"She's been saying crap like that all day," said Alex, dismissively. "Ignore her. Yeah, someone had the sense to report it and it got taken away. God knows who it was, though. They found the body under campus where they were digging, right?"

"Yep," said Sarah. "Someone stole it. It's so messed up."

*Yeah.* But was Rachel just talking nonsense, or… something else?

"Tell me about it," said Alex. "People steal signs from campus when they're on bar crawls, yeah, but a dead body? Ugh. There's a limit." She shuddered.

"I don't think it was a drunk student," said Rachel, absently.

"Huh?" I said, looking at her. She scribbled on a scrap of paper, like she had this morning. An uncomfortable feeling crept up my spine.

"I think *he* put it there."

Silence fell. Alex rolled her eyes, but even she looked a little freaked out. "Okay, I'm going to pretend it's a normal day and nothing crazy just happened. It's the only way I'm ever gonna get this bloody assignment finished."

"Agreed," I said, quietly, though my head was anything but. My unfinished work couldn't pull my attention away from the paper Rachel was scribbling on. I found my eyes drawn toward it, over and over again. She'd written one line, over and over again, "There are no angels".

Shivers danced up and down my arms. Sensitive to the Darkworld or not, she had some awareness of what was going on. Perhaps even more than I did.

It didn't bode well.

## 12

### DOUBLE SELF

I dreaded the night. The instant I tried to sleep, the images waiting behind my eyes replayed in a gory slide-show. Conrad, the body, the blood-stained graves. The message scrawled in the old church: THERE ARE NO ANGELS.

It hurt to keep my eyes open, but I couldn't deal with those thoughts right now. I opened my laptop and typed a barely coherent email to Cyrus, giving a rundown of the events of that weekend.

His response came almost immediately: **"Holy. Crap. Okay. It's gonna take me a while to process all that."**

Of course, being in a different time zone, six or seven hours behind, Cyrus would think this a reasonable time. I guessed he'd replied from his phone; it would be too much of a coincidence that he'd be at a computer the exact same time my message arrived. What did it matter, anyway? My brain was so tired I overthought everything and twisted the tiniest thing into a knot.

**"I know, right? I never thought the harpies**

would turn on the *venators*. I honestly thought they had them under control."

"What did the *venators* do?" Cyrus replied. "Please tell me they reported it to the Inner Circle."

"Yeah, but they didn't do a thing. Claudia and I went to talk to them and they just said they'd relied on the harpies for so long they wouldn't stop using them after a freak accident, or whatever."

"Freak accident? That was an attack. They need to get their priorities in order. Did dear old Dad have anything to say?"

"Mr Blake? Shit, I forgot he was your dad for a minute there. That was stupid. Yeah, Claudia and I saw him sneaking off into the tunnels yesterday actually. I don't know what he was doing or where he was going. It got too dark for us to follow."

"I don't trust him. Hell, I've never trusted him since he joined the higher-ups. There's something up with the Inner Circle. It'd serve him right if one of the harpies took *his* eyes out. Man, Leo's gonna freak."

My heart did this ridiculous flip. *For God's sake.*

"You're going to tell him?"

"'Course I am. He'll want to know. What were the other Inner Circle members like, anyway?"

"There was this woman who was like Dr Philips, only scarier. Ms Constantine, she said her name was. And this blond guy who didn't say much. I don't know whether he agreed with the others or not."

"Might be Mr Fraser? He used to be a good guy. Well, for one of them. Came round to our

**house a couple of times. Leo used to make trouble, as you can imagine."**

Those words caused my chest to tighten painfully, and I tried to shut my mind to the rush of memories. As I was already trying to suppress so much, I only partially succeeded.

**"Anyway. I gotta go. You take care of yourself, Ash. You sure you want to carry on working for them?"**

**"I want to know more about Lucifer, about all the shit that's going on. I think they're the only people who can tell me."**

**"Keep your enemies closer. I get it. Stay safe. Talk later."**

**"Sure thing."**

I shut my laptop. Now I needed something else to distract me from sleep. If I could escape to another universe even for a minute, it'd be a blessing. So I ignored all my unfinished work and lost myself in a book for the first time in weeks.

LIGHT SPILLED ACROSS MY VISION, painful against my tired eyes. I'd dozed off after all, leaning against the wall in bed with the book in my lap.

I eased out a crick in my neck, putting the book to one side. The light streaming through the curtains told me that the sun had risen. I felt like I hadn't slept at all. Groaning, I moved into a more comfortable position—and froze as my eyes found someone else in the middle of the room, looking right at me. The doppelgänger.

*"Miss me, Ash?"*

The last time I'd seen her had been months ago, the

night before my life had fallen apart. She'd been the one to ask when I'd last spoken to my parents. Even though she'd only voiced what I'd been suppressing, I still felt a spark of anger at my double for igniting the fire that had destroyed everything.

"How are you still here?" I said. "You're dead." The real doppelgänger had been killed that night in the sepulchre. Not that she'd really been living anyway. She'd been a kind of ghost, a half-demon remnant of a human-demon killed twenty years ago, brought back by the energy channelled in Jude's experiments. But the higher demon Belphegor, also drawn to the hole Jude had ripped in the Darkworld, had killed her. I still saw her image in dreams, but I imagined it to be a manifestation of my subconscious, not a demon.

*"You're right. I never claimed to be her. It's easy to take on a form you recognise, but I don't think you want to speak to a demon who looks like one of your friends, am I right?"*

"So you are a demon? Are you working for Lucifer?"

*"I have no love of Lucifer. He might claim to rule the Darkworld, but he's no demon. Many of my kin are in agreement. We are on your side, Ashlyn."*

"A likely story."

*"We want to help you. You may be the last hope for the Darkworld."*

"Like I want anything to do with you."

*"You need my help, Ashlyn. If you fall to Lucifer, all will be lost —for humans and demons alike."*

"Lucifer doesn't want to kill me. He wants me on his side—right? That's what Mephistopheles said."

*"And you'd choose to support a crazed human sorcerer rather than listening to reason? You need to overcome your prejudice, Ashlyn. Not all demons are out to cause you harm. You are our equal."*

"You kill people. You read people's minds and try to trick them. You're evil."

*"Evil?"* A laugh. *"You think humans are free of what they call evil?"*

"No. Lucifer's evil, too."

*"I'm glad we agree on that, at least. Come on, Ashlyn. Are you not curious to learn what I have to say?"*

"Why do you need to ask? You can read my thoughts, can't you?"

*"I prefer not to be intrusive. Besides, I can't penetrate your shield. It's too strong for any other than a true demon."*

"So how are you speaking to me?"

*"Selective mind-communication. You've a lot to learn, Ashlyn."*

"How d'you mean?"

*"You need to learn what you are. What you can do. You have some idea, but a large part of yourself is locked away. You deny yourself."*

"I don't want the demon inside me to start killing people. I'm not like that." No. I wasn't. Sure, she'd tried to defend me before, but I could control her. I had to, to avoid a repeat of what happened with Mephistopheles.

*"What makes you think your other side has evil intents?"*

"She… she tried to kill Leo. And almost succeeded."

*"She was trying to kill the demon inside him, Mephistopheles. Demons might not distinguish between friend and foe, but wouldn't your friends at the Venantium prioritise the loss of one life over the potential loss of many?"*

My chest grew tight, tears springing to my eyes. I couldn't deny it. If Mephistopheles had triumphed, he'd have gone on a killing spree, and Leo wouldn't have been the only casualty. The demon inside me had been trying to avoid that.

Maybe it had been me all along.

*"You can't deny it, Ashlyn. Humans and demons alike rest on a*

*balance that can tip either way. You might not be dependent on magical energy as an anchor, as true demons are, but it is something that affects you whether you like it or not. Take your demon heart."*

My hand closed on the crystal around my neck before I remembered it was a fake. I picked up my black jacket instead, the one with the hidden pocket I'd picked as the perfect hiding place. Of course, I'd had to wear the coat constantly, removing the crystal only when I did my laundry. My friends joked that I must sleep in it.

The amethyst gleamed in my hands, deceptively innocuous.

*"You've never tried to access its power yourself, have you?"*

"I don't know what you mean."

*"Clearly, your mother has told you nothing about how to draw on your power. But you can draw on it anytime you like. You do it subconsciously, when you connect to the Darkworld, but in order to make full use of your powers, you need to learn to control it."*

"You seriously expect me to want to take lessons from you?"

*"Have you ever wondered, Ashlyn, why it is that when your connection to the Darkworld opened, you could no longer feel the temperature change? And why you can, now?"*

"Huh? How did you know about that?" Since when did demons care about human concerns?

*"It's what happens when a human-demon comes to consciousness of their true self. You are part of the Darkworld, and the Darkworld is a place free from light and warmth. You had your feet in two worlds, for a time. But then what happened?"*

"I don't know. I don't know what you mean."

*"You fell in love."*

Darts pierced my heart. The doppelgänger was right; I'd first noticed that I could feel warmth again that night in the sepulchre, when Leo had kissed me...

*"Love is the most complex of human emotions. You opened your-*

*self to another, and in doing so… you began to take energy from him. As a demon would."*

*No.* It couldn't be—I hadn't taken anything from Leo. I couldn't have. I would have known—wouldn't I? *I'm not a demon. It can't be true!* I didn't speak the thoughts aloud, but I knew the doppelgänger read them from me anyway.

*"You didn't mean to do it, I know that. It didn't happen on a large scale, either, not enough to be noticeable to anyone who wouldn't recognise the signs. But it's true. You take energy from the people around you. And if you wanted, you could take more."*

The world span. I shut my eyes. "You… you mean I could kill. Like a real demon."

*"No. You're not strong enough, and it would kill you besides. Human-demons are not meant for taking power. But Lucifer may force you to do it. That's why you must learn to control it."*

"How do *you* know?" I said. "You said most people wouldn't recognise the signs—but *you* did."

*"How indeed? To be honest, I don't entirely trust you, Ashlyn. If I reveal my true identity, there's nothing to stop him or any other demon from reading it from you. But I can teach you to control the energy you take from those around you."*

I felt ice-cold already. *I can't. I can't risk it. I…*

*"The power is already there, waiting to be claimed. You don't need to take much. Just a taste."*

My fist remained closed around the amethyst, and I could feel the power lurking at the edge of consciousness. Despite myself, I touched it, as I did when I reached out to the Darkworld, feeling the edges curl around my fingers like trails of silk. With the touch came coldness, awareness of a vast store of energy—and something shot through me, making every bone tremble. It took a moment to recognise the emotion. Anger.

Energy coursed through me, wiping all tiredness from my mind and body, revitalising as fresh air. But with it came a murderous rage, sharp as a flood of ice-cold water. I gasped, and my vision flickered to purple and back again.

The demon inside me was furious.

*Why?* I asked, but there was no answer, only wave after wave of pure rage. I let the crystal drop and felt my hand sear. It had actually burned me.

I looked up. The doppelgänger had vanished.

"I don't understand," I whispered.

The rage had gone, to be replaced by confusion.

"I don't understand," I said, again, looking down at my burned hand.

No one answered.

## 13

---

### AUNT EVE'S HOUSE

The one upside to touching the crystal was that I was no longer tired; if anything, I felt more energised than I had in weeks. But I didn't know what to do with that energy. No doubt the Venantium would call on me again. I still wasn't sure whether I wanted to go back.

But when my phone vibrated, it wasn't the Venantium or even Claudia, but a number with no name. **"I am in the area, but I fear to set foot in Blackstone. If it is not too much to ask, are you able to come to my old house in Windermere? I will give you directions if you don't remember the way."**

"You've got to be shitting me," I muttered. She dared to invite me to her house—the house she'd lived in for fifteen years when she'd been my aunt Eve?

I didn't know what to do. She hadn't said it was urgent, which made me think that she only wanted to talk.

Like I wanted to spend any quality time with my so-called mother. I ignored the text and decided to tell Claudia about my eventful night.

First I had to get through lectures. I was falling behind on the reading, but it was go to the lectures unprepared or risk falling even further behind. Didn't help that whenever I let my thoughts stray, they inevitably landed on the doppelgänger, the demon inside me, that sharp anger. I was completely restless, unable to keep still in my seat, like I'd drunk a litre of cheap, shitty energy drink. In my seminar, I skim-read the required reading surreptitiously under the desk, whilst my fellow students debated about Victorian gender roles. Like I could think about stuff like that right now.

Claudia met me in the library, after I'd muttered some feeble excuse to my friends and slipped away.

"What gives?" she said.

"Too many weird things happening lately," I said, and gave her the gist of what the doppelgänger had told me—leaving out the part about me taking energy from people; I couldn't even begin to process how I felt about that. I also told her about Rachel, and the girl who'd killed herself.

"You think the demons had something to do with it?" said Claudia, biting her lip. "I don't know…"

"I just figured it seems too weird to be a coincidence. Especially with it being in the flat where Terrence was up to crazy shit. And Rachel definitely knows there's something going on. She was drawing demon eyes and writing something I saw in a dream." I didn't mention I'd seen it at the cathedral, too.

Claudia's concerned gaze met mine. "You're dreaming again?"

"Yeah." I pulled out my phone. "My dreams have always been crazy, but last time it was the fortune-teller doing it."

Claudia's eyes flashed toward the lit-up screen of my iPhone. "You heard from her?"

I'd left the message open on the screen. I lowered my gaze. "Yeah."

Silence thickened between us. Claudia clearly didn't know what to say, and I couldn't blame her. I didn't know what to think. If anyone could give me answers, Madame Persephone could—and yet the last time, the sting in the tail had been too much. If she kept any other life-shattering secret from me, I'd break.

"I think you should go," Claudia said quietly.

"Why?" I said. "I have nothing to say to her." I was aware that I sounded like a child, but she'd seriously screwed up in the parenting department. What more could I say to her?

"She might have important information about Lucifer, though. She's more likely to tell us stuff than the Venantium, let's face it."

"Yeah, but she also lies. Hell, her whole life's a lie. She's possessing the body of a comatose woman. Does that not creep you out?"

"Ugh. Forgot about that. Yeah, it is creepy. But still. She might be the only person who can give us some answers."

She had a point. "Yeah, but... I don't know. She wants me to go to the old house in the Lake District. The place where... where Terrence died."

Claudia frowned at me. "Why?"

"I guess because it was where we spent time together when she was my aunt Eve. It's all mixed up in my head now. She used to tell stories..." A lump rose in my throat, threatening to choke me, when I thought of those happy, carefree days when I still had parents.

I thought of Aunt Eve and her cosy cottage in the middle of the woods. I thought of the dark trees clustering around as though guarding a secret, luring me inside. Ten-year-old Ash ran through the woods, delighting in the limitless freedom, until she realised she'd wandered too far and was in an unfamiliar place, filled with dark shadows. The time I got lost in the woods was a scene I still visited in nightmares occasionally—I'd wandered around for hours, shivering and sobbing, panicking as the sky darkened and shadows swept the forest, until I turned a corner and found Aunt Eve waiting for me. As if she knew where I was.

Of course she had.

I FELT no happiness or freedom as I walked uphill through Windermere this time, head bent against the chilly wind. Claudia walked alongside me; in a fit of paranoia, she'd refused to let me go alone. The lake was a rippling blue carpet, visible through gaps between the houses and little shops as we climbed the hill, each step triggering another memory of that snowbound night. The night I'd both learned who I was and had been deceived again.

I had only one lecture on a Wednesday and it wasn't particularly important, so I felt no guilt about skiving in order to leave as early as possible to avoid having to come home at night.

We followed the fortune-teller's unusually clear directions. Usually she went out of her way to be cryptic, but her response to my blunt **"Okay"** sent in reply to her last text was a plain list of directions from Windermere to the cottage in the woods.

I had a strange sense of déjà vu, walking along the winding country lanes lined with cheerful cottages belonging to holidaymakers and retired people. This time of year, there were few people about. Boats still ran trips on the lake, but most of the passengers hid inside, looking out at the mountains through grimy windows, and those who sat on the open roofs of the boats were huddled in thick layers.

Then the lake disappeared from view as the cottages were replaced by trees, a thick wall that spread alongside the hill. I shuddered at the memory of standing in a bank of snow, struggling to push a minibus up the ice-coated slope, before a figure had beckoned me into the woods.

I'd had no will of my own then. Terrence had had my demon heart, and it had not been my decision to follow him into the dark woods but an irresistible pull.

This time I was even more reluctant. But I knew I had to do it. I nodded at Claudia and led the way off the road and onto the barely defined path through the thick trees.

I kept reaching to touch the fake pendant around my neck to reassure myself that it was still there, even though I could feel the weight of the genuine one against my chest from my jacket's inside pocket. I held my phone open to messages to check the fortune-teller's directions, not trusting in my ability to remember them.

The forest seemed like a left-behind relic from a time in the long-past when the world was covered beneath vast forests that never seemed to end. A patch of nature left untouched. Our feet whispered over the carpet of autumn leaves. It couldn't be more different from the forbidding, snow-coated wilderness I'd stumbled through last time—yet fear still lurked beneath the surface. It was too quiet. If not for Claudia beside me, a reassuringly human presence, I'd probably have flat-out ran through the forest to get it over with.

To distract myself, I told Claudia all about Aunt Eve, including the last conversation we'd had here when she'd revealed herself to be the fortune-teller. I'd never gone into details about that night; not with Claudia, anyway.

"And you had no idea she was your mother?"

"Of course not. I don't think I even really believed her at first." No. I'd been focused on what she'd told me about *me*—about being part demon. I hadn't thought even then she played mind games with me. I'd thought she was *helping* me. On my side. The regret left a sour taste in my mouth.

A pause. "Yeah. I've never heard of another magic-user who could change their appearance like that. But... well, I guess it was the first clue, you know." Claudia dug her hands in her pockets.

"That she was a liar," I said, and an angry voice in my head awoke, asking why I followed the directions of someone I'd sworn never to speak to again. "It's stupid. I should have realised something was wrong from the start. Why would she have had the demon heart in the first place if we weren't related? She was the one who sent it to me." The clues were all there, really. I'd been as blinded as when Terrence doctored my memories. But that was the point of mind-magic, wasn't it?

"You couldn't have known," said Claudia, consolingly.

"She said..." I cast my mind back to that fateful night. "She said mine was the only true demon heart. She even said it was a family heirloom. I should have made the connection."

"Who would? You'd been through enough crap that night."

"I could have asked later. I did think about it some-times, but I never questioned why. Maybe she messed with my mind to stop me from raising the question." And that was worse than erasing my memories: she'd even stopped me *asking*. She'd taken my free will away, and there was no getting around that.

"Would it have been any easier knowing the full truth

back then? Maybe she was waiting for the right moment to tell you."

I sighed heavily. "I guess. I just feel stupid. It's all coming back to me now. *No one has had the connection to the Darkworld in your family for over a hundred years…*"

"She said that? What a—"

"Total bitch," I said. "She's all half-truths and evasions. Why are we even here?" I dug my feet into the ground.

"Too late to go back now," said Claudia, pointing ahead.

Through the branches, I glimpsed the clearing where my aunt's old house sat nestled in the trees. Our soft footsteps made the only sound as we approached. Nature had reclaimed the cottage in the years it had been vacant. Ivy snaked up the walls and over the cobwebbed windows, almost obscuring the door entirely. I drew in a deep breath, glancing around to make sure we were truly alone.

The wooden door had once been red but was now rust-coloured; the colour had bled out in age. It creaked loudly, protesting as I forced it open. I pushed aside a wreath of cobwebs, squinting into the hall. The lightbulb swinging overhead had long-since died, and dusty silence pervaded.

The living room was on the left, the door slightly ajar. Three moth-chewed armchairs grouped around an empty grate where a fire used to burn whenever I visited. Last time, even in the aftermath of the demon attack, the fortune-teller had told me this was a place of refuge, a place I'd always be safe—the seat of my demon heart's power. Now that I focused, I could feel the power thrumming at the edges of my perception, a connection waiting to be awoken. The pendant vibrated in my pocket like a beating heart.

But laced with that power, I also felt the same searing

anger as before, anger that didn't belong to me, and I knew that if I touched it, I would burn.

"Where is she?" said Claudia, moving forward into the clearly empty living room. She shook her head.

"I don't know." A prickling of misgiving danced up my spine. *She told you to come. She's always honest when it matters.*

We backed out of the living room and tried another door. The smell of spoiled food drifted out of the kitchen, but again, I saw no one in there.

A *creak*, like a footstep on the stairs, made me pause. Another. My heart started beating fast.

Why would anyone be upstairs?

*Thunk.*

I spun around, hearing something drop from the ceiling and clatter onto the bare floorboards. Dust rose in plumes around me, and I squinted into the gloom, the hairs rising on my arms.

Hands came out of the shadows and closed around my neck. I choked on a scream, falling backwards into Claudia. Heat seared my arm as she aimed a fireball at whatever had hold of me—a ghoul, hideous and grey-skinned with grasping fingers.

It let go of me with a piteous whine, skittering away from the fire. I massaged my neck and croaked, "Someone set us up. Let's get out—"

Black fog rose from the floor, surrounding us. I felt the pendant burn, and the Darkworld's chill rushed through me.

Claudia swore violently. The flash of a conjured light, instantly extinguished. I couldn't see the way out, and wherever I stumbled, I never made contact with anything solid. The walls on either side of the hallway seemed to have blinked out of existence. It was like we were no longer in the house at all.

Panic constricted my chest at the thought. *No. It's a trick —the Darkworld is messing with us.*

"Summon a light, you idiot!" yelled Claudia. "I can't—"

I cursed my own stupidity, instantly calling a light to my hand. The darkness receded somewhat, but the light was dim, not the blazing orb I could usually summon.

"It's working for you!" Claudia's voice came from somewhere behind me. "I can't do it."

"What's—what's going on?"

I took a few cautious steps forward, but could see a couple of feet in front of me, and the door remained in shadow.

A breeze lifted the hair from my head, and with it came a whisper, *"Be careful what you say aloud, Ashlyn, for we can always hear. Give us your demon heart."*

Despite the light, I didn't see the hands until they'd seized me. Human hands, but wrong somehow, worn away at the edges. I struggled, reaching to the Darkworld, and felt my mind brush that vast store of power. It thrummed through my body, breaking the hands' grip on my shoulders. I wriggled free and turned to face my attacker.

It was a guy around my own age, a head taller than me. Dark hair flopped into his violet eyes, masking the demon heart gleaming beneath.

The demon looked up at me and smiled.

## 14

POWER

"*S*uch power, Ashlyn!*" the demon said, almost gleefully. *"Such glorious strength! Why did I not see it before? If I had taken your heart myself!"*

"Who *are* you?" I said, fighting for balance. The floor swayed beneath me, increasing my fear that we really did stand in some Darkworld-conjured illusion.

*"You don't recognise me in this body, do you, Ashlyn?"*

"Evidently not." My hands shook, but I met the demon's stare evenly. "I don't make a list of demons' names."

"Ash, come on!" Claudia tugged at my arm, her face a mask of terror under the dimming light.

I stepped back, away from the demon.

*"After all the trouble I took to lure you here? Come, now Ashlyn, I'm offering you a deal."*

"I have no idea who the hell you are. And I'm not interested!"

I backed farther away, but the darkness came with me, obscuring my path. The demon moved closer, half in the darkness.

*"I don't think you quite understand the situation, Ashlyn. The Seven are coming. You will not be spared. Join Lucifer and myself. We will protect you from the Venantium. From your father."*

"I don't—the Venantium? What do you mean?"

"For God's sake, Ash, he's trying to distract you!" Claudia succeeded in summoning a feeble flame, but it winked out almost immediately. "How're you doing that?" she said to the demon.

*"I am doing nothing. It is this place. It feeds on the power of others. But it gives strength to those who feed on the shadows."*

*"Who are you?"* The question came from my mouth at the same time that my mind flooded with an intense surge of pure rage. My vision flickered to purple, and I fought to keep the demon back because if I let her out, something terrible would happen.

*"You should know who I am. You sent me back to the Darkworld almost on this very spot."*

Shock warred with anger, and the anger slowly receded, my vision returning to normal. I took a shuddering breath.

"You're..." I swallowed, my mouth dry. "You're the demon who possessed Terrence. Aren't you?"

*"My name is Vassago, for future reference, human-demon."*

I blinked. Since when did demons have a sense of humour?

*"I admit this host disappointed me. I expected more of one of the venators' kin, but his magic is weaker than his ambition. Pity. But Lucifer will provide me a better host..."*

"Ash..." Claudia's urgent voice pulled me back to reality. I'd unconsciously been backing farther away, right up to the door. One second and I could open it...

But no sooner had that thought crossed my mind than Vassago's hand lashed out, grabbing for the pendant. The string snapped. He pulled back in triumph, the fake crystal glinting in the beam of light which still hovered overhead. *"There, now, that wasn't so difficult, was it, human-demon?"*

I didn't dare breathe. He had the fake pendant—but it was only a matter of time now…

*"You lie!"*

The demon's cry reverberated in my ears, and he prepared to lunge again. I concentrated on the power at the edge of my consciousness and let it pour into my hand, ice-fire solidifying, paradoxically cold and searing hot. As his fingers brushed my coat, I stabbed him between the eyes with a dagger of flaming ice.

The demon screamed. The house shook around us, walls quaking, the Darkworld fracturing. As the darkness dissipated, I saw the walls crumple inwards—a chunk of ceiling fell down and hit the floor inches from where I stood.

*"Ash!"* Claudia screamed.

But I couldn't stop the power. *I'm doing it*, I realised. The power was both inside me and outside me, shattering the windows, splintering the floor, bringing the walls down around us. I was trapped in my own body, fixed in place whilst a monster looked through my eyes and—

*Stop!*

Someone seized me around the middle, and then I was tumbling over the threshold just in time to avoid being buried under the collapsed house.

I came to awareness, facedown on the ground, forehead pressed to the earth, dead leaves brushing my hair. I moved my hands, feeling for injuries. Other than a few bruises, I was okay. Alive.

I twisted, searching for Claudia. My eyes roved over the ruined house, a pile of splintered wood and crumbled bricks. Claudia stood a few feet away, regarding me warily. It was the first time I'd seen her look *afraid* of me.

I didn't blame her. I was scared of me, too.

~

CLAUDIA SAID nothing the whole journey back to Blackstone. My mind reeled, and it kept coming back to the knowledge that someone had set us up—someone who had my mobile number. Even now, I'd only given the number to a handful of people. Just friends. And the fortune-teller. And someone at the Venantium had it, too, of course.

Which brought me back to the second worry: what had the demon implied?

*"The Seven are coming. You will not be spared. Join Lucifer and myself. We will protect you from the Venantium. From your father."*

*Protect you from the Venantium.* Did that mean they were on the verge of discovering my secret—or did it mean something else?

*The Seven are coming.* The seven Higher Demons. No one could summon them without suffering instant death, as far as I knew. I'd seen one, Belphegor, that night Jude and the doppelgänger had attacked in the sepulchre. He'd undone the damage Jude had done to the Barrier—and killed the doppelgänger for straying outside the Darkworld. The doppelgänger hadn't really been alive anyway, but it struck me as callous in the extreme to punish her and not Jude. Not that I'd expect anything less from a demon.

*Your father,* the demon had said. Lucifer, the higher demon. Their leader, or so people believed. Between him and the sorcerer who also called himself Lucifer, I couldn't see any way I'd make it out of this unscathed.

Someone must have summoned Vassago. The same person who'd set a trap for us. Someone had my number—and also the mobile phone the fortune-teller was using, I guessed. *Lucifer?* Melivia Blackstone had been involved with both Lucifers at some point in the past. One had tricked her and bound her to him. The other had fathered me. Neither was on my side.

I hugged my arms to myself. I'd never felt more alone. And, though part of me was ashamed at the very idea, I feared for the fortune-teller's safety.

*If Lucifer really can summon a higher demon—or all seven— we're screwed,* I thought dismally. It didn't take reading between the lines to work out that was what the demon had implied. What all my visions meant. Lucifer had lived in the Darkworld for so long he'd probably at least had contact with one or more of the higher demons. If the doppelgänger had attracted their attention in our world, then a human sorcerer living in the world of demons would surely be noticed. Jude had known about him, had tried to contact him, even, to find out how to give humans the power of the Darkworld. The power only demons had.

The Seven made ordinary demons look like a minor threat. If they sided with this lunatic human sorcerer, everyone would die.

*The great Seven will rise, with Lucifer at the helm, and all will be cast into darkness.*

Claudia finally spoke when we disembarked in Redthorne, ready to get the bus back to campus.

"We'll have to report this. Someone needs to know about it."

"I know." But that meant going back underground, where Conrad was imprisoned, where the Inner Circle prioritised tradition over human life. "I just wonder who the guy was. The one Vassago possessed. Did he summon it?"

"God knows. Probably someone Lucifer influenced."

I looked at her. "You really think that?"

"I don't know." She stopped talking as a group of tourists walked past, ready to board a train to the Lakes. Ordinary people enjoying a day out. A spike of envy lodged itself in my heart. To be carefree again…

"Vassago was definitely carrying Lucifer's message," I said quietly. "Lucifer's planning something big—obviously. But he had the fortune-teller's mobile phone. It… sounded like her." Not that I'd ever seen her use a phone, but she had to have sent those other messages somehow. I'd been able to send a reply to her from Redthorne, when Mephistopheles had attacked Leo and me. And demons didn't use technology.

"Yeah, but…" She paused, biting her lip, glancing at me out of the corner of her eye. It meant she wanted to say something, but didn't know how I'd take it.

"Yes?" I prompted.

"She said she was bound to Lucifer in some way, didn't she?" said Claudia. "Well… I don't know, I haven't seen her in forever, but it's looking like he has her in his clutches either way."

"You mean she joined him willingly." My tone came out flat. I didn't even want to think about the implications. To think I'd been prepared to give her a chance. Instead, we'd almost got killed—well, Claudia had. As if I needed another reason to avoid my real mother.

"Not necessarily. But suppose you're right—suppose Lucifer *can* influence people from the Darkworld, like a demon can."

I'd thought of the same thing myself, more than once. None of the usual rules seemed to apply to Lucifer. Hell, the Darkworld was practically his playground. A human who could run circles around demons.

"It wouldn't surprise me," I said. "I'm starting to think… Well, it sounds like Lucifer's had influence over the

Darkworld for a while. For all we know, he *is* the one who's telling people to summon demons."

"Like an evil voice whispering in your ear. Yeah, that's what demons do. But you still have free will. If the demon's in the Darkworld, it can't actually harm you. Basic knowledge."

"What if…" I voiced something else that had crossed my mind during the long train journey. "What if it could?"

Rachel. That girl in our old flat. Even Pete. And that body on campus. Clues stacked up, threatening to topple the last of my sanity. *Let's face it; it's answers I wanted from her.* But instead, we'd landed in a worse mess than before.

Now Claudia stared at me. "Huh? Look, if you're suggesting demons can break through the Barrier at any time, then why haven't they already?"

"Not… not exactly. But think how many people Lucifer's got on his side. He must have something other demons don't have. He's human. He *could* leave the Dark-world any time, right? He did it before, twenty years ago." Voicing the fear aloud didn't make it go away. *He's coming,* Rachel had said. Maybe Lucifer could speak to anyone from the Darkworld. Even on campus, where nothing could get through the Barrier.

Maybe we were living on borrowed time, after all.

Night hadn't fallen yet, but shadows crept over the ground as we walked from the bus stop to the cemetery. The dark spires of the cathedral made me uneasy, remembering that collapsed church at the other graveyard. My skin prickled.

No one was in the entrance hall. I could, however, hear a commotion coming from behind the door that led to the cells. An uneasy feeling skittered down my spine. Muffled shouts and thuds greeted us, and I hesitated, wondering whether it'd be a stupid idea to head that way.

The door flew open before we could decide, and David ran out, almost crashing into me.

"David!" said Claudia. "What gives?"

"Have either of you seen Mr Fraser?" He breathed heavily, leaning on the wall for support as though he'd run a long distance.

"Who?"

"Never mind." He made to run for the iron doors at the back of the hall, but Claudia seized his arm.

"Hold it," she said. "What's happening? We need to make a report."

"The prisoner's escaped. Conrad got out."

"Conrad's escaped?" I said, blankly. "But he's not a prisoner."

"Doesn't matter. He's dangerous, and only Mr Fraser knows the tunnels best. He's one of the Inner Circle."

"We need to go to the Inner Circle," I said quickly. Crap. Like we needed anything else to worry about.

Claudia nodded. "We'll come with you."

David was already half running toward the oak doors. As Claudia and I entered the hallway, we found him knocking at the door that led to the Inner Circle's meeting room. It figured that he'd obey the rules to the letter even with a vampire loose in the cells.

There was plainly a meeting in full motion. Six people sat around the table this time, but Mr Blake was noticeably absent. In his place at the head of the table sat the woman from before, Ms Constantine. A broad-shouldered, dark-skinned man was on her right, next to a petite woman with a dark bob of hair and thick-framed glasses. I recognised the man Cyrus had called Mr Fraser, sat between a steel-haired man and a woman who could have been Dr Philip's double, perhaps a few years older.

Six pairs of sharp eyes pinned us to the spot.

David recovered first. "Um. I need to speak to Mr Fraser. It's urgent. The vampire's escaped."

The blond-haired man was already on his feet, concern flickering across his face. "Carry on without me," he told Ms Constantine.

"But we have seven items to complete," said Ms Constantine.

He stared at her, and so did the youngish, bob-haired woman. "Surely this is more important?" he said.

None of the others said a word, simply looked on, disinterested. *What the hell?*

"I have to go," said Mr Fraser. He met Ms Constantine's glassy stare. "I trust Hayley to take notes for me."

The bob-haired woman nodded. She looked as uncomfortable as I felt.

"Fine," said Ms Constantine. "You two. What did you want?"

My voice dried up in my throat.

"We—we want to report a demon attack," said Claudia.

"Do you?" Ms Constantine's tone was flat.

"Ash and I were attacked today. She—Ash got these messages. We thought they were from the fortune-teller."

I took over. "She said she wanted to meet me at her old house in the Lakes. I didn't think anything of it. Claudia came with me. But the fortune-teller wasn't there, and this guy—he was possessed, and attacked us. I killed the demon—sent it back to the Darkworld."

"Might I ask why you trusted the word of this woman?" said Ms Constantine.

"I…" Of course, to the Venantium, she was a rogue

sorceress who'd escaped their headquarters earlier this year. They'd tolerated her before, but now she was a fugitive. "I trust her. But I don't think it was her. I think someone else has my number."

"Give me your phone." It wasn't a request. I swallowed and pulled my iPhone out of my pocket. She all but snatched it from my hand.

"You should have informed us that you were in contact with that woman," said the dark-skinned man. The others were nodding.

"Dr Fenton is right. You withheld vital information from us during your time working for us."

I noted the usage of the past tense.

"You may file a report if you wish; forms are in the cabinet at the back. But don't expect an investigation any time soon. We have too many reports coming in, and without further evidence we cannot afford to waste our resources on tracking down this woman."

"I don't think it was her!" I said, again. "I think someone else was using her phone."

"We will investigate this." She waved my phone. I had the sinking feeling I wouldn't be seeing it again for a while, if ever.

"Is there anything else you wanted to report?"

"Um. Well," I said hesitantly. "The demon also said he was working for Lucifer. He said his name was Vassago. Does that mean anything to any of you?"

Six pairs of eyes turned on me. I noticed, in a detached sort of way, that only the woman—Hayley—and Mr Fraser, the fair-haired man, had any humanlike quality to their expressions. The others looked through glass-marble eyes that made me feel as though I were being stripped to the core.

"Vassago," the dark-skinned man repeated. "It is unusual for a demon to give a name."

"I've seen him… it… before," I said—then realised I'd said too much. The Venantium had never found out about the time Terrence had attacked me; the fortune-teller had decided that it would lead to risky questions about why I'd been targeted in the first place, and why I hadn't been registered. Somehow it had been swept under the rug.

"Have you?" said Ms Constantine. "You have had dealings with this demon?"

"No, he—it—just said we'd met before. I wouldn't know. I mean, all demons look the same…"

*Quiet,* a voice whispered in my head.

"Never mind," said Claudia, loudly. "It wasn't important, anyway. The demon's gone."

"Fine. You may make your report as you wish." But I still felt six pairs of eyes on my back as we left the room. *Idiot. You'll be lucky you don't get an invite back into the Angel Box.*

We walked swiftly back to the entrance hall and out into the graveyard, not speaking. Urgency hurried my steps. *They're not going to do anything,* I thought. *They'll arrest you before they actually do anything useful.* Frustration clawed at me, and my anger rose as the demon inside me roared.

"Ash." Claudia grabbed my arm, then let go as though she'd been electrocuted. "Sweet Jesus, you're like an icicle. How can you be that cold?"

*Well, it had to happen sooner or later.* "The demon," I muttered. "She's angry."

"Whoa, there." Claudia edged away. "Keep her reined in. Are you sure you're okay?"

"Not like I can control her," I said. "The one person I might have asked about it is gone. Maybe even dead."

I hadn't meant to say that, but the words hung in the

air, a physical presence. Claudia moved closer to me, hesitant.

"You can't know that," she said. "Ash… you know the fortune-teller. She's probably working on a plan. She wouldn't give in to Lucifer."

I knew she was only trying to reassure me. I wished I could believe her, just to have something to hold on to, something to tell me everything was going to be okay.

God, I missed my parents.

**15**

## LUCIFER'S WARNING

Days passed. I walked through everyday life as though in a dream, going to lectures, spending as little time as possible in the company of others for fear they'd realise something was wrong.

Each time something out of the ordinary happened, however insignificant, it set my mind whirling. The girl who'd discovered her friend had hanged herself was institutionalised. People whispered that she'd been raving about monsters. Two of the other people in that flat requested to move, including Pete.

I didn't return to the Venantium's Headquarters. They couldn't text me now they had my phone, anyway. Whenever I met with Claudia, we talked about other things, like we could avoid the elephant in the room. Stupid expression. More like a freaking *demon* in the room. The fortune-teller had gone. Conrad was presumably still missing. And it felt like the world was breaking apart.

One rare night when Alex and Sarah weren't occupied, we went for a drink at the union bar, and found Pete asleep at the table we usually sat at. All the other tables were occupied, so Alex, with a grimace, reached out and shook him awake.

Pete shot upright with a yelp. "Shit, man, what's with you?"

"You were sleeping," said Alex, sitting down. I didn't particularly want to join Pete, who smelled like he hadn't showered for a month, but Alex would probably send him packing in a minute. I sat in the chair farthest from him, Sarah next to me.

"Yeah. I'm not fucking going back to my room."

"Why not?" said Alex.

"Because there's fucking *voices* in there."

"Are you okay?" said Alex. "Because that doesn't sound normal."

"No one believes me," he muttered, shifting in his seat. "I'm going to get a drink."

"I don't think that's a good idea."

"If you lived in a room with voices, you'd need to get hammered, too." He stood up, swaying slightly, and sank back down again.

"I'm gonna go get us drinks," said Alex over her shoulder. "You guys stay here."

"*Why?*" said Sarah, jerking her head toward Pete. She mouthed, "He's lost it."

"We'll move as soon as another table's free. The queue's just gone down."

And she rushed off to claim her place in line at the bar before another group of people came in.

I turned to Sarah, who'd edged her chair as far away from Pete as she could. Pete muttered something about voices again.

Someone else sat down in Alex's seat, startling me. Rachel. She wore her paint-splattered overalls and even had clumps of green paint in her hair.

"Hi, guys!" she said.

Sarah looked like she wished the floor would rise up and swallow her. I couldn't blame her. As for Rachel, I could only conclude she was high as a kite again.

"Who are you?" Pete said. "I wish you'd all go away. I've got a hangover, and I've been sleeping in the fucking bar for three days."

"Have you?" said Rachel, blinking at him. "That doesn't sound very nice."

"I'd rather that than have voices in my head all the bloody time."

"You hear them, too?" Rachel leaned forward over the table.

I glanced at Sarah, who looked like she was thinking, *Oh God, the freaks are all here.*

But the old suspicions rose. Rachel knew something about what was going on…

"Yeah, man," said Pete. "They're in my head whenever I'm in my room, but I can't hear what they're saying. All these angry voices."

"The voice I heard isn't angry," said Rachel, as offhand as though commenting on the weather. "It keeps telling me he's coming."

"Who?" said Pete, suddenly giving her his full attention. I'd never seen him look this serious.

"Lucifer."

The breath seemed to stop in my chest, the air thickening so I couldn't draw it in. Dizzying thoughts spiralled through my mind.

"Seriously, Ash," Sarah whispered in my ear. "I'm moving. I don't care what Alex says."

I nodded absently, but kept my eyes on Rachel and Pete.

"Sure, I'll be with you in a sec."

As Sarah moved away, I hesitated, ducking on the pretence of retying my shoelace.

"Lucifer the Devil?" Pete asked Rachel.

"He's more than that." A strange giggle escaped her mouth. "He's going to be our leader."

"That so?" Even Pete seemed to decide Rachel wasn't all there. "Tell him to get these damn voices out of my head."

"Oh, he won't listen. I'm just a conduit." She laughed again and turned to face me. "Ash knows what I'm talking about. He wants to speak to you, but you're well-guarded, aren't you?"

Goose bumps broke out on my arms. I couldn't believe I was witnessing this. The world had gone mad.

She moved closer, whispering in my ear. "He told me what your friends did to me. They took my memories away. That wasn't very nice, was it?"

"I don't know what you're talking about."

"I saw something I wasn't supposed to, so they erased my memories. You know how violating that feels, don't you, Ash?"

Coldness pressed on me, inside and out. *She can't know about that. No way.*

"I have no idea what you're talking about," I said, again. "I'm going to join my friends."

Sarah and Alex were both calling my name. I rushed over to join them, mind spinning as though in freefall.

I DIDN'T SLEEP that night. I only had to close my eyes for the nightmares to start, replaying the horrific events of the past few weeks over and over again.

And now... Rachel knew about Lucifer. She was under

his influence. I had to talk to her, alone, without my friends there. But I couldn't begin to think about where to start.

*Ignorance would be a blessing*, I thought, staring at my ceiling. I'd even dragged out my old photo albums to entertain myself late at night. Well, it wasn't much as far as entertainment went, but I'd hung on to them in the hope that I might be able to piece my own memories together, even if I couldn't have that old life back. But even without the change, I'd felt ever since coming here that my life before was a dream. My life before I'd seen my first demon, and my own demon had awoken in the back of my mind. The smiling human girl in the photos wasn't me.

I slammed the album shut, rubbing my eyes. I was still fully dressed, tiredness dragging at the corners of my mind. *I can't live like this.*

I was nodding off over the pages of a book when a sudden sharp *tap* jolted me awake. I rushed to the door to peek through the spyhole, but no one was outside.

*Tap.*

How could someone be tapping on my third-floor window? I pushed back the curtains, and jumped back, my heart leaping into my throat. A harpy hovered outside, its crone-like face inches from the glass. I bit back a scream, letting the curtain drop.

*What the hell's that thing doing here?*

The harpy tapped on the glass again. The memory of Conrad writhing and bleeding flashed into my mind. Not knowing what else to do, I made for my phone, before remembering the Venantium had taken it from me. *Damn.*

I couldn't sit here, knowing one of those abominations was right outside my window. My connection to the Dark-world was, as usual, one step ahead of my conscious thoughts, and ice-fire had already sprung up in my palm. Fighting paralysing fear, I inched the curtains open and held out the fire towards the harpy, hoping I looked threatening rather than terrified. My other hand moved to open the window.

The harpy let out a *caw*, and the fire suddenly became ice once more, receding until it melted to harmless water that dripped from my palm. The window flew open and the harpy perched on the ledge as I backed away, its sunken eyes meeting mine. I saw something evil gleaming in those black pits, something that went far beyond the usual intelligence of the crone-birds.

The harpy was possessed.

*"Ashlyn Temple,"* came the same soul-piercing voice of a true demon, but with a different tone. Cold, but also curiously gloating.

*"Do not think that you have been forgotten. As a human-demon, you will be immensely valuable in my coming plan. So please try not to get yourself killed."*

I stumbled back against the bed, feeling like something big clawed its way up my throat. My heart jackhammered in my ears.

*What—or who—are you?*

Before I could even voice the question aloud, the reply came. *"You have heard my name, have you not?"*

"Lucifer?" I whispered, disbelieving.

*"There is no need to speak aloud. Your thoughts are transparent as glass."*

It had to be a true demon, or at least a powerful ghoul, if it could read my thoughts. A shudder went through me, rocking my entire body. It wasn't possible—demons couldn't get past the Barrier...

*"Oh, I'm no demon. I'm much more than that... but you have an inkling of what it means to be part of the Darkworld, do you not? I could teach you to separate your consciousness at will, to inhabit an*

*object or even a living thing… but I can tell from your mind that you are resolute about retaining your humanity. Pity."*

"What do you want with me?" I knew he could read my thoughts, but speaking out loud gave me some semblance of control. Not much, though, admittedly.

*"Merely your cooperation. I'd hate to have to kill the last child of the Seven. You have too much to offer."*

"So you expect me to sit back and let you… summon demons, and whatever it is you're planning?"

*"People have been sitting back and letting me influence them for generations. Of course, humans are malleable as clay. When the time comes to reveal myself, I will tell you my true goal. I'm sure that you will come around to my viewpoint… or at least, part of you will."*

I felt the demon in me stir, and dread settled in my heart.

*"We'll speak again soon, Ashlyn. Try not to let your demons fracture your mind before then."*

And the harpy exploded, feathers scattering like confetti.

I let the curtain drop and sank back onto my bed, trying not to have a panic attack. My breath came out in sharp gasps, like something was squeezing the air out of my lungs. I gripped the bed to ground myself and focused on taking one breath after another. After a minute, it became easier.

The day my life fell apart, the fortune-teller had said my life had been in danger from the instant I was born, because of Lucifer. She'd said he'd want to kill me, absorb my magic, or use me as a weapon. I was half higher demon, the child of the true Lucifer.

*But he didn't say anything about that. He just wants me to stay out of his way. It couldn't have been him.*

But who else could have got past the Barrier? A true demon couldn't even appear as an image. And I hadn't even known it was possible to possess harpies. I didn't know what Lucifer was capable of. Hell, I knew next to nothing about him, other than that he was a powerful sorcerer who had secluded himself in the Darkworld.

*I'll have to ask the Venantium.* I lay down on my bed, suddenly overcome with exhaustion. My limbs trembled. *Crap. Did that just happen?*

*Tell someone,* the voice in my head insisted. *Tell Cyrus. Tell Claudia.*

Not that Cyrus could do a thing, but I needed to do something. Otherwise I'd collapse in panic again. I pulled out my laptop and typed a shaky email.

The reply came instantly: **"WTF?"**

**"I know, right?"**

**"Ash, you've got to tell the Venantium. If Lucifer really is getting past the Barrier, they have to know. You can't fight him alone."**

**"I know. I just don't know if that was really him. There's no way to tell."**

**"Who else could get past the Barrier? If he's still human, the usual rules don't apply."**

**"Yeah, but it doesn't explain why he's chosen *now* to come back. He's been speaking to other students, too. My flatmate Rachel."**

**"That's bad. He's involving non-magic-users?"**

**"Looks that way. But I don't think he can actually manifest or do anything else. He did say something about being able to teach me how to inhabit objects and other living creatures…"**

**"You've got to tell someone, Ash. Seriously."**

**"Claudia and I are going to talk about it tomorrow."**

**"Yeah, but you know what I mean."**

**"The *venators* haven't been particularly**

**helpful so far, but okay. I'll go back and talk to them."**

**"Good. Keep yourself safe, Ash."**

~

By the early hours of the morning, I'd decided not having a phone was going to drive me crazy before Lucifer did. I was forced to hang about in the flat kitchen all day, looking out the window to see if Claudia left the building, and jumping out of my seat every time I heard someone come downstairs. Alex and Sarah, luckily, were out—Alex at archery club, Sarah at work—but I kept an eye out for Rachel.

Claudia finally left the building around midday, and I only just remembered my keys as I pelted downstairs to catch up with her.

"I need to talk to you," I gasped, clutching a stitch in my side, as the door to the block slammed shut behind me. "Urgently."

"I got an urgent message from Berenice, too," said Claudia, flicking her hair over her shoulder. "She's coming in from town to talk. She's on the bus now."

"Um… I'm not sure Berenice wants to see me," I said. Honestly, I'd sort of forgotten about her in the wake of the recent insanity. "Last time I saw her, she punched me in the face."

"Ouch," said Claudia, wincing. "I didn't think she was too pleased with me, either, but she seems really freaked."

"So am I," I said, with a glance back at the building. Too many people were wandering about the student village. This really wasn't the place to tell her about last night. "I have to talk to you somewhere quiet."

"C'mon," said Claudia, beckoning me in the direction

of the bus stop. A strong wind swept up the hill, flattening my hair and making me shiver. Winter was on the way, and the last leaves had fallen from the trees lining the path. The dark clouds in the sky hovered directly over Blackstone like a harbinger of doom, and my heart jumped as the bus appeared round a bend, rattling to a stop. Berenice hurried off cloaked in Influence, and walked swiftly towards us.

I looked at Berenice warily, wondering if she was going to hit me again. But she didn't look confrontational. She looked scared.

She wasn't the only one. Panic squeezed my chest again. I wanted to vent, and I also wanted to run for my life. To tell everyone to clear off campus because it wasn't safe. But I knew better. I'd be dismissed, like Rachel. *Holy crap. She was right.*

"Come on." Claudia led the way to the woodland path, where we could talk uninterrupted. "Right," she said. "Not gonna lie, I'm kind of freaked out by the pair of you right now."

"I couldn't say it in the message!" said Berenice tremulously, folding her arms. "They might have tapped the phone lines."

"The Venantium don't do that," said Claudia.

"They took *my* phone," I pointed out.

At the same time, Berenice said, "I wasn't talking about the Venantium. Look, I just wanted to talk to you guys. You won't believe…"

"Lucifer?" I said quickly. I dug my hands in my pockets, fists clenched.

"What?" said Claudia, her forehead wrinkled in confusion.

"He talked to you, too," said Berenice. "I thought so." But her voice was free of its usual snide tone. "Did he… What did he say?"

*He talked to her?* My heart rate kicked up, and my hands started shaking again. It wasn't a whacked-out dream on my part. What had Lucifer been doing last night—visiting every available sorcerer? No. Claudia didn't know. So why choose Berenice and me?

And what about Leo and Cyrus? They were on the other side of the world. I couldn't protect them if Lucifer decided to hop over there. He was in the Darkworld. No space could confine him. *Oh, God. Please not them.*

I clenched my shaking hands. "He—he told me not to interfere with his plans, that he was planning on recruiting me when the time was right. Something like that." I looked at Berenice. "What did he say to you?"

Berenice closed her eyes, biting her lip, as though it pained her to remember. "He... he said that I'd be his. Soon."

Claudia looked from her to me, mouth agape.

"What did he mean by that?" I said.

Berenice met my stare defiantly. "There are things you don't know about me."

"Maybe we can help." It crossed my mind to mention I'd seen her tormented in a dream, but I could tell that wasn't the right thing to say.

"Like hell you can. I'm contracted to a demon." She drew in a breath. "Yeah. You could say life sucks when you know a demon could end your life at any time."

Claudia stared at her. "You're... what?"

I kept quiet. I knew this already. Maybe that was why Lucifer had chosen her... because in his eyes, we were both doomed. *Oh, God.*

"Mephistopheles. It was either die or become his willing vessel at any time." She closed her eyes again, then opened them and gave an entirely unconvincing shrug. "I regret it most of the time, but it's done. And

Mephistopheles works for Lucifer. So they both have a claim on me."

"Shit," Claudia whispered. *Yeah. Tell me about it.*

Berenice averted her eyes. "Yeah. He said my time was coming soon, or some shit like that."

"Maybe he was trying to mess with your head," I said, but the chill spreading through my body, the memory of that dream, told me this was the most honest she'd ever been with us. "He did that to me."

"Yeah, I know demons are fond of mind-fuckery," said Berenice. "I thought he was a demon at first. I mean, it's only a matter of time before they get in here."

"What makes you say that?" I said, though I'd wondered the same thing, more than once. Lucifer had come right through the Venantium's barriers as if they didn't exist. If he could do that, could his army of demons be far behind?

Berenice raised an eyebrow. "Hello?" she said, back to her snarky self. "You been working for someone else? The Venantium are useless, their defences are full of holes. Trust me, Lucifer's been in the Darkworld a very long time. He's clever, far cleverer than us lowly humans, anyway."

My heart sank, but I knew panicking or lying down and accepting our fate wouldn't help any of us now. "What do you know about him that I don't?" I said. *What else did he say to her?*

"Nothing. I tried to look in the Venantium's library, seeing as they've generously decided to open to the public," said Berenice. "But it's a load of crap. Found absolute jack shit. But I nearly ran into Mr Creepy Blake on the way out."

"Seriously?" I glanced at Claudia. Not that I cared much about the Inner Circle at this point. Had he been skiving off in there instead of helping the Venantium?

What the hell was wrong with those people? *We have to tell them about this. They have to listen.*

"What was he doing in there?" said Claudia. "We ran into him in the tunnels a while back, too."

"He was in the section with all the creepy stuff, by the look of it. Well, I know everything's creepy in there, but the *real* stuff. *Seven Princes* and books like that. I just got this seriously bad vibe. I'd get out while you can."

"I don't work for them anymore," I said, "but... I think we need to tell them about this." And it said something, really, that the authority figures ranked *last* on our list of people to consult in an emergency.

"They'll kill me if they know," said Berenice, flatly. "They won't take any chances. And they'd kill *you*, too."

"Maybe they'd listen if we told them there's a serious threat to security," I said.

Berenice narrowed her eyes at me. "Like hell they care. If you ask me, half of them are in his pocket already. That Mr Blake, for one."

I gawked at her. "What?"

"Come on. Sneaking around in tunnels? And in the demon summoning section of the library?"

"Didn't he ditch his family to get revenge on demons?" I said. "Why would he throw all that away just for whatever Lucifer's offering?"

"Well, if what you think about Lucifer is true, maybe he didn't have a choice," said Berenice. "The Inner Circle are right at the heart of the Venantium. It'd be the perfect plan."

"Well, true," I said, "but..."

*Oh, God. What if it is true?*

"We have to chance it," Claudia said. "I don't like putting our faith in them, but who else is there to talk about it? If Lucifer comes here, we're powerless no matter what. At least we'd give them a head start."

"Well, don't come crying to me when you're a demon's bitch, too," said Berenice, and she departed to the bus stop with a toss of her hair.

~

"THIS IS A BAD IDEA," I said, as once again, we found ourselves walking through Blackstone. It had already begun to get dark even though it was barely five, and shadows striped the cobblestones. "At best, they'll ignore us. At worst, they'll lock us up."

"Positive thinking, Ash," said Claudia, as we crossed the square.

Someone ran towards us, right at me. Two more figures followed behind, and I stopped dead as they rushed past me. All three had come from the direction of the graveyard.

"Is something happening down there?"

We hurried down the alleyway alongside the cathedral. I knew as soon as we climbed over the cemetery wall that something was wrong. Someone had opened the hidden entrance to the tunnels, inside the gargoyle statue, and it hung open like a hinged jaw. Claudia looked at me, eyes wide.

"We'll go in the front door," I said.

We stepped into the open grave, side by side, and entered the hall to a scene of total chaos.

People were everywhere, running, shouting, fighting, and the hall rang with discordant clamour. Screams echoed from the doors to the tunnels, now open, and I saw one *venator* jump at someone hurrying out of the door that led to the cells, fire in hand. Harpies swooped overhead, screeching and dive-bombing certain people—people who weren't wearing the Venantium's uniform, and who were attacking the *venators*.

"What the hell?" said Claudia, eyes widening.

I scanned the crowd for the source of the chaos and saw several more *venators* fall. Their attackers all wore filthy rags and most had long, tangled hair, but they looked human. There were none of the telltale signs that someone had summoned something from the Darkworld. *Oh my God. Who are they?* Nobody had spotted us yet, but I didn't dare move for fear of getting caught in the melee.

"Shit," said Claudia. "They're prisoners. They must have escaped from the cells."

She was right. And they'd clearly taken the *venators* by surprise, not to mention outnumbered them. The hall was a mass of writhing bodies and sparks of magic. One man brandished a candleholder still burning with a blue flame, while three *venators* warily approached him.

"You took away everything," he growled at them. "You left me to die." He smiled, revealing cracked, rotting teeth. "You're the real monsters. You will burn!" And he threw the candleholder, the Darkworld-conjured fire spilling over. The *venators* ducked, and the flames rose higher, scorching the plush carpet.

How was something like this even possible?

"Conrad," I gasped. "Did he let them out?"

Shouts rang out and echoed, drowning my voice. Combined with the apocalyptic scenarios painted on the walls, the scene looked like the end of the world. And we could only look on in horror.

"Hell," Claudia whispered. "We're in trouble."

## 16

---

## THE BEGINNING OF THE END

No one had noticed us, but still more people were running out of the tunnels, and the crowd grew bigger, sweeping us up. A pack of struggling *venators*, who were trying to subdue a large man making a bid for freedom, separated Claudia and me. With a roar, he broke free and ran for one of the doors—the same door that led to the cells. I wondered why he was running back underground—perhaps because there was no obvious way out of here. How long had it been since these people had seen daylight?

Bursts of fire lit the air. None of the escapees used magic. Of course, the prisoners' Darkworld connections must have been blocked. Dr Philips had done the same thing to me during the brief time I'd been put in the cells, accused of crimes committed by the doppelgänger. But the *venators* had no such handicap. One threw a handful of fire at a prisoner; the victim's scream was lost in the general noise. Claudia grabbed my hand and pulled me into an alcove.

"We have to get out of here. We don't want to get caught up in this."

I nodded, but someone tackled me, knocking me off my feet. A woman with filthy hair and filthier grey rags. Her over-long nails dug into my arms as she bent over me, and I tried not to choke on the stale smell.

"Have you seen my son?"

I shook my head. She was a large woman, and her strong hands squeezed all the air from my lungs.

"No," I choked. "I haven't seen anyone—"

"You work for these scum?" She indicated the hall. "They killed my husband. You work for them?"

I shook my head frantically. The woman looked half-deranged, and I didn't want to do anything to provoke her further.

"No," I whispered. "No, I don't work for them."

She relaxed, which was even more disastrous, as I was now pinned under her full body weight. She looked barely capable of keeping herself upright.

"Good." She leaned forward and whispered in my ear, her stale breath wafting over my face. "I'm going to kill them all. If you see Howard, tell him to come and find me in the place where the devil rises."

She staggered away from me and into the crowd, whooping loudly.

"Ash! You okay?" Claudia rushed over to me.

"Yeah, I think." I got to my feet gingerly. I felt bruised, but nothing was broken.

"Who in seven hells was that?"

I coughed, looking around, but she'd gone. "I think it was Howard's mother."

Claudia's jaw dropped. "You're shitting me."

"Never mind that, let's get out of here."

The route through the tunnels was blocked by a stream

of people running in and out, *venators* and prisoners alike. Claudia nodded to me when there was a gap, and we ran for the door. In the tunnel, chaos reigned. Screams and shouts rang out, and a flash of terror shot through me when a harpy flew low over my head. *Those foul things are still down here?*

"Come on!" she yelled over her shoulder.

We ran into the corridor that led to the interrogation room. This time, *my* jaw dropped. Someone had smashed the Angel Box, shattered it like cheap glass. Fragments lay scattered on the ground, some edged with blood. But whose blood, we didn't stop to find out.

"This is bad," said Claudia, her voice hushed.

We had to climb over a body sprawled across the floor in front of the first cells. I didn't look too closely, but I could tell a *venator* by the uniform. Guilt warred with fear. Should we really be running away? I had no idea what crimes these people had committed, but I felt like we should be doing *something.* Claudia, however, was all about self-preservation. She barely waited for me to catch up before taking off again.

A handful of prisoners remained in the cells. Some looked too weak to move, dragging their limbs towards freedom at a tortured pace. I could still hear a commotion up ahead. Horrible shrieks echoed around us. Harpies. *Shit. We're going to run right into them.*

Claudia swore, out of breath. "I'm going to conjure fire," she said. "You do…whatever it is you do. It's not important. We need to kill those things."

I nodded, dry-throated with fear.

We rounded the corner and faced pandemonium. Harpies flew in circles, dive-bombing a huddle of prisoners, most of whom lay inert on the ground. Razor claws slashed at anyone who came near. The chill of the Darkworld raced up my arms, and ice-fire in hand, I moved just in time to avoid a harpy's attack.

Fire exploded over my head, thrown expertly by Claudia. The harpy burned away, feathers stripped from bone, but there were more coming, drawn to the moving targets. I threw a handful of ice-fire into the air and knew from the screeching that I'd hit at least one, but we couldn't stop. We ran flat-out through the melee, striking out a path for the stairs that led to the surface.

Claudia was ahead of me, her feet pounding up the stairs to freedom—but before I could take another step, someone seized me and dragged me to the ground. My knees scraped rock, and I fell down the few stairs I'd climbed, back into the tunnel, pulled by a strong grip. Strong arms crushed my chest, and I yelled, trying to connect to the Darkworld.

"Don't even try it." Mr Blake held me with a strength I could never hope to break. His black-marble eyes glared into mine. I twisted, trying to escape his grip.

"You should have given in when you had the chance. Now give me your heart… human-demon."

The word *human-demon* rang in my ears like it was foreign, something that didn't belong to me. Numbness spread through me, pure disbelief. *I can't have heard right. No way.*

But Mr Blake's eyes were glowing, not like a demon's but with a black sheen like the night sky reflected on a lake. The Darkworld seized me with icy hands, every inch of me growing numb. Shadows rose around us, masking the tunnel walls, smothering the stairs, cocooning me and Mr Blake. But it wasn't Mr Blake. He was a host… for a higher demon.

*"Did it come as a surprise, Ashlyn? The great Inner Circle,*

*hosting the highest of demons? I am known as Mammon, third of the Seven."*

I didn't answer. I couldn't answer. My tongue was frozen to the roof of my mouth. The Darkworld itself spoke through Mr Blake, and I knew that the real man was long-gone. No one could survive possession by a higher demon.

*"The human sorcerer has been busy… I confess that I would much prefer to have created a body of my own, but it has been enter-taining, pulling the strings of the Venantium. You are aware, I am sure, Ashlyn, that they have all but dug their own grave?"*

"Why," I whispered. "Why are you on Lucifer's side?"

*"The human sorcerer plans to give us exactly what we need. It is not my wish to answer to the whims of a human, but the false Lucifer's vision mirrors our own. This world will be ours, human-demon."*

"What—what do you want from me?"

*"Merely your cooperation. And your heart, human-demon, to ensure obedience."*

"I won't give it to you." Anger broke through the paralysis in my veins.

*"I won't give it to you!"* the demon in me cried.

*"Human-demon, I need not tell you that things will be very diffi-cult for you if you refuse to cooperate. You will not be safe from friend or foe unless you stand beside us at the brink of hell."*

*"I won't."* The demon spoke through my mouth, looked through my eyes, yet our thoughts were in conjunction, and her rage stilled the fear in my heart. I looked calmly into Mammon's eyes, the eyes of the Darkworld, and my own death.

"Stop."

A figure had appeared on the steps above. My heart leapt into my throat. *It's her. It's actually her.*

The fortune-teller. Once again, she'd appeared just in time.

"Leave her," she said. "This was not part of the agreement. Leave my daughter alone."

It was the first time I'd ever heard her call me her daughter. It sounded wrong coming from her mouth, but then again, so did everything else she'd said. Even now, numb with terror, I couldn't forgive her.

*"You know that the human-demon is the crux. We need her heart."*

Mr Blake reached for the pocket of my jacket, the place where I'd hidden the true demon heart. I'd never had the chance to buy a replacement for the fake I'd lost at the old house.

"Don't," said the fortune-teller quietly. "Don't do anything you might regret, Third. You don't know the extent of what Lucifer is planning. And you know he holds your heart, too."

*"You're lucky you're under his protection, Melivia Blackstone. Very well. If Lucifer reprimands me for failing to obey his command, on your head be it."*

The fortune-teller met the demon's eyes. She looked as forbidding as ever, even in the face of a higher demon.

"Then let it be so. Leave."

Mr Blake's deadened eyes turned onto me. *"Tell my host's sons that I'll be coming for them shortly."*

And he let go of me, the darkness receding from his eyes. I stared, numbly, as he gave us a curt nod, as if dismissing us, and walked away down the tunnel.

I stood frozen to the spot, the demon's anger receding from my mind to leave only numbness.

"I'd suggest the two of you leave, too," said the fortune-teller to Claudia and me. "It is not safe here."

I heard, but my feet refused to obey.

"Ash!" Claudia stumbled past the fortune-teller, down the stairs. She grabbed my arm and pulled me after her. My feet kicked into action, and I ran, shoes pounding against stone. I didn't stop at the surface; leaving Claudia behind, I vaulted the cemetery wall and I'd reached the town square before I stopped to catch my breath.

The angel statue in the centre of the square had been defaced. The words "*There are no angels*" were scrawled in blood along the foot of the pedestal, and the stone back of the angel was split down the middle. Blood pooled on the cobblestones, but I could see no one fleeing. It was eerily quiet.

"Those who made arrangements will have got away by now," said the fortune-teller, appearing behind me like a ghost. "The others…"

"What's your game this time?" Claudia ran to join us, panting. "You're pretending to work for Lucifer now?"

"Don't lie to me again," I added. The demon inside me had withdrawn, but my anger at the woman who had ruined my life still burned strong.

The fortune-teller bowed her head. "I had hoped to avoid this as long as possible… but the fact is, Ashlyn, I belonged to Lucifer long before I brought you into the world. Now I am his to command, and disobedience means death… for both of us."

"You… belong to him?" I said, my heart still racing. *No. It can't be that.*

"It's hard to explain. When I went with him into the Darkworld, our spirits were somehow conjoined. Part of him is in me… and part of me is in him. It may not be obvious, and yet it is true. I can no sooner betray him than cut off my own arm."

"So you're saying you can never help us again?" I said

hollowly. "Wait—*did* you send those messages? The ones luring me to your house?"

Her silence said it all. I couldn't believe it. *I trusted you*—and I had, despite everything. I'd trusted she had a plan.

"You—"

"Demon lover," Claudia finished. She was white-faced, clearly almost as appalled as I was.

But she'd picked the wrong thing to say—possibly the worst thing she could have said. The fortune-teller turned on her, and I thought for a minute that that was it for Claudia.

"You know nothing of this life," she spat. "You know nothing of what it means to pay for your crimes repeatedly for a hundred years. There was a time when I believed in salvation, that I could atone for my sins. But there is no salvation. There is only the Darkworld. And I have made my choice."

"You're going to let him win?" I said.

"I am going to do everything I can to ensure our survival."

"Even serve *him*."

"The world has been under Lucifer's sway for longer than most people know. The Inner Circle, for instance… five of the seven have fallen. That is Lucifer's plan: he intends to replace them with the Seven Higher Demons. I do not know how long they have been in place, but Mr Blake has not been himself for some time, and neither has Ms Constantine. She is now under Leviathan's control. Mr Dyson is now hosting Asmodeus; Mrs Wilcox plays host to Beezlebub—and the demon known as Satan has Dr Fenton in his thrall."

"Why are you telling us this?" And so casually. So hopelessly. *Stop it. Please.*

"It makes no difference," said the fortune-teller bitterly.

"The two free Inner Circle members are Hayley Fairfax and Benjamin Fraser, but I have no doubt that when Lucifer and Belphegor make an appearance, it will be the end for them, too. The Venantium has fallen. You should return to campus. It remains under the protective barriers, for now at least."

"Why?" I said. "Why should we run away? We have to warn them—warn the last of the *venators.*"

But it couldn't be true. The Venantium couldn't be finished. The skies weren't falling. The darkness hadn't filled the streets. The world hadn't twisted into a Boschian version of Hell.

"They will know. It cannot be helped. This was inevitable. The important thing is to save yourself, Ashlyn. You are too valuable to Lucifer, but if you can keep your heart safe from him, he will not be able to use you as a weapon, too."

And that was it. Defeated, we watched the last hope walk away, across the blood-stained cobbles of Blackstone.

## 17

BEFORE THE STORM

Silence hung over Blackstone, low and heavy, like a storm cloud. On the long walk uphill back to campus, my limbs dragged. All the same, we hurried as fast as we could, barely speaking. The fortune-teller's words had opened a gulf inside me, and every hope I'd had disappeared inside it.

She'd destroyed my past. And now she'd destroyed my hopes for the future, too. It was either death, enslavement to Lucifer, or a life in hiding. What kind of choice was that?

No sooner had I lay down in bed and shut my eyes than the real darkness rushed in to claim me. In this dream, I ran through a narrow passage that twisted and turned, following my own shadow. The doppelgänger always stayed several metres ahead, and whenever I rounded a corner, I saw her slipping out of sight.

I had to catch up with her, because she had something important to tell me. The corridor became narrower and narrower, until my hands brushed the walls on either side and I ducked my head to avoid hitting it on the low ceiling.

Then the voices came. Whispers. First, my name, over and over again, in the icy tones of a demon. *"Ash. Ash."*

*"We want you, Ash. We need you."*

"Go away," I whispered.

*"Come to us, Ash."*

I had no idea where the voices came from, but I couldn't stop running. The doppelgänger was always just ahead, always unreachable.

"Not much further, Ash!" Her voice echoed back to me, and I ran harder, feet barely touching the ground. But the faster I ran, the more I felt a presence inside me, pulling me back. My demon half. She didn't want to catch up to the doppelgänger. I could feel what she felt, somehow separate and yet conjoined with my own feelings.

I'd never felt this connected with her before. When her emotions were strong, they'd sometimes rushed into me, unwanted and overpowering. But this time I was consciously aware of our connection. It wasn't an invasion. She was truly part of me.

And yet… I was afraid. I didn't know whose instincts to trust—hers or mine. I knew I had to get to the doppel-gänger. Why, I didn't know. But the demon was determined to pull away.

I became aware that the tunnel was sloping down-wards, and now the walls were earth, not stone. I heard a dripping sound nearby, and my feet skidded on the damp ground. It started to look familiar. I don't know how I knew, but somehow, I could visualise taking this exact path before.

It was the underground passage to Crowley.

But I couldn't stop, wouldn't stop. The tunnel widened, and with a sinking heart, I knew we'd reached the sepul-chre. I followed the doppelgänger into the vast chamber. A chill rushed through me at the sight of the rows of graves, and the memory of an army of skeletons, digging their way out of the ground.

The doppelgänger stood, waiting for me, near the door at the far end of the room. Her wild hair and too-pale face matched my own.

"Are you ready, Ash?"

"For what?"

"To see the truth?"

"Of course I am!"

"Then look on your fate, *human-demon*."

And she changed. Before my eyes, the doppelgänger became Mr Blake, not as himself but possessed, eyes flat and pitch-black. Mr Blake beckoned me closer and threw the door open wide.

What I saw outside that door made me scream, keep screaming, unable to stop. My chest constricted, body paralysed in terror, as Mammon's laughter echoed around me.

Then I was falling backwards, my legs giving way. Hands caught me, cold, dead hands. I twisted around and found myself facing a grinning skull.

A Skele-Ghoul.

The chamber was no longer empty. Skeletons filled the spaces between the graves, violet eyes glowing.

*"Come to us, Ash. See what they've done to us."*

But they weren't alone. Coffins lay all around them, on top of the graves. The graves that terrified me even more than the demon did, that drew screams from my lungs, because I knew, somehow I knew…

And yet I couldn't help it. I lowered my gaze to look into the nearest one. There was a body inside, inert, stained with blood. A girl with curly hair. Claudia.

A cry caught in my throat. All of them contained bodies. I ran to the next coffin. It was Berenice.

The next was Howard. Then Cyrus. Then…

"*No!*"

Leo's eyes were open, but no light burned in them. Dead.

I dropped to my knees, the impact shuddering through my entire body.

*"I hope you enjoyed the preview, Ashlyn. Now, wake, and witness the main event!"*

My eyes flew open. I gasped, as though surfacing from deep water, and gripped the edges of my bed. *It wasn't real. Just one of Lucifer's tricks.*

But if he could get in my head, how long before he could get through the Barrier?

*There is no Barrier,* I thought. A higher demon walked in Blackstone—*five* higher demons. If they had broken through, then anything could come here. Nowhere was safe.

The truth hit me like a vast wave. If there was one thing I'd been told repeatedly since I'd learned the Darkworld existed, it was that *nothing* could break through the Barrier alone. It had to be summoned, and in any case, the defences around Blackstone were amongst the strongest in the world. If higher demons walked here, then nowhere in the *world* was safe.

In other words, however far I ran, Lucifer would always be able to find me.

IN THE END, I left Claudia a message using my room phone, since my mobile was still with the Venantium. I had to talk to someone, and I knew everyday conversation would be impossible after the past twenty-four hours. Hell, I wondered if I'd ever worry about trivial things again.

Even my room didn't feel like a safe haven. Not when Lucifer could swoop in as a harpy. Not when five of the Seven walked the earth. *God, I need to get out.*

The lights in the hallway didn't come on immediately as I left the room, like they usually did, so I almost fell over someone lying in front of my door. Rachel.

"Ouch!" She sat up, blinking her overlarge eyes at me. A sheen of sweat glazed her forehead, and her face looked faintly green.

"Shit! Sorry," I said. "What're you doing out here?"

"I went for a walk, and then I wanted to sleep, and I saw... things." She shuddered. "I don't want to. I won't..." She pressed her hands to her head. "Always there... won't get out. Says he's coming soon."

"Lucifer," I said. "You were right. I do know something. But you have to fight him off."

It might be reckless, but what did it matter if I told Rachel? No one could reprimand me for telling her; no voice of authority remained.

"I can't... I can't get away," she moaned. "Ash, be careful..."

"Kinda hard." I looked at her. "There's something dangerous in Blackstone. I don't know if it'll come to campus, but... someone's after me. I might have to leave soon."

I'd come to that conclusion a long time ago. I'd have to leave. The least I could do was ensure that none of my friends were dragged into this mess.

But Blackstone itself was right at the centre of everything...

"Okay," said Rachel. "I think your friend wants to talk to you."

My phone rang inside my room, and I jumped.

"How'd you know that?"

"He tells me things. He talks to me… I can't stop the voice. I can't get away from it."

A chill danced down my spine. "Do you think he's possessing you?"

"I'm scared," said Rachel. "He's not interested in me. He only wants to keep an eye on you. But soon…" Her head dropped, and when she looked up again, her eyes were blank, black pits. *"Soon, I'll come for you, Ashlyn. Don't even think about leaving."*

"Lucifer," I whispered. "Get away from her."

*"I am doing her no harm. You should be more concerned for your own life, Ashlyn. Soon."*

And the dark faded from her eyes. Rachel swayed on the spot, dropped to the ground. She curled into the foetal position, whimpering. I hesitated, torn about whether to call someone for help. *They'd lock her away. But she's not mad.*

She'd just gotten too close to the Darkworld. Close enough for Lucifer to pick out. Perhaps he'd been drawn by the block in her memory, where Leo and the others had erased her witnessing magic. Perhaps he'd picked her at random. Who knew how that crazy sorcerer's mind worked?

My phone rang again. I dashed back into my room.

"I'm on my way," I whispered. "My flatmate's hurt. I think—*he*—tried to get into her head."

I hoped my flatmates couldn't hear.

"Crap," said Claudia, her voice staticky on the other end. "Could you buzz me in?"

I glanced at Rachel. She'd quietened; now she looked to be just sleeping.

"I think she's okay. I'll come down."

Claudia didn't waste any time launching into her theories.

"It's here," she said the instant I opened the door and

let her in. Her voice was unnaturally high pitched, and there were dark circles under her makeup-less eyes. "It's happening beneath our feet. Lucifer must have got to the heart of the Venantium—of the Barrier. All the top-secret stuff's miles underground, even below the main headquarters. Lucifer must have found his way in."

I rubbed my forehead, glancing back upstairs as though someone might appear and explain all this madness away. "I don't get why Mr Blake—I mean, Mammon—showed himself yesterday. If he'd stayed hidden, he could have kept fooling everyone. No one suspected. I mean, we saw him underground, but I'd never have thought he was controlled by a *higher demon*. I thought higher demons killed everyone who summoned them."

"Very few people *could* summon one," said Claudia, clutching her phone convulsively. "You need to be an uncommonly strong magic-user, and have amassed a huge amount of magical power inside the demon heart you use as an anchor. That's kind of what Jude was trying to do… for *fuck's* sake. I can't believe we have another effing group of nutjobs here."

"Tell me about it," I said lamely, my hand twitching toward my own demon heart. I *had* one, but didn't know enough about it to be any use. I'd been offered answers, more than once. But accepting a demon's offer, even though I *was* one, seemed like a surefire way to get everyone I knew killed. Even if *I* couldn't die.

*Stop that.* Like it mattered now. My flatmates were upstairs, with no idea the world outside had gone totally batshit.

"They used to have books in the library," Claudia said. "Jack said—ages ago. He said they checked all the books' content and took away the ones that might give people ideas when they opened to the public."

"I'm not surprised." But right now, I wished I'd hung on to what books I had. I doubted I'd be able to get into the library again and walk out alive. "Lucifer—I can't believe he summoned *five* higher demons without anyone noticing." Even voicing it aloud didn't make the situation seem any less absurd. "God. *How* could no one notice that?" But I'd seen them up close, and though I'd had that nagging sense something wasn't right about the Inner Circle, the idea that demons might be possessing them was as far from my thoughts as possible. *The Barrier's gone.* No matter how many times I repeated it to myself, a large part of me refused to accept it.

"My guess is that he wormed his way into the Venantium first," said Claudia. "Maybe he already had influence over one of the Inner Circle—oh, never mind that. We need to find out if anyone survived, but Jack's not picking up his phone." She glanced around, then said, "I reckon Conrad let the prisoners out. He's the only new prisoner. That we know of, anyway."

"I didn't see him." But he was less dangerous than the alternative—unless Lucifer had got to him, too. "Maybe Lucifer wanted a diversion."

"Why the hell would Lucifer want to create a diversion when he has practically the whole Venantium under his control already?" said Claudia. Her overly high-pitched tone told me *she* was trying to rationalise a way out of this madness as much as I was.

"Because then any weird shit would get blamed on the prisoners?" I suggested. "Even demon summonings. I mean, these people must have done something pretty serious to get locked up."

"Um, not necessarily. Look at what happened to you. And Howard's parents."

"Oh shit," I said. "Howard's mum…"*Oh, God. I haven't told Berenice.* Or Howard.

"Shit, I forgot she jumped on you. What was that about?"

"She wanted to know if I'd seen her son. She said…" I swallowed. In everything else that had happened, I'd forgotten. "She said the Venantium killed her husband. Then she said something like, tell my son to meet me where the devil walks. Something like that."

"Okay." Claudia gave a nervous laugh. "She's cracked. That temper on her's just like Howard, though. Guess that's where he gets it from."

"Maybe we should talk to him," I said. "She seemed lucid when she said her husband was dead…"

"What, you want to break that news?" said Claudia sceptically.

"Not really, but… I don't know. How about Berenice?" We had to do *something.* Even if now was the worst possible time to ignite Howard's grudge against the Venantium.

"Good call," said Claudia. "Okay. Well, I have her number—oh, shit."

She stared at her phone, frowning. "I have about six missed calls from Cyrus last night when we were in the tunnels."

I moved to look at her phone, too. "Cyrus?"

"Yeah. I'll call him back."

My heart did an unpleasant somersault. If something had happened to Cyrus—and Leo…

"He's not picking up. Not even voice mail. I'll check Facebook."

Her fingers raced over the touch screen. "Nothing. You heard anything?"

"No phone," I reminded her, my heart now thudding

against my ribs. "And I barely go on Facebook these days."
*No. Not Leo. Please.*

"Never mind. Anyway. Berenice." She moved away,
phone pressed to her ear, talking quietly.

I looked around. Another cold, grey-skied morning.
The faint sound of clubhouse music still coming from
some hard-core partier's flat. Birdsong drifting over the
treetops. Normality on the surface. Chaos beneath.

Claudia hung up. "She'll meet us in town, in the café
opposite the Coach and Horses."

"Town?" I said. "But—but the fortune-teller said not to
leave campus. Town's not exactly safe at the moment."

"Well, Berenice didn't even know about what
happened last night until I just told her. She and Howard
were out in Redthorne, and things were pretty quiet when
they got back."

I could barely fathom that. How could they not have
noticed how wrong everything was? Even Rachel had, and
she didn't even have a Darkworld connection. Maybe some
people were more sensitive to it than others, but still. It just
seemed so absurd that Berenice and Howard had been out
partying when Mammon the higher demon had cornered
me.

"I don't get it." I shook my head. "Lucifer could
appear at any moment."

"A concrete block could fall from the sky and crush you
at any moment," said Claudia. "Theoretically, anything's
possible. That doesn't mean you can't leave your house in
case some disaster strikes you on the way to work. The
world goes on whether you want it to or not. We're always
on the brink of disaster. It's human nature."

It was one of Claudia's rare profound moments, and I
didn't have any counterarguments to hand. I just nodded.
"Okay. To Blackstone it is, then."

I thought Berenice would have brought Howard with her, but she met us alone outside the café.

"He's got a killer hangover. I left him to sleep it off," she said.

I glanced at Claudia, wondering how much she'd told her over the phone.

"Well," said Claudia. "He's probably not going to want to hear what we have to say."

"What?" said Berenice. "I'm hungover, too, you know. I need coffee."

She ordered a double espresso from the café. I went with hot chocolate, more to have something to do with my hands than anything. We were almost the only people in there, apart from a man in a balaclava sitting in the corner. That might have struck me as odd, were it not for the more pressing matters.

Claudia finally broke the silence. "Okay. Well, it might not look like it here, but the end of the world is kind of upon us."

Berenice gave me a suspicious look, as if to accuse *me*

of yanking her chain. I looked stonily back. Like she could intimidate me now.

"Um, well, not exactly," Claudia amended. "But Lucifer's taken over the Venantium. Five of the Inner Circle are under the control of higher demons. Including Mr Blake, who tried to attack us yesterday. Also, the fortune-teller's given up and gone over to the Dark Side. And all the prisoners have escaped. And we got attacked in the Lake District. I think that's it."

Berenice sat, mouth agape, her coffee forgotten.

Claudia fidgeted. "Okay. Maybe I should have worded that better. But, yeah, that's what happened."

Berenice's eyes narrowed, and she glared at me. "Why," she said, "is it always you?"

"Because I'm a *human-demon*," I snarled, having had about enough. "It means the whole world wants me dead, so I really couldn't give a crap what you think. Someone who has it in for me tried to get me killed at my aunt's old house the other day. Then we went to report it, and the Inner Circle wouldn't listen. Then someone let the prisoners out of the cells, and I got attacked by Howard's rabid mother. We tried to run away through the tunnels, and Mr Blake tried to take my demon heart, and it turns out he's possessed by a higher demon. The fortune-teller showed up and convinced him to go away, but she's on Lucifer's side now because he has some kind of hold over her. She told us five of the Inner Circle had already fallen and we were all doomed, and then she buggered off. Tell me what part of that is *my* fault?"

Berenice did a goldfish impersonation again. The first words to come out of her mouth were, "Howard's mother?"

*Typical. She would put Howard first. Not like Armageddon's upon us or anything.*

"Yes," I said, through gritted teeth. "She escaped from prison."

I told her in more detail about my encounter with the crazy woman.

"His dad's dead?" said Berenice.

"Well, that's what his mum said, no idea whether it's true or not. We figured that you ought to be the one to break the news to him."

"I can't," said Berenice. "He'd run off and get himself killed."

"Kind of my thoughts exactly," said Claudia. "But it's up to you. Doesn't he deserve to know?"

"I guess," said Berenice. "But if the Venantium's really out of bounds, and his mum didn't say where she was going—"

"She only said a riddle that didn't make sense," I said.

"Right. Well, that's no use." She narrowed her eyes at me. *Like it's my fault.*

"I don't understand how you couldn't tell something happened here yesterday," I said. "I mean, there were so many prisoners they ran out in the streets. And someone wrecked that angel statue in Blackstone, too."

"I'm not a psychic," Berenice snapped. "I haven't even been to the town square. What was I supposed to do, anyway, recapture the prisoners? You two are the ones who work for those tosspots. I never had anything to do with them."

"I didn't mean—"

"There's probably no one left, anyway," said Berenice dismissively. "Five higher demons underground, no one's gonna get out alive." Her hands shook, rattling her coffee cup, and she looked away.

"Your optimism is infectious," said Claudia. "Anyway, what the hell are we going to tell Howard?"

"Tell me what?"

Claudia swore under her breath.

"Hi, Howard," said Berenice, a touch too brightly. She moved her shaking hands under the table.

"You left your phone," said Howard, looking suspiciously from me to Claudia.

"Oh yeah. Thanks." Berenice took it and frowned at the screen. "I have a missed call from Cyrus?"

"I just talked to him," said Howard. "He and Leo just flew into Manchester. They're coming back here."

My heart kick-started so fast I felt light-headed. Leo was back. I hadn't prepared for this. I had no idea what to say, how to react—with over-the-moon happiness or wordless rage. I clenched my hands on the table, head ducking under everyone's stares.

"Do you think he knows what happened?" said Claudia, in an obvious effort to divert the others' attention.

"Not if he was on a flight," said Berenice.

"*What* happened?" Howard demanded. "Am I missing something here?"

"Um, kind of." Berenice took a deep breath.

"It's the end of the world as we know it," Claudia interrupted.

Berenice looked daggers at her, but Claudia just blinked, unruffled. I knew why she'd said it; Lucifer's domination of the Venantium was paramount, and the quicker as many people as possible knew, the better.

"Uh. What?"

"Lucifer's taken the Venantium," I said. "Five of the Inner Circle members are under the control of higher demons. I don't know how it happened, but by now, there might not *be* a Venantium left."

"You're having me on," said Howard. "I saw a group of those *venators* earlier. They looked okay to me."

"Really? Who?"

"I dunno. I think one was that David kid. Does it matter?"

"That can't be right," I said. "Yesterday the place was in chaos, all the prisoners got out, and Mr Blake was possessed by a higher demon. The fortune-teller's gone onto Lucifer's side, too. She's given up."

Howard stared at me for a good half minute. "The prisoners," he said slowly. "You'd better not be bullshitting me. They got out?"

"Yeah," said Berenice quickly. "Your mum's free. She said to tell you to meet her at the place where… what was it?"

"The devil rises," I said. "It might not mean anything. She was a bit… um…"

"What about my dad?" said Howard.

There was a very awkward silence.

"Um," said Berenice, "your mum said he didn't make it."

Howard stared at her blankly. His fists began to clench.

I don't know what would have happened, but a sudden crash made everyone in the café jump. The door had been thrown back so violently that it almost came off its hinges. Several people marched into the café and right over to our table.

"Miss Temple." It was Dr Philips, and her eyes were ablaze with anger. "Come with us."

Her companions moved in, three male *venators* I didn't know.

"What—why?" I said. I hadn't even expected that she'd be alive, much less walking around Blackstone.

"You have made a serious confession. I need you to report it to the Venantium."

"I thought——" I looked from her to the other *venators* and back again.

"You are a danger to everyone around you, Miss Temple. If you do not come with me right now, I will be forced to restrain you."

*Is she working for Lucifer?* There was no flicker of a demon in her eyes…

Another possibility hit me. I'd assumed that the Venantium was finished, but what if Mr Blake had only revealed himself to me? What if the rest of the *venators* were still under the impression that things were normal, apart from the prisoners escaping? That they still believed they had a fighting chance against Lucifer, and remained oblivious to the poison at the heart of the organisation?

Then I was totally screwed.

"I knew you were lying," Berenice hissed as I stood. I didn't see a viable alternative. Dr Philip put her hand firmly on my back and pushed me towards the exit.

"I'll need to question the three of you, too," Dr Philips said. "You were here when she made the confession."

"What confession?" I said, bewildered.

"My colleague overheard you admit to being an abomination," she said, indicating one of the other *venators*. He was the man who'd been wearing the balaclava, I realised, as an icy shudder went down my spine. *I admitted to being a human-demon,* I thought. *I said it straight out. God, I'm an idiot.*

My judgment had come at last.

## 19

## CAPTURED

The three *venators* advanced on me. I took a step back, debating what to do. What if was a trap, constructed by Lucifer? Now that I knew the truth, I couldn't be sure whether the *venators* acted of their own volition, or if they were being manipulated.

Maybe it didn't matter. As long as Lucifer was in control, he could do whatever he wanted, regardless of whether the Venantium's employees were aware of it or not.

Hands grabbed my shoulders. The Darkworld rose to defend me, coldness piercing me. My vision flashed to purple, and the three men recoiled.

"Demon," one of them said. "It's a mother-fucking *demon.*"

"I told you what to expect!" Dr Philips shouted, her body tensed. "Take her!"

But I wouldn't give in without a fight. Ice coated my hands and moved down my limbs, like liquid, spreading out across the ground from my feet. The *venators* jumped back with shouts of alarm as the floor beneath them became slippery. The flow of ice climbed the walls, frosting the windows of the café. Icicles formed along the ledges and above the door. Fractured light danced off the planes of glittering ice, tinted purple through my demon eyes. In the centre of it all, I stood, feeling the waves of anger wash through my demon half. *They won't take me.*

The ice had already started to coat the men's feet. Even Dr Philips looked momentarily lost for words. Then she shouted, "Don't underestimate her! Seize her, quickly!"

Fires sprang up around the *venators,* melting the ice, and they lunged at me. One of them slipped on the ground and fell. I dodged the other two, running past at a speed I'd never have managed in my normal state. It scared me shit-less, not knowing what the demon inside me was capable of —but I had to rely on her now. It was the only chance I had.

The demon took control and propelled me up the street, but one of the *venators* grabbed my ankles and pulled me over. I hit the cobbles hard, pain shooting up my knees. I tried to stand, but he pinned me down.

The demon rose in me again. *No! Don't kill him!* I shouted, horrified at the rage, the desire to destroy every-thing that came near. It was both a part of me and completely alien. Ice surged from my hands like glass shards, and the man jerked back, bleeding from the hands and face. I wriggled free, willing the demon to stop —*enough!*

As the man fell sideways, dazed but not dead, I ran again, sheer panic taking over. They'd catch me wherever I ran, and yet I had no choice. If I were caught, I'd lose my last chance to get the hell out of Lucifer's way. *I should have left when I had the chance…*

"Shit!"

I'd run into a dead end, and there were two figures waiting at the end. A trap.

I stopped, looking to either side. Two high brick walls: no hope there. But the demon was still in control. The world blurred and darkened; I felt the wind rush past—and suddenly I wasn't in Blackstone anymore but on the country lane leading to campus. My head spun. *I can't have moved that fast.* Yet somehow, I had. Demons could travel at unnatural speeds… break matter down… what else had my other side been hiding?

*Don't stop.* I ran for the woods, past the old Blackstone house. My eyes roved over its ruined walls and the scorched earth around it. Was Blackstone about to face another tragedy?

*"Ash."*

I recognised that voice. It stopped me dead in my tracks.

The fortune-teller stepped out of the shadow of the house, regarding me with that pitying stare I'd grown to loathe.

"Ashlyn," she said quietly. "Don't run. They'll find you."

"I'm not interested in quitting now," I said. "I won't give myself up."

"It's the safest place," she said. "Under the watch of the Venantium, you'll be out of the way of Lucifer's plans."

"I'll be in the middle of them!" I said, incredulous. "You're the one who saved me from Mr Blake. I'll be right under their noses if I let them take me in."

"They won't harm you. I have enough influence over Lucifer to ensure that much."

"I don't believe you." I shook my head. "You said it yourself: the Venantium's finished."

"Be that as it may, their headquarters is the safest place from the other sorcerers and demons joining Lucifer's cause. Blackstone will soon be fortified as Lucifer's stronghold. No one will be able to enter or leave. You'll be safe."

"Like hell," I said. I couldn't stay there any longer. Dr Philips would come for me soon. "Just because you've given up on me and on the world, doesn't mean I have."

The demon rose, without warning. *"Think on it, Melivia Blackstone,"* she spoke through my mouth.

The fortune-teller stared, lost for words. Yet another first.

And I ran. My feet tore up the undergrowth as I pelted through the forest, not sticking to any path. When the buildings of campus started to appear through gaps in the trees, I began to wonder. What was my plan now? Pack up what I could and leave? Where? My flat in Manchester was still vacant, but I couldn't hide forever. I had to warn my friends, at least. Get everyone away from here. How, I had no idea.

*"Use Influence."*

It took me a minute to realise it was the demon who had spoken.

*I can't do that.*

But did I have a choice? It was the quickest way to convince people...

*It's not right. You know it's not.*

The demon didn't answer, but I knew what she was thinking all the same.

*Okay. What now? Back to the flat? Or...*

I had no way of contacting Claudia, but I guessed that she was still in Blackstone with Berenice and Howard. The rest of the Venantium couldn't be trusted. Which left...

*Cyrus. And Leo.*

They were back in the country—and coming here. But

they wouldn't know about any of this. They wouldn't know Blackstone was no longer a safe haven.

*CAW!*

The screech ripped through the silence. Wing-beats rustled the tree branches, and I ducked just in time to avoid the harpy's dive. Its wing clipped my face, drawing blood.

*Shit!* I threw a handful of ice-fire, but my aim was off, and the bird avoided it. Another flew down to join it, and the two circled my head, cawing loudly.

"Shut up!" I hissed, directing ice-fire at one, then the other. One hit, the bird falling to ashes; the second missed —and two more birds swooped down to join the surviving one. I backed away, and narrowly avoided the talons of another, jabbing the air inches away from my face. I thought of Conrad's ruined eyes and felt dread coil around my heart.

And the demon woke. The world flashed purple, and ice fanned out from my hands in spears, piercing the harpies one after another. Frost crept up the trees, branches cracking; the earth froze beneath my feet, and still the power kept flowing.

*Stop it! Stop—they'll catch us!*

But it was too late. The undergrowth rustled and three men emerged—the *venators* from earlier. I had to hand it to them for stealthy movement; I'd thought I was alone.

Fire sprang up, igniting the undergrowth and barring my way. It was either run towards the fire or take my chances with the *venators*.

The demon took control and the scene blurred; seconds later, I was several feet away and running—

My body stopped. Everything stopped around me, like time had drawn to a standstill. I couldn't move my limbs.

*What's happening?*

Darkness clouded my vision, washing out the purple tint. I felt the demon withdraw, my mind becoming fully my own, and the ground rushed up to pull me under.

~

MY EYES FLICKERED OPEN. There was a foul taste in my mouth, and when I moved my hands, I felt ice crack, cold and sharp.

Light dazzled my eyes, and at once I knew where I was. In the Angel Box. My first thought was: *impossible.* I'd seen it broken, shattered on the floor. Yet nowhere else had the same white, glaring light, so bright it made me dizzy. I tried to move, but my limbs felt limp and heavy. I half sat, slumped against the glass wall. What had they done to me?

"Miss Temple."

I blinked. Dr Philips stood before me, flanked by two other *venators*, two of the men from before. I struggled to sit up again, but couldn't manage to move more than an inch. I felt a cold, suffocating pressure all over: my connection to the Darkworld was blocked.

"Human-demon," said Dr Philips. "You used demonic magic. Do you deny it?"

I shook my head slowly. My tongue felt glued to the roof of my mouth. Not that anything I said would change anything. I was well and truly trapped.

"You will answer my questions," said Dr Philips. "Then you will be taken to the cells whilst the Inner Circle decide on your punishment."

*This can't be happening.* After everything, I was going back to the cells.

I forced myself to speak past the numbness. The words came out in a jumbled mess. I backtracked, tried again. "Look. I need to tell you something."

"You will speak only when you are spoken to, abomination."

"It's important!" Desperation fought the paralysing sensation, and I managed to move into a sitting position. "The Venantium are under Lucifer's control."

"I will not listen to your lies, human-demon. Tell me. Are you working for Lucifer?"

"No!"

The light increased in intensity until all I could see were black spots before my eyes.

"The Angel Box is responding in the negative," she said, and through the haze, I saw her scribble something on her clipboard. "Very well. Have you ever communicated with another demon?"

"If you mean speaking to them, then yes, they won't leave me alone!" The light pounded at my head, turning my thoughts to fragments.

"Affirmative... And have you ever knowingly assisted a demon?"

"I don't think so." I forced my legs to stand up. "Have *you*?"

"How dare you!" She moved right up close to the glass, like she wanted to hit me. Her lips were white.

"I'm telling the truth!" Anger filled every inch of me, made it easier to speak. "Lucifer has control of the Inner Circle. If you put me in the cells, you'll just be handing me over to him. He wants to use me as a pawn, but I'm not on his side!" I gasped for breath, willing my legs to stay upright. The light continued to pulse bright.

"I will not listen to any more of this." Dr Philips motioned to the others. "Take her to the cells. I've found out everything I need to know. Her connection is blocked; there is no danger. She's helpless as a regular human." She was breathing fast. "Miss Temple, you have done

EMMA L. ADAMS

"Look under your own noses! The Inner Circle—"

"Will be overseeing your trial!" she said. "You will wait in the cells until that date. I need not say that visitors are forbidden. You will learn, Miss Temple, that we are less tolerant than you apparently believe."

*No. Not now. Please.* "Please."

The glass walls fell away, and the two men seized my arms instantly, as though expecting me to make a bid for freedom.

"Please," I said again, as they manhandled me across the room. "I'm not your enemy. I might be part demon, but I never asked for any of this. Lucifer's the real villain, and he's coming—he might already be here!"

But Dr Philips had already turned her back. Even trying to appeal to her humanity had failed.

The corridors bore no sign of the struggle the day before, and the tunnels were deserted. No prisoners remained in the cells. I'd be alone down here in the darkness. My flesh crept at the thought. *I have to get out.*

They pulled me past the first corridor of cells, down into deeper darkness. I made myself go limp, letting my feet drag, but out of the corners of my eyes, I was searching for a way out. We turned a corner and began to descend a long tunnel, leading deeper into the dark.

*"I'm still here, Ash."*

I looked up, as though the voice had come from somewhere nearby, and not in my own head.

*How?*

*"They made a mistake. They didn't take your demon heart."*

I felt it burn through my jacket pocket, and energy began to course through me. Slowly, the suffocating pressure receded. Neither of the *venators* reacted.

*But I thought my connection was blocked?*

"*They are not strong enough to keep me out. I'm part of you.*"

*Should I run?*

"*When I say.*"

We slowed down, reaching the foot of the tunnel. I glimpsed more cells, smaller and more cramped than the others. My heart thundered against my ribs, and I was sure the others must have heard her—sure it was too late.

"*NOW!*"

Another surge of energy broke through the block, and I reached out to the Darkworld, pulling handfuls of shadows out of the air. The two men were sent flying. One hit the wall hard and didn't get up; the second sprawled on the ground. He lunged for me, but I kicked out, my foot coated in solid ice. It was effective as a blow with a heavy object, and he crumpled instantly. *At least those self-defence classes came in handy.*

I felt kind of bad, as those guys clearly *weren't* working for Lucifer, but now wasn't the time to worry about that. Pounding footsteps ahead told me someone else was coming, and I had nowhere to hide. I pulled the shadows closer to me, fumbling to make a shield, but too late. Two people came into the tunnel. The two people I'd least expected to see.

"Looks like we don't need to beat anyone up after all," said Cyrus, moving into the candlelight.

The second remained in the shadows, dead-still, just looking at me. Leo.

## 20

---

### REUNION

I couldn't say a word. Shock and disbelief warred with joy and relief so intense it hurt. It was too much, on top of everything that had already happened. Tears pricked my eyes, and my whole body started shaking.

"Ash," said Cyrus. "You okay?"

I merely nodded. I wasn't sure how to define "okay" when everything had gone to shit, but right now I'd settle for "alive."

"Thank God," said another voice. Claudia appeared behind the other two—along with Berenice and Howard.

"What—" I gaped at them all. The entire Circle of Sinners had come to rescue me.

"We went looking for you at campus, and ran into these two," Claudia explained. "Well, I didn't know where you'd gone. You moved so damn fast."

Leo said nothing, but his stare didn't make me as uncomfortable as the weight of things unsaid. I didn't even know where to start.

"Well, the gang's all here," said Berenice, her tone flat. "Now can we get the hell out?"

"Not till I find out what happened to my parents," snarled Howard.

"Shh! Fine. But don't get us caught."

"I'm afraid it's too late for that," said another voice, and someone else stepped into the candlelight.

Dr Philips's eyes blazed. Her lips were in such a tight line they looked sewn together, as though suppressing a blinding rage. "You are all under arrest for aiding in the escape of a prisoner. How dare you come here and assault my colleagues!"

"I think your prisoner had already dealt with your colleagues," said Leo, and I felt the urge to laugh tempered with the equally strong urge to throw my arms around him and cry. I clenched my fists, refusing to look at him. *I don't want to look you in the eye:* those were the last words he'd said to me. I couldn't forget that. I couldn't forgive him.

"Get out of the way," Cyrus told Dr Philips. "It'll go better for you that way, trust me."

"You dare to threaten me?"

Even I was shocked that the threat came from Cyrus of all people. "Your incompetence is going to get a load more people killed if you don't start listening to the people who are trying to tell you what's right in front of you. There are demons in your organisation. Face it, you're in over your head."

"I will *not* be spoken to like this!"

"Ash?" said Cyrus. "Do the honours."

I reached for the Darkworld and let ice flow from my fingertips, directing it around the others and towards Dr Philips. In seconds it coated her, stapling her mouth shut before she could make a noise of protest.

"You really have a knack for that," said Cyrus.

"C'mon, already," said Berenice. "This place gives me the creeps."

It was weird beyond belief, being together as a group again. I still couldn't look at Leo, even with the unsaid words clogging my throat. Out of the corner of my eye, I saw him biting his lower lip as if nervous, but it was difficult to tell whether that was down to the mess we'd landed ourselves in or from being around me again. He'd never really opened up to anyone before. Except me.

I heard a noise up ahead, and paused.

"What's up?" whispered Cyrus, from just behind me.

"I thought I heard someone."

"Well, it's a good bet that it's an enemy," said Cyrus. "Let's move on."

*Use Influence,* the demon told me. I drew the Darkworld closer to me, letting the shadows envelop us. Cyrus nodded, grasping my plan. The others let their lights dim, too. No *venator* would be able to see us now, at least.

The noise became louder. It wasn't human noise, but an odd rumbling in the ground. I felt the hairs on my arms rise. *The Darkworld.*

"Shit," said Cyrus. "Come on. We have to get out."

But before we could take another step, someone stumbled down the tunnel from the stairs leading to the surface. Conrad.

"Help!" he cried. "Is there someone there? Help me get out!"

"Oh, shit," said Claudia.

"Ash?"

*Damn.*

"Don't leave me!" he said. "I can't get out—he won't get out my head!"

He lurched forwards, hands outstretched. "Please help me. He's going to kill me. He's going to make me get— demon hearts."

He let out a strangled cry and fell to his knees. His head tipped back, and his ruined eyes glowed black.

*"Ashlyn. I never expected you to come to me."*

*Lucifer.*

I heard several sharp intakes of breath, but I couldn't look at the others. I couldn't take my eyes off the demon speaking through Conrad.

"How?" I choked. "How did you—"

*"I have been here a long time, Ashlyn. I am everywhere. And I see your little group is all together now—just in time to witness this momentous occasion."*

"What do you mean by that?" I said. My words came out steady, but adrenaline coursed through my veins, my pulse racing.

*"Today, my friends, I am going to break the Barrier."*

My heart dropped. I knew we weren't getting out of that tunnel. Not alive. I felt the demon stir under the surface, the slight flicker of purple at the edges of my vision. *No. Have to get out…*

"What?" said Howard. "What the hell are you?"

*"I am Lucifer. You might have heard my name. I have met some of you before. Your girlfriend, for one. You might say I have a special interest in her, belonging to Mephistopheles as she does."*

Berenice made a choked sound, her eyes bugging out, her face chalk-white.

"You stay the hell away from her, whoever you are," snarled Howard, stepping in front of her.

*"Space has no consequence in the Darkworld. Just assume that I am everywhere. Now come with me."*

"What?" Howard laughed humourlessly. "You expect us to just do whatever you say?"

*"I thought you might need an incentive, Howard Lloyd."*

Berenice screamed.

"Berenice! What's wrong?" Howard's expression changed entirely—I'd never seen him look so concerned.

"He's—" she choked. "He's in my head." She let out a wail of pain. "Get out! Get him out!"

"Bastard! Let her go!"

*"You don't want to miss the show, Howard. You of all people must want to watch the great Venantium fall."*

Berenice screamed again.

"Let her go!" Howard grabbed Conrad by the throat, his other fist clenched.

*"Humans are so fragile, so easy to manipulate. If you don't want to see your girlfriend damaged beyond repair, I would give in to me now."*

"Fine," said Howard, dropping Conrad. All the fight seemed to have gone out of him. "Fine. I'll come with you. Happy?"

*"I knew you would see things my way. It wouldn't do to let you slip away now, would it?"*

"You're sick," Berenice choked. "You're not human—whatever you used to be."

*"Oh, I'm more than human, far more. But enough of that. Come."*

The ground fell away around us, and there was suddenly nothing beneath my feet. Before I could let out a scream, my knees buckled as we hit solid ground again—just like dropping into the Venantium's Headquarters.

*"It's a bit of a waste of a demon heart…but I have not the patience to wait for you humans to stumble through the labyrinth to your doom."*

I blinked. The scene had changed entirely, and we were now in a wide chamber with soaring pillars supporting a high ceiling. One of the catacombs.

Five people stood in the centre of the chamber. It took a minute for me to recognise them as five of the Inner

Circle. Their faces were identically blank. Mr Blake stood in the centre, above a prone figure: Conrad.

Many other people gathered around the outskirts of the room. I couldn't make out their faces, but I recognised the uniform of the Venantium on almost all of them.

Conrad lifted his head, and his face twisted into a painful smile. *"You're all here! Now the show can really begin."*

He pulled himself to his feet, holding out a small, gleaming object. A demon heart.

The five Inner Circle members lifted their hands, in which they, too, held demon hearts.

*"In order for me to manifest, a large amount of power is necessary,"* said Lucifer, through Conrad. *"An unfortunate but necessary consequence of being tied to the Darkworld for as long as I have. No matter, for the energy gathered will allow me infinite use of my powers. All I need is a sacrifice, one capable of absorbing a high amount of magical energy. Unfortunately, my powers are such that even a human-demon would die."* He looked at me, and an icy shiver danced up my spine.

*"Luckily, I found another volunteer, one who has acted as a higher demon's conduit before."*

Conrad's hand jerked into the air in a little wave. *"This young vampire has generously volunteered himself."*

"Conrad," I whispered, terror coursing through my bones. A sacrifice?

*"Mr Melmoth, your esteemed colleague, never told you why he neglected to act on his theories about a cure for the Vampire's Curse, why he destroyed all evidence of his experiments. But I found out the truth through the eyes of my demons. He realised their potential. A vampire can take in infinite energy. They could become a valuable weapon. Melmoth saw that a war was coming, a war that the Venantium couldn't hope to win. It is a pity that he was brutally killed before he was able to share this revelation with the rest of you. Other-*

*wise, you might have been able to prevent your Inner Circle from being compromised."*

"You're lying!" Leo shouted. "Melmoth would never have sacrificed innocent lives. He gave his whole life to finding the cure."

*"Apparently you didn't know your guardian as well as you thought."*

"Stop screwing with us," said Leo.

*Don't,* I thought. *Don't provoke him.*

*"Oh, I'm quite serious. Time to say your last goodbyes,"* said Lucifer, making Conrad wave again, his hand sickeningly limp.

Then his head twisted with a horrible *snap.*

I tasted bile. My head swam. I'd thought I'd reached the limit of pure terror, but a fresh wave took me. My own head felt detached, as though I watched through someone else's eyes, a screen of events that weren't real. A waking nightmare.

*"Better. Now: witness my revival. I have looked forward to walking this world once again."*

In unison, the demon hearts began to glow. My heart pounded, and despite the terror paralysing my body, I tried to contact the Darkworld. Nothing answered. Whether Lucifer had done something to prevent interference, I didn't know. But I could only watch as Conrad's body began to change.

He grew in stature, twisting grotesquely into a shapeless mass no longer recognisable as human. Elongated claws sprouted. Black shadows massed around him, swirling, and when they cleared, a terrible creature emerged. It was humanoid, covered in black fur, and long-clawed. The trademark violet eyes glowed, and a grin twisted its gaping mouth.

*"Fear me, humans."*

Right then, I knew we were going to die.

*"Now for the second stage: the Barrier. Come, Melivia."*

Someone came forward out of the shadows: the fortune-teller. Her head was bowed, and she held out a giant glass-like demon heart, bigger than her hands.

*"This demon heart can hold the strength of thousands. A good job there are so many of you, isn't it?"*

"He's going to sacrifice us," Claudia whispered. "All of us."

I couldn't even nod, but I knew she was right.

*Help,* I whispered to the darkness. *You want free rein, I'll give it to you. Just stop him. Save my friends.*

## 21

### END OF DAYS

S till, no answer came. Helplessness dragged me down. Who could stand up to five higher demons? To say nothing of the energy revolving around the giant demon heart; malevolent, strong, and utterly paralysing.

We were finished.

I glanced sideways. Perhaps it was stupid, but I felt a surge of gladness that I wasn't going to be alone when I died. I'd offer myself for any of them in an instant, but Lucifer didn't do bargaining. His plan was far bigger than any of us, and we were just sacrifices in his game. One that would end the world.

The fortune-teller held out the demon heart, and the monster, Lucifer, stroked it with one massive paw.

*"I have amassed the magical energy from a thousand dead* vena-tors *already,"* he declared. *"This place is a treasure trove of untapped magical potential. You should have taken better care of your dead."*

No one said anything. None of the *venators* had moved

the whole time. I wondered if they were even aware of what was happening. They couldn't all be in shock, surely. *They're supposed to be fighters.* How could so many powerful magic-users stand there and let this happen?

*"First, I believe it only right that the first victims should be the adopted sons of the man who gave me so much trouble twenty years ago."*

He gestured. Horror rooted me to the spot. He couldn't mean—

*"Come, Cyrus, Leo. Your father awaits!"*

Mr Blake looked up. *"Come, children,"* Mammon said through his mouth.

No one moved. I felt like someone had pounded a stake into my heart, pinning me to the spot. *No. Please. Please don't —not him.*

Whatever had happened between us, whatever wounds had been inflicted, that was nothing compared to this. And I couldn't do a damn thing to save him.

*"Oh, there's something you could do. Are you willing to take a gamble?"*

The demon hovered behind my eyes. I felt her yearning to break free, cold and sharp, astonishingly *alive.* But she couldn't beat Lucifer. No one could.

*"I can,"* she whispered.

Was she lying? I knew from bitter experience how easy it was to lie to oneself—but with an alternative personality, did that apply? How could I know she was telling the truth? She'd tried to *kill* Leo before—

But she hadn't. She wasn't my enemy. Maybe I should trust her. Lucifer wasn't even looking at me. His eye was on his prize.

*"Come forth, brothers! You don't want me to inflict any further harm on your friends, do you?"*

A force slammed into me, almost knocking me off my feet—the same ripple went through everyone else. Shadows snaked around the group, pinning each of us in place.

*"Any one of these people could die at any second. It's like a lottery. Are you feeling lucky?"*

"Leave them!" said a tremulous voice. Cyrus. Out of the corner of my eye, I saw him move, straining against the shadows which restrained him. "All right. What do you want from us? Neither of us care that you killed our father, you know."

"The jerk-ass deserved it," said Leo. "Cheers."

Lucifer apparently didn't know what to make of his brazen attitude in the face of death.

*"Arrogant human,"* he said. *"I like it. As much as I enjoy conducting human screams of pain, it's refreshing when someone stands up to me. More satisfying when I destroy every ounce of hope you had."*

The demon's presence flooded me. Somehow, despite the crushing darkness, she'd broken through. And I let her take me over.

The world was bathed in violet light, making even the shadowy strands of the Darkworld look oddly beautiful. I wondered briefly if this would be the last thing I ever saw.

Then cold anger took over. Once again, it coursed through every inch of me, more potent than anything I'd felt before. Though I knew that anger was powerful, could define a person, make them do terrible things, it was alien to me. Did the demon inside me really possess that much hate?

Out of the corners of my eyes, I saw figures in the darkness—not my friends, but a line of shadowy people, forming a circle in front of us. Half people, insubstantial.

The demon whispered to me, and I understood. The rage I felt came from these half shadows, from these beings of the Darkworld. They hated Lucifer. They wanted him dead.

And they'd help me.

Waves of darkness rushed from Lucifer, towards Leo and Cyrus... and stopped, repelled by another wall of shadows, a solid barrier that cloaked my friends and me from all sides. A demon shield. But there was something different about this one. As I looked closer, through the demon's eyes, she whispered the truth to me, and I understood.

Shadowy figures formed the entire shield, overlapping spots of darkness. They weren't ghouls, weren't even regular demons. They were something else entirely, and somehow strangely familiar.

*You took everything from us, Lucifer,* they whispered. *But we waited. You might have hidden yourself in the deepest recesses of the Darkworld, but we have been waiting all this time for you to return. You won't succeed.*

Lucifer stared at the barrier, his monstrous face etched with disbelief. I wasn't sure if he could see the figures or not, but he looked nonplussed that anything could have stopped him.

But something had. The demon had done the impossible.

The fortune-teller, too, stared at us. Our eyes met, and she looked away, as if ashamed.

Lucifer recovered. *"You cannot stop me. The Barrier will break at my hands, and you will know it, humans."*

The five Inner Circle members held up their demon hearts.

*"These are no ordinary demon hearts,"* said Lucifer. *"It's taken*

*me a while to work out the mechanics of your Barrier. It's very cleverly done. Who would have thought of using demon hearts to repel the very forces that once controlled them? But it has always been about power with you. As it is with demons, so it is with the Venantium."*

The five demon hearts glowed: one blue, one red, one green, one white, one gold.

*"Hiding your central demon heart amongst the regular demon hearts was a bold move. I admit it had me fooled for a while. It was only when I used one of your lackeys to steal a heart for my servant Mephistopheles that I began to consider the potential of a source of untapped magic. When you tell your recruits that the Barrier's source is hidden deep underground, I imagine they envision some kind of wondrous machine. But it seems that the great Venantium has not advanced far since their genesis. You do not progress with the times, and for that you pay the ultimate price."*

The shadows rose, this time enveloping the five Inner Circle members and the demon hearts.

*"This is the end of days the original Venantium foresaw, humans."*

I felt it in the air, like the stillness before a storm. The Barrier all around us trembled, threatening to break with the finality of a peal of thunder.

*"It is quite possible that many of you will die the instant it breaks. I feel it only fair to warn you."* My blood chilled at his tone, as calm as a doctor reeling off a list of potential side-effects.

*"Demons do not experience emotions like you and me, but they never forget, and there are some who will take any chance at instant vengeance on the Venantium. My loyal servant Mephistopheles harbours a grudge against certain humans, for instance."*

Another chill to the heart. Mephistopheles had reason enough to despise Leo and me, if just because we were still alive.

*"Most of your deaths are likely to be painless, if it is any consolation. It is strange how fragile the boundaries of the human mind are. I, of course, have cloaked my mind against penetration, but one alone of your number shares that with me."*

My body numbed as the beast looked at me. The shadowy wall looked fragile and insubstantial in the face of this unspeakable evil.

*"She will not be alone for much longer. The Seven are notoriously virile, and will doubtless take advantage of their new corporeality to create more remarkable creatures like Ashlyn here. All will, naturally, be taken under my wing. They have their uses, however inconveniently... combustible they are."*

He was going to kill me. I knew it in every part of me, and yet I was no longer afraid. The anger stirred again, in and around me, and the wall of shadows seemed to tighten, as though the invisible creatures making it up drew closer together.

*"Ashlyn,"* Lucifer whispered. *"Even as I explored the depths of the Darkworld, I heard your name whispered amongst demonkind. You are quite something, for a human who has only been aware of her connection for such a short time. I have seen every thought in your mind, and it amazes me how unaware of your potential you remain. You have lost everything at the hands of those you trusted, had your very place in existence called into question, yet you have not given yourself over to your other side. These are qualities that would serve as valuable in my most trusted companions... but not in my enemy. You are too unstable, Ashlyn, and therefore, you must give yourself over to me, or face a death reserved only for the children of the Seven."*

Pure rage radiated through me, through the very walls. The shadows bristled and quivered, a rumbling sound rising like distant thunder. I could hear words in it, but the only one I could make out was, *"Die!"*

Lucifer seemed unaware of the other presence in the

room. He must be able to see that something blocked his way, but not the shadowy, raging figures. Somehow, this provided a brief flash of comfort.

*"I expect you are tired of hearing this by now, Ashlyn, but I am afraid I must be the last to ask you to hand over your demon heart."*

## 22

### THE FALL OF EVE

I didn't move. The darkness held me in place. *This is it.* I felt strangely calm, but the anger still brewing around me left no room for any other emotion in my heart.

*"I suspected as much. Pity. Very well. Melivia, bring her to me."*

A cold shudder ran through the Darkworld, and the fortune-teller looked up, her eyes blank. She moved towards me, right through the defensive barrier, and inexplicably, rage rose within me—not at Lucifer, but at her. Would she really sacrifice me?

*"Whatever force defends you works only on demons; I suspected as much. It feels like one of Melivia's little deceptions. No matter. She is mine now, and does as I command."*

A hand found mine and squeezed. *Leo.* I became aware of my heart pounding in my ears, as the demon drew back, letting my own consciousness seep into my body. But I couldn't face the deluge of emotions. There was no time. It was too late.

But Melivia had stopped, several feet away. Was I imagining it, or was there a flicker of her old will in her eyes? *No.* I turned away, to Lucifer, whose attention was fixed on the fortune-teller. And I knew: to him, this was more about her than me. He didn't care about me; he only cared about dominating her, like he had most of her life. Making her do his bidding, like a puppet.

He didn't even notice my demon, and the shadows quietly raging in the background. We were united against Lucifer.

A faint chanting rose in my ears. I couldn't make out any words, but it sounded like Latin. A chorus of a thousand whispers, joined in song. I felt the power in it, although nothing had visibly changed. A shift in the Dark-world. I didn't know when I'd become aware of the ways power moved through the shadow-world, but I could tell that it was now concentrated on this room—and not on Lucifer's side. He held a power of his own, but his came almost entirely from the demon hearts. It might have bothered me that I knew this, like it came from some sixth sense I'd acquired, but all I could do was pray I could use it, somehow, and get us out alive.

The fortune-teller faltered, just as she crossed through the barrier.

*Fight it,* I thought. *What happened to that indomitable spirit?*

She *was* fighting. I didn't know if she heard the chanting, but something had halted her progress. She turned the demon heart over in her hands as if unsure why she was holding it.

Then she looked me in the eye and gave me a faint nod. Her voice spoke in my head, clear as though she'd spoken aloud: *You're my legacy. I won't let you die.*

She turned to face Lucifer. "I will not hand my daughter over to you."

Lucifer plainly hadn't expected any resistance. He slammed a paw into the ground, sending another ripple through the Darkworld. My heart thudded. *I'm her legacy?* Even to her, I wasn't a person, but a means to fight back against the demon who'd ruined her life.

My hand slipped out of Leo's as ice flowed to my fingertips, and Lucifer didn't even notice. Of course he didn't.

The shadows moved in, and this time, I knew for certain: the chanting, the depthless anger, came from them.

And I had plenty of anger of my own to join with theirs.

*"You are mine,"* he said to the fortune-teller. *"You agreed to bring her to me without a fight. I do not wish to harm you, Melivia. You are far more entertaining than any other human I have drawn into my grasp."*

"I am not your toy," said Melivia quietly. "Do not presume that I have any more desire to do your will than the demons you think you can command."

No. But she couldn't see past her hatred of Lucifer to consider I might be able to speak for myself. The pair of them had engineered my life—them, and the real Lucifer. She'd even doctored my *memories.* Whether she acted in my favour or not, I knew beyond a shadow of a doubt that part of me would never forgive her for that.

My body trembled all over, my rage at the fortune-teller and what she'd done mingling with the fury at Lucifer, for trapping us here. The collective fury of the shadows pulsed through me like the heartbeat of the Darkworld itself.

*"I see that I did a less thorough job of breaking your spirit that I thought. It seems that the frivolous, idiotic girl I tamed has not disappeared after all."*

"We cannot change our basic nature. That is one thing you, Lucifer, have failed to grasp, in all your years of stolen life."

*"Oh, you have never ceased to be a foolish girl in my eyes, whatever you might have learned since your dalliance with the higher demon who shares my name. Interesting that he has never rushed to your aid, is it not?"*

The fortune-teller held his gaze. "As I keep telling you, the higher demons do not answer to the whims of humans. They take what would give them an advantage, but even you cannot command them indefinitely. Make no mistake, they serve you now... but they will be your undoing, Lucifer."

*"No,"* my demon whispered in my ear. *"We will be your undoing."* Though I couldn't tell whether she directed the words at Lucifer or the fortune-teller, in that moment, I didn't care.

*"You dare to lecture me?"* Lucifer himself appeared not to have heard the demon. He had eyes only for Melivia.

"I only tell you the truths you are too blind to acknowledge. Humanity is not something one can erase from one's makeup. You are still only a human mortal in their eyes, whatever you might have achieved in the Darkworld."

*"I am not human! Humans are weak. They will fall immediately when the demons rise."*

The demon spoke in my ear again: *"No. You will fall, false Lucifer."* The shadows edged closer to him, and again, he didn't seem to notice. Now I made out faint outlines— shaped like people. Humans. Or...

A shadow moved alongside me, then another. They were more than a shield against Lucifer: they were fighting on our side. With me.

The shadow folded over us, a film over my vision. Keeping Lucifer out.

Keeping even the fortune-teller out.

"If twenty years has taught me anything, it's that human life continually adapts to the most adverse conditions. Life may not be as it has been in the past, and yet you underestimate the forces of change, of history. This isn't something you can appreciate in the Darkworld, where life, such as it may be called, is unchanging."

*"Enough. Your words mean nothing. Bring me the human-demon, Melivia."*

"I will not."

*"Part of me is forever lodged in your heart, Melivia. You cannot escape it."*

"You are wrong."

*"Then so be it."*

The demon heart in the fortune-teller's hands began to glow. She let out a sharp gasp, as if it burned her hands.

Lucifer changed, again. Right now, he resembled a medium-sized shadow-beast, covered in shadows bristling like fur. But as he reared on his hind legs, he began to grow, becoming something sinewy and humanoid, tall enough to blot out the ceiling above me. His eyes were red pits, and cruel fangs curved over his mouth.

Fear should have frozen me. But underneath the anger pulsing through the shadows came a flood of... reassurance.

Somehow, they—we—had shut Lucifer out. Stopped him getting at the others. But he was on the other side, and so was—

"You waste your power, Lucifer." The fortune-teller's voice was, to my amazement, still calm, measured. Could she see the shadows? Why wouldn't she withdraw behind the shield, like the rest of us? Unless...

*"I will break the Barrier, and then I will kill your daughter, Melivia. And you will live on and help me to rule the Darkworld and human worlds alike."*

"You are simply a deluded psychopath," said Melivia. "I might have made excuses for you when I was a naïve child, but I have spent my life trying to undo your work. You can't bind me to your will any more. I would rather die."

*"Then die."*

He surged forwards—and with a jarring smack, met the barrier surrounding us.

The sensation was more discomfort than pain: like someone lightly bumping into me. No, into the demon. We were one, and aligned with the shadows keeping Lucifer out—but how could we use this to beat him? Around me, the shadowy figures still chanted, and incredible as it seemed, they were holding Lucifer back. The beast roared, moving its head to see what was blocking its path.

And the fortune-teller started chanting, too.

Her voice was soft, yet I heard it clearly in my mind. At first it wavered, as though Melivia was working to stop her fear from seeping through, and then it grew more confident, into a melody that reverberated in my very bones. It wasn't English, wasn't even Latin, but something else entirely. A song of the Darkworld. Through my demon, I sensed the meaning rather than understood it—a meaning beyond words.

Lucifer shook his head.

*"What is this, Melivia?"*

Her response was to raise her voice, the melody thickening as the other voices rose to support her. The monster was stopped in its tracks and started to shrink back to its normal size. The melody rose and swelled, moving like the flow of the tide. Wave after wave broke over us, rippling through the Darkworld, even through *my* demon, and it held everyone in the chamber transfixed. Even the five Inner Circle members didn't move, although they'd barely shown any signs of life since we'd entered.

*"What have you done?"* Lucifer shook himself, as though

trying to free himself from a net. He was back to the size he'd been beforehand—still grotesque, but no longer gigantic. He lunged for Melivia, but still couldn't break through the barrier.

*"What devilry is this, Melivia? Who defends you?"*

"There are some whose anger lives on even after their mortal deaths. Think on those you have wronged, Lucifer, and you will know who ended you."

*"What…?"*

The chanting rose up again, harsher this time. I felt anger wash over me, the anger of thousands. I knew the shadows were the ghosts of Lucifer's past victims. Human-demons like the doppelgänger. Like me.

We would end Lucifer.

As Lucifer's attention focused on Melivia, shock distorting his expression, I moved forward, out of the shadows.

The Darkworld answered, its anger fuelling my own, as ice-fire surged to my hands. Shadows draped around me, formed of the spirits lost, forsaken by everyone, abandoned to the Darkworld. Eager for revenge.

The fortune-teller remained amongst them, but I paid her no notice. This would be my victory. Lucifer had ruined more lives than hers, and the Darkworld was—had always been—on my side.

The shadowy hands joined with mine as the ice-fire formed a long shape. A sword. Violet tinged the world, the demon moving forward, taking control.

But I was still there, still in control of my body. As Lucifer stared at Melivia, I lunged forwards and stabbed the shadow-beast through the flank.

Some part of me expected pain, but instead, anger raged through me once again. For these lost spirits, it would never be satiated. Lucifer spun around, pieces of shadow falling away, face twisting with rage. His teeth bared, biting at the shadows, but closed on nothing.

He couldn't harm me behind the shadows.

The demon and I moved as one, the whispering anger of the Darkworld hovering over my shoulder like a second shadow. One sword became two, and I slashed at Lucifer's face. No blood poured out—instead, he changed form, to a shadow-fox-sized creature.

"You stay away from me," I snarled, the Darkworld amplifying my ordinary-human voice so it echoed around the chamber. "You don't get to control my life."

I didn't look to the fortune-teller for her reaction. All my attention was focused on the ever-shrinking form of Lucifer. He was far outnumbered by the lost spirits whose lives he'd ruined.

The song became an inhuman scream—both from the Darkworld and my own mouth. Two swords merged into one, an icicle I hurled at Lucifer. With the shadows holding him back, he couldn't avoid it.

The shadow-creature collapsed in on itself, barely visible now. *That can't be right.* Lucifer was holding back...

What the hell was he doing?

As the floor trembled under my feet, the truth hit me. He'd been conserving his power, and now new shadows climbed the walls and spread across the ceiling. Not the shadowy creatures defending me.

"He's going to bring the ceiling down!" I shouted over my shoulder. *The others. You have to get them out.*

But the demon's ever-burning rage refused to be quenched. I stepped forward even as fear for the others pulled me back—the shadowy figures moved alongside me, adding their anger to the ice re-forming in my hands and fanning out from my feet.

Ice flowed across the floor, reaching the walls where

Lucifer's shadows climbed. A furious wave of noise went through the Darkworld, like a thousand voices whispering at once. And my demon joined them: *"Die, Lucifer."*

A human-sized piece of rock fell and shattered on the ground, breaking the trance. I scrambled back, feet skidding on the ice rink I'd created—*oh, hell. Not again.* Dust obscured my vision, making it impossible to see if my friends had listened and run—and that second was enough to give Lucifer the chance to leap at me again. The shadow-beast met once again with an invisible wall, and now I directed every ounce of fury into the ice flowing to my hands.

And at Lucifer.

The shadows kept him hemmed in, and I almost thought I saw fear in those violet eyes. Then the shadow-beast shrank, clawing and screeching, under a waterfall of ice. I raised my hands, the ice flowing from my fingertips and pushing him down... until nothing remained but ice.

Within, Lucifer beat against the walls, a horrible yowling sound echoing through the Darkworld. I walked closer, anger simmering. Dust stung my eyes, the slippery floor slowed me, and worry for the others beat at the door. *Stop, demon. Leave him.* But deep down, I knew I couldn't. Lucifer wasn't dead. *Could* he die? He was effectively a demon himself...

"You can't kill him, Ashlyn."

The fortune-teller spoke to me without looking in my direction, advancing towards Lucifer's now-frozen shadow form.

*What the hell is she doing?* I tried to move forward, but this time the shadows pushed *me* back.

*What?* "Hey!" I shouted after her, but she ignored me.

"Lucifer," Melivia said. "You forget that my heart is my own. You might have bound my power, but you cannot stop me from giving it away." She reached into her coat and pulled out another palm-sized white crystal. "You gave me this when you restored me to life. You made it so I could never access the power inside, even if I could use extraordinary magic. But the Darkworld can awaken it, and so can the dead."

"*What...?*" The voice came from all around us—from the ground underneath our feet, the ceiling above our heads. Dust rained down, obscuring even the shadows.

The chanting roared up again, and this time, Melivia joined in. She rotated on the spot, lifting the two demon hearts so they were raised over her head. She looked as powerful as I'd ever seen her, in that moment, her silver-fair hair flowing behind her, raised like a halo.

And the tips of her hair alighted.

*Fire.* It flickered around her, ghosting up from the ground, outlining the figure of the fortune-teller. Her mouth continued to form words, but the song faltered and died, and I saw real pain flash in her eyes. Not pain —agony.

She was burning.

*No.* I stepped forward, but again, the shadows pushed me back.

The flames circled her, leaping over her body, and the demon hearts in her hands began to smoke. She threw back her head and screamed.

But her scream was nothing compared to Lucifer's. The monster's howl shook the chamber itself, and a chunk of rock fell from the ceiling shattering amongst the *venators* still crowded at the back.

Panic brewed, the spell of the chanting finally broken, and people started running. I saw shapes in the fog, frantically stumbling around, but it was the fortune-teller, ablaze and beautiful, that held my attention. Her, and Lucifer, who was now burning, too, back in his shadow-beast form. The ice imprisoning him had melted away, turning to steam.

Sensation came back to my hands as they dropped to my sides. *No. God, no.*

"Get out!" I yelled at the others. "It's not going to stop —we'll die."

She'd die. The Darkworld raged, but the demon had retreated inside me as more pieces of rock fell from the ceiling and the ground trembled beneath my feet.

"Leo!" I yelled, running towards him. "Get out—all of you."

Claudia moved in and clutched my arm. "Holy shit. Holy shit. She has his demon heart." She'd voiced my exact thoughts. The fortune-teller was destroying Lucifer's demon heart—at the cost of her own, and her life. That was the price to return to life, and Lucifer had fixed it so that the energy contained within her own demon heart was off-limits to her. But she'd worked around it, clearly, and now the Darkworld rippled around us, strengthened by the power emanating from the heart in her hands. The shadows pushed us all back to the room's edges, and the monster was now a flaming mass, orange-yellow fire eating away at it. *Real* fire, death to demons, even me. I swore over and over, hands clenching, desperately calling for ice-fire that was no longer there.

*"I will not die!"* Lucifer screamed.

The fortune-teller drew a shuddering breath and screamed again. Her voice echoed in my mind, *"Forgive me, Ashlyn. You bear a terrible burden. But Lucifer is finished. We are bound, and if one dies, so will the other. Destroying his heart will prevent him from ever returning."*

Another piece of the ceiling fell, closer this time. I tried to call out to her, shout a futile warning, but arms grabbed me and pulled me back.

"We have to leave!" Leo shouted.

"She's—" Sacrificing herself, without trusting me to finish the job. And what of the other spirits? They'd pushed me out, too. I moved forward, but common sense took over. *Get the others out. Get them out.*

Leo's hand rested on my shoulder. "She knows what she's doing. I'm sorry. We have to get out of here; otherwise we'll be trapped."

He was right, I knew, but I couldn't take my eyes off the fortune-teller. Aunt Eve. Melivia. Burning like a torch. Burning for all of us.

Another shower of rock fell, blocking her from view, and then we were running.

## 23

### AFTERMATH

I couldn't see anything for the falling rock, throwing dust clouds into the air as it struck the floor. Was the entire chamber collapsing? I conjured a light, but there was so much dust that I could see little even with it held above my head. Leo's hand came out of the darkness and held mine tight. Together we dodged and ducked the falling rubble and made for the point everyone seemed to be heading for: the tunnel leading out of the chamber. I only hoped that the tunnels weren't collapsing, too.

But we made it. Leo pulled me after him, out of the door, and into the mass of people running up and down, as if unsure which way led out.

"This way!" he shouted.

I didn't hesitate, but followed him. Where were the others? I looked back, but there was too much dust to make out more than indistinct shapes. Shouts rang out. Someone was sobbing.

*Claudia? Cyrus?* We couldn't just leave them.

"Come on, Ash! The others are smart. They'll figure a way out."

I had to believe him. We had to get out.

All the same, a horrible ache pierced my chest, from the pressure of emotions I couldn't yet allow myself to feel. For the fortune-teller, and her sacrifice. It got worse as we left the chamber behind. Melivia's face, outlined in flame, kept coming to the front of my mind. I could only hope that Lucifer was truly dead. Could I have killed him? I didn't know. All I could do was push the feelings down and run for my life.

The noise of falling rock echoed behind us, intermixed with screams. We ran faster. My breath came out in sharp gasps. *Keep running. Come on…*

And finally, stairs leading upwards into light like the stairs to heaven. Our feet pounded on stone. The light grew bigger, brighter, until—

I had no idea where we were, only that it was outside. The light came from a cottage a few metres away, surrounded by fields. It looked like somewhere between Blackstone and Crowley, although I couldn't be certain. Night had fallen, and a sliver of a crescent moon hung in a wide sky flecked with endless stars.

I sucked in a breath of fresh, cold air, exhaled, and turned to Leo.

"Any clue?"

"No. This must be one of the hidden entrances to the tunnels."

"I thought people didn't know about them," I said, gesturing towards the cottage. "It's right out in the open."

"I reckon that place belongs to one of the *venators.*"

"Ah. I guess there won't be anyone there."

I had no idea how many Venantium members had been in the tunnels, but it had seemed like a lot. All of them, maybe. No more than a hundred. Leo looked at me, and I could tell he was wondering, same as me, how many of them had managed to escape.

*And the higher demons were still there*, I thought, with a sick feeling. Even if Lucifer was gone, there were still five higher demons in our world...

"Ash. You okay?"

*What kind of stupid question is that?* "Of course I'm not okay," I said quietly. "I just lost my mother, not that she ever—ever acted like it. And we don't know where the others are."

"I only meant, are you not hurt," said Leo, contrite. "I know. If we could just get our bearings...I think I might remember seeing this cottage on the train to Crowley..."

"We could follow the train line?" I suggested. *Take practical steps. Don't remember. Don't think.*

"Good call."

I spotted the line, snaking between two fields in the distance, and we set off at a brisk pace despite our aching feet.

The silence between us was palpable, even though most of me was in emotional turmoil from the rapid succession of events. I was scared for the others, too. But Leo... this wasn't how I'd imagined our reunion. Strange how I'd always expected, deep down, that there would *be* a reunion, even though six months felt as long as a lifetime, and everything had changed.

Now the world had shifted again, and Leo was the only familiar thing I could hold on to.

We met the rail track eventually, where it twisted between grassy banks. We probably weren't supposed to be trespassing in this field, but I hardly cared at this point.

Leo said his instinct told him we should follow them east, and I went along with it. He knew the area better than I did, after all, even though he'd been absent for so long.

The silence stretched, seemingly never-ending.

*I don't want to look you in the eyes.*

Leo finally turned to me. "I know this is a bad time," he said, his quiet voice clear in the pervading hush. "But I missed you."

My heart contracted. I didn't say anything. I couldn't say it back—couldn't say *I missed you, too.* "Missed" was too inadequate a word for the empty darkness that had filled me ever since he'd left me at the worst possible time, when I'd lost too much already. When Melivia had died, because —*oh, God. Don't think.*

"I know an apology isn't enough—"

*Damn straight it's not.*

"But I really did. I wanted to come back, but I just couldn't. I couldn't."

"That's no excuse," I said, my voice hoarse from the dust and the silence.

"I wanted to email you, call you, a million times, but I... I didn't think you'd appreciate it. I just wanted to hear your voice."

"Well, you can hear it now," I said coldly. "Your brother *did* email me. For months."

He flinched. "I told him to check on you," he said. "I wanted to check you were okay."

"You waited a while," I said.

"I... I know. I used to check your Facebook page, but you stopped updating, and then you disappeared for ages. I got worried."

Seriously? "I'm gratified," I said. "So I should feel privileged that you cyber-stalked me but couldn't get up the courage to actually speak to me?"

"That's not what I—" He swallowed. "Look, I'm

saying this all wrong. I made a mistake, a bad one. I shouldn't have left. There's no excuse."

"That's better," I said, the words coming out before I could stop them. Somewhere inside, the demon's anger still raged along with the others' underground. Our arguments seemed petty by comparison.

"I'm sorry. It was the only way I could think to deal with the situation, and I wasn't thinking clearly at all. Having that monster inside me…"

"Welcome to the club," I said bitterly. "Do you think it's all fun and games having a split personality?"

"Is that what it is? I thought she was someone different. Not you."

"Oh no, she's me," I said, and realised it was true. "She's just less driven by emotion. An advantage sometimes, really."

"She's a demon, though, right? What she did down there… I've never seen a human sorcerer do anything like that. Ever."

"I'm not entirely sure," I said. "It's not like I know any other human-demons to compare with. She has emotions. Like the doppelgänger."

Leo gave me a quizzical look. *I didn't tell him.* It had totally slipped my mind, but I'd never mentioned what the doppelgänger really was. At the time, I'd been determined not to give myself away as a human-demon.

Maybe lies would have always come between us.

"The doppelgänger was like me," I said. "A human-demon, but Lucifer killed her. My demon told me."

"Did you see those… shadows? They looked like people."

I swallowed, my heart thudding. "Yeah. They were the remains of the human-demons Lucifer killed. They used to live around here."

One had died on campus. The demon had whispered to me that the body dug up during construction had been one of them, too. An angry spirit.

"Wait, so they're—what, ghosts?"

"Not exactly. They're fuelled by anger and can draw on the Darkworld to give them power. They were there, in that chamber. They helped me…" *They could have killed Lucifer.* But could they? The fortune-teller had thought the only way to win was with her sacrifice. *Of course she did. She couldn't see things any other way.*

I gritted my teeth, tears blurring my eyes. *Damn her. Damn Lucifer.*

"The—the fortune-teller must have known," said Leo quietly. "She said something about anger living on after mortal death, and I felt how angry those spirits were. And then when he said something about—killing you, like any child of the Seven—that was when they started threatening him, even though he couldn't hear."

"I thought… I thought only I could hear them," I whispered.

"I don't know what you heard, but they kept whispering about revenge for their deaths. What she said… I mean, if she didn't mean actual ghosts, then maybe with human-demons, the demon part survives after you die."

"What, so you think I'm immortal?" I'd shied away from contemplating it before, but it made sense. Too much sense.

"I don't know. Demons can't die, they just… exist. What that means for you…"

"Don't say any more," I said. "I've had about enough already. It's bad enough that I carry the anger of thousands. I've felt them before."

"They're only angry at Lucifer. Can you still feel them?"

I thought. Now that he mentioned it, the anger had disappeared sometime since we'd started talking. I felt nothing beside my own turbulent emotions—which were all-consuming enough on their own.

"No. But that doesn't mean…"

I had to know if Lucifer was really dead—and if the others had escaped. Somehow, we'd got side-tracked, but I could feel the panic pressing in on me, like the suffocating, collapsing tunnel—if they were dead… like her…

"The doppelgänger was like them? She tried to kill us."

I fought to recall what the first other human-demon I'd met had said, a lifetime ago. "She was killed by the *venators*. They thought she was a monster."

Leo sucked in a breath. "God… I thought it was exaggerating."

"What?" I said. My head throbbed. I just wanted to lie down at the roadside and collapse, but I couldn't do that. Not now the one person who might have stood a chance against the Darkworld had gone. Not with the Barrier gone, and… *Stop it. Please, stop it.*

"I did some background reading when I was away," he said. "Cy and I ran into some people like us. Long story, but they spotted our shields. Anyway, I found this book in a library in New York City—about Lucifer. It said that— well, there were a lot of stories, but he's known to have used human-demons in the past. Built an army, actually, and slaughtered every one of them himself when they turned out not to be useful to him."

I felt sick. Hadn't I seen enough slaughter tonight? Conrad… the fortune-teller… the many who'd doubtless been killed trying to escape the tunnels…

"Shit!" Leo exclaimed. "I'm a fucking idiot."

"First sensible thing you've said for a while," I said, the words slipping out before I could reel them in.

"My phone," he said. "It wouldn't work underground, but maybe…"

He waved it around, searching for a signal.

"Hell—missed call from Cyrus—five minutes ago!" He stared at me, wide eyes bright in the moonlight.

"Come on," I said.

We forced ourselves to run, just hoping that we headed the right way. The only landmarks were the occasional cottage and stone walls dividing the fields. But eventually we saw the gleam of a number of lights in the distance.

"Blackstone," Leo breathed. "Thank hell."

My heart tightened with dread for what waited for us there. But we had to know. And so we walked on, faster. Leo took my hand again, and I didn't protest. We had bigger things to worry about—like our friends.

I saw the first bodies as we reached the top of a hill, looking down into the valley where Blackstone was nestled. There was an abandoned mine shaft near the path that led around the town to the coast, and from here, black dots moved, dragging unmoving figures from inside the mine. Or tunnel. Some people had found another way out. But not everyone had made it.

We took off down the hillside at a run.

*Venators.* Some in uniform. Some not. Row after row, lined up in the field. David was one of them. I saw Freya sobbing over her brother, who lay pale and unmoving. Next to him, Dr Philips lay unmoving at the end of the row, her body twisted horribly. She must have been in the sepulchre with the other *venators*, after all.

"Ash! Leo!"

Claudia came running towards us. Her face was streaked with tears, and she threw herself on me. "I thought you were dead!" she sobbed.

"We're okay," said Leo, quickly. "The others?"

"They're fine. Berenice got trapped under rubble on the way out, but Howard saved her. Come on."

We half ran, half skidded the rest of the way down the hillside, where Cyrus embraced us both.

"Fucking hell," he said. "Never do that to me again, bro."

"How'd you all get out at the same time?" said Leo, patting his brother's shoulder. "We've just walked miles from the middle of nowhere."

"Typical!" said Claudia, rolling her red-rimmed eyes at me. "Some of the *venators* helped us—pointed us in the right direction. We owe them massively. They—well—" She gave a sweeping gesture at the corpses around us. They must have died fighting Lucifer's servants.

I blinked, feeling tears trembling at the edge of my vision. "They've lost a lot."

"I'm sorry, Ash," said Claudia. "There—there wasn't a body."

I'd known it already, but it was like her words wrenched open something inside me, the dam suppressing everything that had happened. I dropped to my knees, barely feeling Leo's arms around me as grief claimed me, sweeping me away.

## 24

PARADISE LOST

For so long I'd been numb, and I would have given anything for that numbness to return now. I hadn't really cried since the day Leo had left, hadn't let myself break down, but it was like everything I'd felt in the interim, and especially over the past few hours, had struck me at once with the force of a tidal wave. All the turmoil I'd felt since I'd had to leave home, since Leo—those two things were inextricably tied together—the loneliness and betrayal, the confusion and desperate longing. Yet that all disappeared as I faced the overwhelming grief for those Lucifer had taken.

The one emotion I didn't feel was anger. It was like it had all been washed out of me, either by the demon or by the death of the woman I'd hated for so long. It felt twisted and wrong to even contemplate that now it sank in: she really was dead. Maybe now I could finally think of her the way she really was—a woman who'd had to make some terrible choices, and was forever punished for an irredeemable error she'd made as a child. Hell, I'd made enough mistakes of my own—like refusing to accept her as my mother. Guilt hollowed the grief already in my heart. I'd been so blind and reckless…

Eventually, Leo gently pulled me away from the bodies. A huddle of survivors from the Venantium had formed, and someone beckoned everyone over. My heart jolted in shock as I recognised Hayley Fairfax—one of the two members of the Inner Circle that the fortune-teller had said weren't possessed by higher demons. She looked, literally, like hell, but I probably didn't look much better.

I stood up shakily, not letting go of Leo, and stumbled over to join the rest of the group. Berenice, Howard, Claudia, and Cyrus stood a little apart from the *venators*. Berenice's face was tear-streaked, and Howard had his arm around her.

"I am sorry," Hayley was saying. Her eyes were bright, her face and hair dirt-streaked. "I suspected something was wrong with my colleagues for some time, but I never could have imagined that Lucifer could have infiltrated the Barrier itself. You have my sincere apologies, and I would not blame any of you who would prefer to leave the Venantium and return to your families."

No one said anything. I couldn't believe that this subdued huddle was all that remained of the Venantium. Hayley wiped a trembling hand on her now-ruined uniform.

"However, I intend to do my utmost to prevent further loss of life. Mr Fraser is currently sending an urgent request for aid to our sister organisation in London, and further emissaries will be sent worldwide. While I do not know if Lucifer survived, the presence of five higher demons is a matter for urgent action, and this meets the criteria for a class-five emergency situation—one step below a declaration of war."

There was an outbreak of muttering at this.

"Um, excuse me?" Cyrus stepped forwards, towards the group. "There may be an emissary from the Venantium in the US already on their way. My brother and I met a group when we were travelling, and I was in contact with Ash, who told me about Lucifer. I thought they ought to know, so they would be able to help fight him if need be. They might've sent out warnings to other groups, too."

Hayley turned to him. "You have my gratitude, Mr…"

"Blake," said Cyrus, with a noticeable flinch.

A ripple went through the group.

Hayley blinked, brushing hair from her dirt-stained face. "You are Mr Blake's son? And your brother, too?"

"Yeah, but we have nothing to do with Lucifer," said Cyrus. "Either of us. Believe me."

"Don't worry. I have no intention of subjecting either of you to further interrogations—if such a thing even exists any more. I have no idea if the Angel Box survived the tunnels' collapse. But I would never dream of punishing you for your father's actions. He treated you abominably, even before he became a demon's slave."

"First reasonable thing I've heard from one of the Inner Circle," said Leo. "There might be hope for you after all."

I mentally groaned. Typical Leo—even now, he insisted on pushing people's buttons.

"You have no reason to stay here," said Hayley. "I won't ask you to fight for us. Those of you who were dragged into this can leave at any time."

"Well, *that's* good news," said Berenice. "Coming, Howard?"

"Wait a minute," said Howard. "Do any of you *venators* know what happened to the escaped prisoners? My parents?"

Hayley shook her head. "I'm sorry. Dr Fenton was in

charge of the prisons. There will be records, but I cannot say whether it's safe to venture underground right now."

"I'm going," said Howard.

Berenice grabbed his arm, stricken. "But Lucifer could still be down there!"

"It's my parents," he said.

Whispers had broken out amongst the *venators* again.

"Please, Howard," said Berenice. "I know it's hard, but I don't want you to get yourself killed. It's too dangerous."

There was a pause. Even Hayley hadn't resumed her speech.

"Okay." Howard bowed his head, and gave Berenice's shoulder a squeeze. "I'll wait."

"I know a lot of you will have questions," said Hayley. "I will do my best to answer, although I cannot confirm anything about the future of our organisation. Anyone who wishes to fight, Mr Fraser and I will be assembling a team in Blackstone Cemetery, by the entrance to our head-quarters, and we will be venturing back into the tunnels to assess the damage. I advise you only to join us if you are absolutely certain—we do not know what might be waiting for us down there."

Another outbreak of muttering. As the *venators* turned to talk amongst themselves, Hayley made her way towards me.

*I should have seen this coming,* I thought as Leo moved closer to me, looking at her defiantly.

"Miss Temple," she said quietly, "I'd advise you to leave. I don't believe you to be a threat, but some of my colleagues may disagree. If you need somewhere to stay, there is a place in London, owned by other independent sorcerers—I only know about it because my brother stayed there, for a time, when he was the target of a rogue sorcerer. It's hidden under a nightclub called Satan's Pit—

it has other branches in different cities, but the one in London is a hub for sorcerers. The owners will help you."

"The place where the devil rises," said Claudia. "Howard —that's what your mum said. She must be hiding there."

Hayley was still looking at me.

"Okay," I said, hollowly. "I'll go."

Leo took my hand in a comforting gesture.

He stayed by my side as we walked back to campus. The others hung a little way back, and I didn't miss the glances that passed between them. But it hardly mattered what Leo and I chose to do now.

Maybe it was a stupid idea to take the woodland path, but there was nothing that could scare me anymore, not after tonight. We walked swiftly all the same, in silence.

The dark trees thinned out, and the cheerful lights of the student village greeted me.

Campus looked normal. Clubhouse music pounded from the student halls, and a large crowd had gathered around the student bar for whatever event was on that night. Life went on as usual, for everyone else. Not for us.

*"The world was all before them, where to choose
    Their place of rest, and Providence their guide;
    They, hand in hand, with wandering steps and slow,
    Through Eden took their solitary way."*

Funny. I could never remember quotes when it mattered, in interviews and exams, but Milton's final lines of *Paradise Lost* came to mind as surprisingly apt, now. Adam and Eve leaving Eden, never to return.

Outside House 23, I dug into my pocket for my key.

Thankfully, even with all the running I'd done, it was still there.

"They're coming with us," Leo said to me, with a glance at the others, who hovered farther back. "We won't leave you."

"Like it matters," I said as we climbed the stairs to the third floor. "The demons are coming for me anyway. I can't be around you—around any of you."

"That's bullshit," said Leo quietly. "I was wrong—so wrong. Lucifer wanted us apart so he could get to you. Mephistopheles manipulated both of us, trying to drive us apart. But in the end, it doesn't matter whether we're together or apart—not to them." His eyes were bright, black sparks. "But it matters to us."

A lump blocked my throat. His last words to me before he left replayed: *I don't want to look you in the eyes.*

"That's not what you said," I whispered, feeling a tear slide down my cheek.

"I'm so sorry. I should never have—" He pulled me into a hug so tight I couldn't breathe, but I didn't care. It was all I could do to stop myself dissolving into tears again. "I love you," he whispered in my ear.

I stiffened. I could hear my heart beating in my ears, but I couldn't say a word—couldn't respond even if I knew how.

He let me go. "It doesn't matter to me if you're a human or a human-demon. It never mattered, and I should never have let it come between us."

I swallowed. His words would have meant everything to me not long ago, but a few short hours had changed it all.

The flat was quiet; my friends had obviously gone out. Maybe they were in the bar. If they'd texted me, I wouldn't know it. My phone was probably buried with the Venantium.

Should I stay and say goodbye to my friends? It didn't feel right just leaving like this.

I flicked the light on in my room. Everything was just where I'd left it, like nothing had changed.

I looked around. There wasn't anything I was particularly bothered about leaving behind, but I felt a pang all the same. I'd hoped this would be my home, but I could never have that, being what I was. Never.

"I lost my phone," I said. "Dr Philips took it."

Dr Philips, who now lay broken on the ground outside Blackstone.

"It's okay," said Leo. "We'll get you a new one."

*Don't help me,* I thought. *You'll only make me feel worse.* It was bad enough owing a debt I could never repay to someone who would never come back.

*She offered me everything. She tried to make it up to me. But I spurned her.*

Another tear dripped down my cheek. I stumbled to the wardrobe, dragged out my most practical-sized rucksack, and began feverishly piling clothes into it.

"Ash, we don't have to leave tonight. We don't know what's going to happen."

"Hello? Lucifer's *here.* Even if he's not, there are five higher demons on the loose, and God knows what else."

"Ash, Lucifer never broke the Barrier."

"There is no Barrier," I said. "The higher demons got through with no trouble. I don't know—maybe the Inner Circle broke it themselves."

"But the world's not overrun with regular demons," said Leo. "I don't think the higher demons have ever followed the rules. They've always been able to get through. Maybe the Venantium just glossed over that part when they told us about the Barrier."

"Pretty damn big thing to gloss over." I felt another sharp pang as I remembered something else. I'd never asked the fortune-teller about my father, the real Lucifer, how she'd met him. Yet another regret to weigh on my heart.

"Ash, it's not your fault, none of this is. I know you tend to blame yourself, but believe me. The Venantium are full of shit. You're more human than most of them. Look what happened to the Inner Circle!"

"I know," I said. "It's just... too much to think about, right now."

"There's... one thing." Leo hesitated. "About those half demons. Why they helped us. Why don't you ask them? Or ask... your demon? Have you ever spoken to her?"

"Not directly," I admitted. "But I guess it couldn't hurt."

He took my hand, and I felt warmth shoot through me. Unbidden, a demon's voice spoke in my ear. *"Love is the most complex of human emotions. You opened yourself to another, and in doing so... you began to take energy from him. As a demon would."*

I shook my head. I'd deal with that thought later. Now...

The Darkworld answered almost immediately, as though it had been awaiting my call. I let ice flow through me, and the room warped before my eyes, becoming distorted. Even the solid presence of Leo beside me felt muted.

The doppelgänger appeared, slipped from the shadows as though she'd been hiding there all along.

"I thought you'd come back, Ash," she said.

"You're not... you're not my demon. I thought..."

"No, I'm not. Your demon occupies the same body as you. You are one."

"So who are you? You can't be the same as the doppelgänger from before."

"She was my sister," whispered the girl. "I am, like the others you glimpsed earlier, one of Lucifer's victims. I was the last human-demon he killed, twenty years ago, before you were born. My sister had already... deteriorated."

I shivered. The human-demon was crying, and it was so strange to see tears falling from my eyes when my own were, at the moment, dry.

"She became a ghoul," she whispered. "She was full of anger, driven by it, consumed. She left her sanity when she departed this world, and became the Death Child. The reason she fought so hard was because she envied you, so much it ate her away from the inside. She and I almost escaped, but Melivia was too late to save us. It was the final straw for her. When she found out she was pregnant with you, she knew that any human-demon would be in danger for their existence as long as Lucifer existed. So she gave you away. I watched you, from the Darkworld, envious of your human life. Mine was cut short at a young age..."

"Is that why you look like me?" Her sister had said as much.

"This is the closest thing to a human form I have." She closed her eyes.

"So would the same thing happen to me, if I died? Would my demon... stay?"

Her eyes opened again. "Yes. The Barrier prevents us from leaving the Darkworld. I will be here forever, if we're lucky."

I'd somehow known it, but that didn't make it any easier to face.

"Lucifer didn't know," said the human-demon girl.

"His attempts to break the Barrier wouldn't have made him immortal. He was wrong. If anything, it'd have the opposite effect. But you can't let him know this."

"He's dead," I said. "Isn't he?" *Please. He has to be. She can't have died for nothing.*

"You don't have to accept my offer," said the half-demon. "But I know Lucifer's alive. He'll try to come back, make no mistake. And other forces are stirring. Melivia lost Mephistopheles's heart."

"Lucifer… is alive? How can that be possible?" How could he—and not her?

"Because part of him is tied to the Darkworld. He is like us: he can't be free. If a demon's heart is destroyed, completely obliterated, they are reduced to the same thing, a shadow. The Barrier is the sum of all demons' energy, and our very essence is bound up in it. If it is destroyed, Lucifer will be, too. He has no humanity left in him."

"Destroying the Barrier?" I said. "But I thought that would set all the demons loose in the world."

"No. It's not true. Yes, removing the Barrier would remove certain restraints, but it would also remove immortality. You can help us, Ash. You can set us free."

"But that would involve…" Breaking the Barrier? How? "It's impossible."

"If you help us," whispered the half-demon, "we will help you fight him. He will return—soon—and the world will be his playground. Accept our help, Ashlyn, or face your own death."

Behind her, I saw legion of shadowy figures, the lost souls of Lucifer's victims. I swallowed, the burden pressing on me. I knew the right choice. It would be hard, nigh on impossible.

But I had to try.

"Okay," I said to the half-demon. "I'll help you."

## ABOUT THE AUTHOR

Emma is the New York Times and USA Today Bestselling author of the Changeling Chronicles urban fantasy series.

Emma spent her childhood creating imaginary worlds to compensate for a disappointingly average reality, so it was probably inevitable that she ended up writing fantasy novels. When she's not immersed in her own fictional universes, Emma can be found with her head in a book or wandering around the world in search of adventure.

Find out more about Emma's books at www.emmaladams.com.

www.ingramcontent.com/pod-product-compliance
Lightning Source LLC
Chambersburg PA
CBHW020317200626
46814CB00006BA/2283